To
Hele.

on her wedding

THE ELECTRIC

Andrew David Barker

Andrew David Barker

Published by
Boo Books
32 Westbury Street
Derby
DE22 3PN
www.boobooks.net

The Electric © Andrew David Barker 2014

Cover by Amanda Plant © 2015

Chapter header image by
Billy Alexander, via www.freeimages.com

Typesetting by
Pinnacle Ltd, Ilkley, West Yorkshire

ISBN: 978-0-9927285-6-4

Printed and bound by CPI Group (UK) Ltd, Croydon, CR0 4YY

ACKNOWLEGEMENTS

My deepest thanks go to Matthew Waldram, who acted as a sounding board, a beta reader, and supporter of this project from day one. I'd also like to thank Amanda Plant, Gareth Watkins, Andrew Jonathon Ord, Danielle Barton, Michael Adams, Ben Waldram, and my publisher, Alex Davis, for taking a chance on this novel. Lastly, I'd like to thank my wife, Kate Horlor, whose support and encouragement are without measure. I could never have written this novel without her.

Andrew David Barker

For Kate

I was fifteen that summer; the summer I discovered the old Electric cinema. It had stood long abandoned and was entwined in green; caught in time as the world moved on around it.

I happened upon it quite by chance, just as the day had fallen into that rusty afterglow left by a sinking sun. When I think back to that first encounter with the Electric, I often picture the deep red light crossing and bending in the broken windows.

Days passed in a seemingly endless, shimmering haze that year; we'd play on the riverbanks and explore the woods and fields around us. By the time I found the old cinema, however, the last days of summer were fast approaching. September had arrived. The leaves were already turning and beginning to fall, and school loomed large in our sights once more. Endless days were coming to an end.

There was David, Emma and I, and the three of us were pretty much inseparable that year. But on the evening I discovered the Electric, I was alone, and that old abandoned building seemed to know it.

That summer I would purposely try and stay away from home for as long as I possibly could. This was something I kept to myself. When David and Emma went home for dinner of an evening, I would pretend to be doing likewise, but in actual fact I'd stay out until dark. My mother didn't care if I was there or not. There wasn't much she did care about anymore.

I circled back once David and Emma had gone, and went down to the river. I sat and watched my shadow cross and stretch around me as the sun bled across the horizon, listening to the country hum with life. After a while, I lay back on the grass and looked to a sky streaked with colour. At one point a heron glided down and stood upon the bank opposite me. It watched the river intently, but then must have noticed my presence, as all at once it took to the air and was gone from my sight in seconds.

The day had been long and hot and I could feel myself drifting off to sleep right there on the riverbank. I closed my eyes and listened as the breeze picked up and sang its song through the trees. Somewhere far off a dog barked.

That was when I heard the laugh.

It was very faint, but in that instant I felt sure it had come from somewhere close by. It had been the laugh of a woman, of that I was almost certain – high and lyrical. I sat up and scanned the river up and down, but saw no one. I got to my feet and walked down to the water's edge. There was nobody around, no one I could see anyway. It occurred to me then that it could be someone spying on me, probably Emma trying to sneak up and give me a fright. She always enjoyed giving people a good scare.

I called her name and immediately felt a little foolish for having done so. There was nobody out there. I told myself I'd just imagined it and pushed it from my mind. Then I walked on along the riverbank.

In time, I would remember the laugh as a kind of marker; a beginning to the strange and incredible events that unfolded at the old Electric cinema.

I drifted away from the river and found myself in a field of tall grass. A ghost moon hung high in the sky. It would be full dark in an hour or less. I walked through the field, gliding my hands over the grass as I went.

I noticed an old wooden shack towards the edge of the field and headed straight for it.

My friends and I must have walked miles upon miles over

the countryside during the summers, but that evening was the first time I'd ever come across the shack.

As I got closer I saw that many of its wooden panels were missing. Light splintered through the structure. The wood itself was weather-worn and eaten away here and there. Part of its roof was missing and it no longer had a door, only an entrance lined with eaten pieces of a doorframe. One good storm would probably raze it to the ground completely. In fact, it looked as if it would really only need one good shove.

To the west, the sun was a bloody arc on the horizon, and as I circled the shack, orange light pierced through the many holes and gaps in the building, changing shade and shape as I moved around it. I went inside.

It took a moment for my eyes to adjust to the dark places between the golden shafts that streamed in. The ground was nothing more than soil, undulating in mounds. If the shack had ever had a floor, it had long since been reclaimed by the earth. I ventured in further, noticing the rubbish strewn here and there. Above me, through the hole in the roof, the ghost moon rode the pale blue and red of the darkening sky.

There was a movie poster on the ground. Well, part of one anyway. It was torn in half and its edges were jagged and sodden, but I could make out the name BOGART written in dull and faded red lettering across the top of the poster, and a hand, possibly Bogart's, gripping a gun. The weapon was silhouetted by a full moon, beneath which lay a winding brook. There was a dead body floating on the water. All I could read from the title were the words NIGHT and CAME. I thought about taking it, but decided against it. It could have been lying in the dirt of that shack for years, and besides, there was hardly anything left of it now.

I kicked around the earth looking for something else of interest, but there was nothing, so I left the shack just in time to see the last of the sun sink behind the world. It left a fiery stain on the horizon.

That was when I noticed the narrow path leading off through the copse. I made straight for it on impulse; any winding path is a curiosity when you're fifteen.

I peered in through the tree line. It looked to be a forgotten path; it clearly hadn't been walked on for years as, for the most part, the woods had reclaimed it. The path would have been easy to miss, but I saw it; a thin trail that led deep into the trees.

I looked back to the shack and the red sky beyond it, then entered the woods and took the path.

The path widened as I went deeper. The trees became less dense, thinning out, allowing great shafts of hazy light to shine through here and there. I glimpsed part of some sort of structure through the trees. That was the moment I first saw the Electric.

What I had caught sight of was part of the marquee, but at that moment I couldn't have told you what I was looking at. I saw black, disjoined lettering – an A and an M, to be specific – on white panelling, which appeared to be raised high up from the ground, but I didn't make the connection. I walked on, heading straight for this new curiosity.

The path narrowed once more, winding around a neat line of trees. The branches were low and I had to duck down to pass through. My t-shirt got caught and I heard a slight tear, but I pushed on regardless. Then I was through, and stood tall before me was the unmistakable structure of a run-down cinema.

Bathed in the red haze of that evening's light, the building still proudly displayed its name high above the marquee – The Electric. None of those letters were missing; the ones on the marquee itself however had long since fallen to the ground. Only the A and M that I had already glimpsed remained, coupled with a lonely N in the right hand corner, and a broken in half F to the left. All the windows were broken, and the jagged edges of the glass that remained caught the light and danced red spectrums through the Electric.

I stood for a long time simply staring in amazement. I never knew of its existence until that moment. Surely an old cinema standing alone and abandoned out here in the countryside would have become the stuff of legend around our town, particularly amongst kids, but I had never heard so much as a rumour about such a place in my entire life. I sensed the thrill of mystery and discovery right away and knew that I had to explore the old Electric.

I stepped closer. Beneath the marquee, the entrance looked dark and uninviting. There was a movie poster just inside the foyer and even at a distance I could read the name of the actor starring in the picture – Humphrey Bogart. I knew right away that it was the same poster I had seen torn up back at the shack.

The poster intrigued me, but I couldn't put my finger on why. I knew about Bogart, even at that age, and had seen quite a few of his movies. My father's favourite film had been *The Treasure of the Sierra Madre*, which he claimed was not only Bogart's best picture, but one of the finest films ever made. I watched it with him one rainy afternoon about three months before he died, and it was indeed a great movie. That film, and the fact that my old man loved Bogart, got me into watching a lot of his pictures, particularly after Dad's death. But there was something strange about this poster. As I got closer, I saw the movie was called *When the Night Came Fallin'*, not one I'd heard of before. But then, he had made a heck of a lot of films during his career, and some may have even had different titles in different countries.

I edged closer and my feet found the cracked and weed-ridden concrete of the Electric's once-grand entrance. The marquee loomed over me and I noticed great cobwebs spanning darkened corners. I wondered who the last person to set foot there had been, and how long ago. Judging by its appearance, mine might have been the first face the Electric had seen for years, possibly decades.

The thought unnerved me and I pushed it from my mind.

The poster for *When the Night Came Fallin'* was inside a glass case, which had protected it from the elements somewhat, but it was still very faded and worn. Dirty water lined the bottom of the case and mould had developed around the edges of the poster itself. Still, it wasn't torn and remained relatively clear and readable.

As I'd suspected back at the shack, the gun cast against the ominous moon was indeed being held by Bogart. He wore a pin-striped suit and was looking off to the side, past his weapon, perhaps towards his quarry. His distinctive profile was as I had seen it many times before, and yet there was also something very different about it. To look at him for too long made me feel incredibly strange, nauseous even. Although that wasn't quite right either. It was a feeling I hadn't felt before. It was like having a mild electric shock on drip feed, that's all I could liken it to: an electric shock that gently pulsed through me. My temples throbbed. I felt dizzy and had to look away. I thought I was going to be sick right there and then, but I wasn't. As soon as I turned from the poster the feeling subsided, and almost in an instant, I felt completely fine again.

I turned my attention to the inside of the lobby. I could see there was a kiosk that long ago would have sold popcorn and drinks, but now just stood barren and crooked. However, it was the grand staircase that caught my eye. It ascended up to the double doors of the theatre itself and was still carpeted in red, although it was faded and sodden. Still, it wasn't difficult to imagine the place in its heyday. Even through its neglect and decay, the Electric still held its grandeur.

The staircase may have been carpeted, but the floor of the lobby was tiled black and white. It had an art deco feel, I suppose, although many of the tiles were cracked; a few even broken in two. They were also, of course, filthy.

I decided to go inside, although I was still unnerved by my reaction to the Bogart poster. There was something about the Electric that made me feel... what? Afraid? Surely it was just my overactive imagination going into overdrive. Decaying and forgotten places will almost always do that to you, especially when you're alone, and especially when you're young. Old places just have a creep, if you've a fertile enough mind. What fear I had, I knew it was irrational, and if David and Emma had been with me, I probably wouldn't have given entering the Electric a second thought. But alone, in the red dusk of the dying day, it certainly took some willpower to step through those lobby doors. But step through I did.

I twisted my ankle almost as soon as I stepped inside. The uneven flooring caught me off guard and I nearly fell, but somehow I managed to right myself in an awkward stumble across the tiles. Pain lanced through the side of my right foot and I yelped, my voice eaten by the deadening silence of the Electric.

I limped around the lobby, testing my foot, challenging the pressure this pain would allow. My ankle often gave out like this; my dad's had been the same, and according to him, both his brothers and his father had also suffered from this plight. Seemed the entire male side of my family possessed weak ankles that would twist at the slightest obstacle. It was family folklore, and had even gained the moniker *the Crowhurst Ankle*. Once, when I was little, my dad sprained his ankle so badly he couldn't walk on it for a month. My longest stretch of ankle agony had been a few days, and that had been bad enough. The episode in the Electric was just a mere twinge, mind. Still, I could have done without it.

The worst of the pain subsiding, I gingerly stepped deeper into the lobby. There was another old poster displayed in cracked and shattered casing. The film was called *Mad Dogs* and starred silent comedian Harold Lloyd. Lloyd, in his trademark round glasses, wore a startled expression and was dressed in a Wee Willie Winkie nightgown. His co-star, stood by his side, appeared to be a large man, but his head and name had long been torn away. While staring at Harold Lloyd, a wave of that same electric nausea returned. I stumbled back, almost going over on the Crowhurst Ankle again. I averted my eyes from Lloyd's comical gape and, once again, the pulse throbbing in my temples faded like dying electricity.

Yet I had to go on. It was getting late. I could see darkness falling rapidly outside, but I couldn't leave. Not yet. Even with the throb in my foot and the strange feelings that came every time I looked at one of the Electric's old movie posters, I still couldn't bring myself to make tracks for home.

I had to see inside the theatre.

I came to stand at the foot of the stairs, looking up at the double doors that remained firmly closed. Someone had long ago closed those doors and walked away from this place, never to return. Had I even been born when this place was last open? It seemed doubtful. The Electric appeared to have stood silent and forgotten for decades, allowing the years to work their gentle decay, and now all that remained was a faded memory of what once was.

I had stumbled upon a mystery all right, and I knew that the few days I had left before school began would now be dedicated to finding out as much as I possibly could about the old Electric. I also knew that Emma would love this place. She loved history and movies, and old things, and she would just lap up a mystery like this. I couldn't wait to bring her here.

I ascended the staircase, the old red carpet worn and thin beneath my soles. There was a plaque above the door, the lettering faded, but not so much that I couldn't make it out. It read **Auditorium** and for some reason I felt a flicker of unnerve. The feeling the old movie posters had given me was, of course, still fresh in my mind, but this sudden fear – for it was definitely fear I felt now – came on in such a wave that I had to grip the banister to steady myself. I paused on the stairs for a moment, trying to regain some composure, but then I suddenly felt convinced someone was watching me from down in the lobby. I turned on the stairs and peered down into the murk. Outside, night was falling fast, and the lobby now appeared to be filled with strange, uneasy shapes and long crooked shadows that cut through dense creases of dark. The imagination can play nasty little tricks on you when looking upon such a scene, but I didn't see anybody down there. Not taking any chances though, I turned around quickly and hopped up the remaining steps to the auditorium doors.

I gripped the handle and pulled, the hinges screeching an awful echo down through the darkened lobby. Then I was through the door, which I left ajar, and came to stand on a balcony overlooking a sea of empty seats. It took a long minute for my eyes to adjust to the darkness. The screen loomed pale in the gloom. The theatre, or auditorium, as the faded plaque had read, smelt fusty and vaguely like sea air. It wasn't altogether unpleasant; it was just the smell of something very old, and very much forgotten. I looked at the screen. It was dirty, but didn't appear to be torn, and the seats also looked to be in quite good condition, considering. I walked further along the balcony, deeper into the auditorium. But then my body snapped rigid, my every hair prickling wildly.

There was a man in one of the seats.

I couldn't move – could only stare at the man sat about a quarter of the way down the rows. I could see the side of his face as he stared up, almost vacantly, at the empty screen. He had a thick, white-peppered black beard and an unkempt head of tangled hair, equally ageing. The coat he wore seemed far too thick and heavy for September – it was a winter's coat, coloured a vibrant, deep red, buttoned up to the neck.

He turned around and looked straight at me, bright green eyes glistening as if wet from tears. My every limb felt wayward. Everything about him seemed incredibly vivid; his ageing hair, his eyes, the coat, all seemed razor-sharp in clarity, as if his very presence was itself a projection; a heightened reality.

He slowly began to stand, never for a moment taking his eyes from me. I remained rooted to the spot, unable to move. I felt sweat run down my face and back, my t-shirt clinging to my flesh in an instant. The man stood straight and tall, as rigid as I. The colours – the deep red of his long coat, his black and white-streaked hair and beard, and those glistening green eyes – all seemed to dance in radiance, the vibrancy almost overwhelming.

He then began to make his way to the end of his row and that was when I finally found my feet. I fled from the auditorium, down the stairs and through the lobby, never once looking back. I stumbled out through the main doors, conscious not to even glance at the Bogart poster, and pushed on, the tenderness in my ankle forgotten. I kept my eyes levelled straight ahead, and put the Electric behind me. I ran through the woodland, and out past the shack and across the fields. The moon was riding high and the sky clear, stars curving over me. I didn't stop running until I reached my house.

I guess most bedrooms could be seen as a kind of window into your entire personality, especially when you're fifteen. With my room, that was certainly the case; a plethora of teenage indulgences piled to tipping point from wall to wall. Comic books, paperbacks, and video tapes were the main offenders, but patchwork clothes mountains also ate up floor space, as did my many drawings that lay strewn about the place. Of course, from time to time, my mother tried to get me to tidy up, but more often than not I'd just adjust a pile of comics to make them look a little neater, or throw a load of clothes into the back of the wardrobe, hidden from sight. She didn't bother asking anymore though. Since Dad's death, her head had been far more messed up than my room could ever be.

On the walls were movie posters and a few pictures of favourite bands – R.E.M., The Cure, Bowie, that kind of thing. The posters were of *Jaws, Dawn of the Dead,* and an old one for *The Maltese Falcon* which my dad had bought me; Bogart stood in *noir* lighting, cigarette in one hand, the statue of the black bird – the film's MacGuffin – in the other. There were also pictures of Phoebe Cates and Molly Ringwald, and one of Madonna that my mother really disapproved of. The only girl I'd ever had in my room – aside from my mother, of course – had been Emma, and when she first came in, she took one look at the walls, and the general mess and clutter, and said, "typical boy's room". And I guess it was.

The morning after I first discovered the old Electric cinema, I lay in bed as the sky lightened outside my window, unable to sleep, my mind going over and over the events of the previous night.

I had come to the conclusion that the man in the cinema must have been a vagrant – the unkempt hair and beard told me that much – who I had unwisely disturbed. He was probably using the Electric as his home. As for the strange feeling the Bogart and Lloyd posters had given me, however, I had no conclusion. That had been the oddest sensation I had ever felt. Yet, in the dawning light of morning, the exact feeling was now hard to recall. It felt dreamlike, otherworldly. I began to even question whether I'd felt anything at all. The only thing that remained clear was the posters themselves. I could still see how Bogart and Harold Lloyd had appeared in their respective pictures with incredible clarity.

A thought crossed my mind then, concerning the Bogart film. I pulled back the bed covers and sat up. I scanned the clutter of my room, trying to remember where I'd put a particular book. I got up off the bed and began to rummage through one of my two bookcases. Paperbacks were doubled-up and piled high and I had to pull dozens off the shelf just to see what lay behind them. There were books back there I'd forgotten I even had, some read, many left unread – one of which was the book I was searching for: a large, thin hardback simply entitled *The Films of Humphrey Bogart*.

I took the book back over to my bed and immediately began scanning through the pages. I caught sight of a sentence in the book's introduction, stating that Bogart made over seventy pictures during his career. I flicked to the index and looked up W, but the only film I found under that letter was a film called *The Wagons Roll at Night*, made in 1941, which I hadn't seen. I then began to go through the entire book, from beginning to end, checking every movie just to see if it said anything about there being any alternative titles. It didn't. Not one film Bogart made appeared to have ever been called *When the Night Came Fallin'*.

Already dressed, I lay on the bed and listened out for my mum leaving for work. She was banging and clattering around in the kitchen below me – she had always been about as deft as an elephant – then I heard her heels clicking down the hallway and out through the front door. As soon as the door banged shut I got up and headed downstairs. My ankle still felt a little tender – a constant reminder of where I'd been the night before.

I made myself some toast, which I neglected to keep an eye on and ended up burning, but ate anyway, and then left the house within minutes. I had to get back to the Electric. I couldn't get it out of my mind. I kept replaying my experience there over and over, questioning and analysing each oddity, each mystery. The fear that had gripped me, particularly with the movie posters, and last off, the vagrant, now felt so distant, so trivial almost, I really began to wonder whether or not any of it had actually happened at all. The only thing I was certain of was that I had to get back there. But even in my complacency of fear, I knew I couldn't again go alone.

I had to let David and Emma in on my discovery.

David levelled his rifle at the old man who lived next door.

Through David's bedroom window I could see the old-timer pottering about in his garden. David knew I had entered his room. He took his left hand away from the barrel briefly, motioning a wave, or possibly a command to stay put, while his eyes remained focused on his target. I stood in the doorway and watched the old man. He was crouched down, his back to the rifle he didn't even know was pointing at him. All around him, in his beloved garden, were a vast array of flowers, their colours multitude and vivid in the morning sun. Right by the old man's head stood what I believed was a marigold – a richly yellow and orange flower standing tall in full bloom. David squeezed the trigger and I heard the rifle – which was nothing more than a simple BB gun – kick as the ball shot, dead centre, into the head of the marigold. The flower exploded right by the old man's head. It was an impressive shot. Yet the old man didn't even flinch, didn't really react at all at first. However, he soon noticed the pieces of flower on his shoulder, and the head of the marigold ripped apart. He looked around in utter confusion. David, who was already sniggering, began to howl with laughter at seeing the old man's bewildered expression.

"Quiet! He'll hear you!" I said.

David ducked down out of sight.

"Ah, old Travis can't hear a thing, Sammy Boy."

"What?"

"The guy's as deaf as a post. Can't see for shit either."

I glanced out of the window again and saw the old man, Travis, now stood looking up at the sky. I closed David's bedroom door behind me and walked across the room, self-consciously ducking low as I passed the windows.

"Don't worry, Sam," said David, "he can't see you, believe me. He's short sighted or somethin'."

I remained low, however, keeping my eye on Travis. He was indeed wearing glasses with huge, thick, lenses, the kind my dad would've called milk bottle ends, which made the old man's eyes look tiny. He crouched down again, inspecting the destroyed marigold. I sat on the floor across from David, leaning my back against his bed.

"What are you loading into that thing?" I asked, motioning to the BB gun cradled in his arms.

David smiled, leaned the gun up against the wall, then dug into his pocket and pulled out a handful of tiny silver balls.

"These bad boys," he said, holding out his hand towards me. "They're steel, coated with zinc or something. Weighty – you feel 'em."

I held out my hand and he upturned his into mine. I had to snap both my hands together to catch them all.

"They are pretty heavy," I said.

I picked one up between my thumb and index finger and squeezed. It was hard all right.

"You get one of them in the head, you'd know about it big time," David said, a touch of pride in his voice.

"Sure," I said, now eyeing the rifle itself. "When did you get it?"

"Got it for my birthday. Dad said he'd had one when he was a kid; gave me a lesson in deadly warfare in the backyard with a row of Coke cans. Mum went mental."

"But now you've moved onto killing flowers and tormenting blind and deaf old gardeners…"

"Yep," he said, beaming.

I handed the ammunition back and then got onto my knees and peered out into next door's garden. Travis was back at work, doing whatever gardeners do with their subjects.

"You wanna go?" David asked, motioning to the rifle.

I said, "I don't know," but what I really felt was a thrill of excitement and longing.

"Ah, come on man, it's well funny," said David. "'The old guy has absolutely no idea what's going on. Must be dense or somethin'."

I looked at the rifle and then out at old Travis. There was a lilting lilac-coloured flower perfectly positioned right by his face. It was a golden opportunity.

"Come on, Sam, I do it all the time!"

I grabbed the rifle.

"Is it loaded?" I asked.

"Locked and loaded, Sergeant Slaughter." He then saluted me.

"Right, Corporal Bad Ass, let me show you how this is done."

I levelled the weapon into my shoulder and looked straight down the sights. It took me a moment to find my target, but then I had it.

"Come on," David said.

"Shut up."

Travis was moving around next to the lilac flower. I was just about to squeeze the trigger when the old man caught the flower with his elbow, sending the head bobbing this way and that. I breathed out and took my eye from the sights.

"What's up?" David asked.

"Nothing. Stand easy, Corporal."

I looked down the barrel once more and got the flower in my sights.

I fired.

I heard the old man yelp before I even realised what had happened.

I looked out and saw Travis ferociously rubbing the back of his neck.

"You idiot!" cried David. He scurried across the room, swung open his door and was out of there in a flash. I peered out. Travis was standing now, seemingly looking straight at me, squinting hard, his hand still rubbing the back of his neck.

I threw the gun on the bed and raced from the room.

I found David in the front room, sprawled out on the sofa, flicking through channels on the TV, sound on mute. He scowled at me as I entered.

"You dick," he said. "You've ruined everything. There's no way I can carry on shooting at his dippy flowers now."

"Sorry, Dave, I just..." I trailed off. He just looked at me.

"I'll probably get in trouble now..." He was in a full-blown sulk.

"Look, Dave, he'll probably just think he was stung by a wasp or something... he ain't gonna think he was shot at. Who would? Like you said, he can't hardly see anything, can't hear anything. He ain't gonna know, man."

David seemed to brighten up a little at this, but then I saw that he wanted to make a point of being mad at me, so he put his sulky face back on and sank deeper into the sofa, flicking from one channel to another, back and forth, back and forth.

I didn't say anything, which was usually what I did when David went into one of his sulks. I just sat completely still, waiting for him to come round. I knew he would. He always did eventually. He couldn't stand the silence.

I could hear David's mother talking on the telephone from the kitchen. She had let me in earlier and had hardly said two words to me, yet she was babbling away like merry hell to some poor soul on the end of the line. David's mother seemed to live for scandal. She was a suburban gossiper to beat them all.

David began to grin, although I noticed he was trying to suppress it as best he could.

"You are Sergeant Slaughter, no doubt about that," he said.

"Take no prisoners," I said.

He laughed, and so did I. It felt good.

"Old fart must've freaked," David said through his laughter.

"Probably thinks all the plants are out to get him now," I said, laughing hard myself, not really thinking about what I was saying.

"Yeah, like they're all turning on him – like them Triffid things…"

"Yeah…" I managed, now laughing so hard I could hardly speak.

My laughter infected David's, and vice versa. If one of us calmed a little, we would immediately be set off again by the other.

Then David said, "Probably thinks his garden is haunted or something, exploding flowers and everythin'… like them polter-gooses…"

It didn't make much sense, but still, David doubled-up at his own fantasy, tears in his eyes.

He then put on a deep voice, as if he were narrating a movie trailer.

"Coming to a cinema near you: GHOST GARDEN! NIGHT OF THE PRUNING DEAD!!"

It was juvenile, nonsensical claptrap he was spouting, but I stopped laughing right away. Suddenly it wasn't funny anymore. David must have seen something in my face because his laughter soon petered out also. He frowned at me.

"What's up?" he asked.

I took a breath, and then said, "You won't believe what I found last night."

I thought about telling David the entire story, but then decided against it. I wanted him, and Emma, to see the Electric with their own eyes. I didn't want them to have any preconceived notions of what they were about to encounter. In the end, all I told him was that I'd found a derelict building out in the countryside, and that it was "way cool". Just enough to spark his interest. David pressed me for more information, but I resisted.

I lingered in the hallway while David raced back upstairs for something. I could hear his mum in the kitchen, still on the phone, still babbling away without coming up for air. David came bounding back down wearing a fresh t-shirt and a pair of black shades like *The Blues Brothers* wore, only David's pair were slightly too big for his face, so they were kind of counter-productive to the desired *cool* he was aiming for. He smiled at me, then went into the kitchen where I heard him say "see ya" to his mum – whose relentless ramblings didn't even cease to return her own son's goodbye – and then returned to the hallway with a biscuit in his mouth. I followed him out the front door.

"Where to first?" he asked with his mouth full.

"Emma's," I said.

I closed the front door behind me and then felt David give my arm a slight tug. I looked at him and he motioned over to next door's front garden. Travis was standing on his porch, his milk bottle ends staring straight at us. I knew we'd have to walk past his house to get to Emma's. If we took the other route, we'd have to cut right round the block, and even though I'd shot the poor guy in the back of the neck, I didn't want to have to take such an out-of-the-way detour. I wanted to find Emma and get back to the Electric as soon as possible.

"What do we do?" asked David.

"Just make like nothing's happened – you start acting weird, he's gonna know we're guilty."

"Right," he said, but he didn't sound very convinced.

I led the way. David walked on my outside, along the kerb, keeping level with me, probably hoping that I would get the brunt of whatever old Travis was planning to dish out. Travis' thick lenses and those tiny eyes followed us as we passed. I gave him a brief look and tried, as casually as I could, to nod a polite greeting. Travis didn't respond. He stood stone still, scowling furiously.

"He knows," I heard David whisper at my side.

I didn't say anything. We passed Travis and headed on down the street. David chanced a glance behind. "He's still looking!"

"Keep going. Don't look back," I said, and we both sped up a little. Finally we turned the corner of David's street and old Travis was out of sight.

David continued to panic about the accidental shooting and how much trouble he was probably going to get in, and truth be told, I was also a little worried. I also knew that if cornered, David would squeal on me in a heartbeat. However, it transpired that old Travis never did confront us about the shooting, nor did he mention it to David's parents, and we soon forgot all about it. David never did use the old man's flowers for target practice again, and both he and I advanced – or regressed, depending on your point of view – to blowing the heads off David's old *He-Man* action figures. They came off pretty easy. We'd even prepare our victims by first removing their heads, filling them with tomato ketchup, and then carefully returning the head to the body. When one of David's silver little balls blew... I don't know, He-Man or Skeletor's head clean off, the ketchup would give us the desired splatter effect. Made a real mess of David's dad's garden shed, I know that. Old Travis did catch us doing it one time and he shouted something that neither one of us could decipher. He then pretty much ran back inside his house. We laughed until we cried.

We crossed the train tracks. Two rusty old lines that snaked through the trees – the wooden sleepers, sodden and eaten away at the ends, were scattered with fallen leaves. The colours, deep reds and ill yellows, were made more vibrant by the splashes of sunlight that leaked through the treetops. I probably wasn't even born when a train last ran these tracks. I wondered if my dad had ever played down here – as we often did – back when the trains did run. It was a throwaway thought, but it seemed to tug at my heart, and I had to bite back a sudden surge of tears. It sometimes happened like that, particularly in those first few years after his death – a thought or a memory would cross my mind, and I'd find myself feeling that hollow part of my heart, and I'd have to fight to gain control again.

I turned away from David, who was busy kicking leaves across the tracks, and wiped my eyes with the back of my hand. We followed the old tracks a little ways, then cut down the bank towards the Car Graveyard. That's what we all called it anyway. Even Emma did. Sometimes we'd refer to it as Corpse Cars as well. It was actually known as the Breakers, and was owned by Emma's dad Al – as in Albert Looms, Car Breakers: if you want its full name.

"You reckon Emma's dad would give me a job here?" David said as we approached the place.

"You want to work here?"

"Sure. How much fun would it be crushing cars all day!"

"I suppose…"

"As long I didn't have to work with old Looms too much…"

"Well, he'd be your boss," I said. "He'd be watching over you all the time."

David fell silent at this.

Albert Looms' Car Breakers stood on a large expanse of waste ground down on the outskirts of town. Beyond it lay the rolling green of the country, but here, there was nothing but crunched metal, and dirt, and rust, and smashed glass, and corpse cars. The place was fenced off, but the fence was so old and crooked that gaining access at night had never been much of a problem – every kid in town knew that. Albert Looms was more-than-likely all too aware of this fact, but he never seemed too interested in security, or safety for that matter. He was a hard guy, and both David and I did our utmost to stay out of his way, as best we could anyway. With Emma though he was a different man. She could really talk to him. In fact, she was probably the only person I'd ever seen him actually have a full conversation with – everyone else who tried to speak to him, myself and David included, would just get monosyllabic grunts and murmurs. But to Emma, he was a true father.

Emma's mother died when she was six years old, and I guess that's why she was so close to her dad. She had no one else. Al, I suppose, thought of Emma as his only link to his dead wife, and therefore gave her every ounce of love and attention he could give. In a way, I kind of admired it – a *screw-the-rest-of-the-world* philosophy, as long as he had his daughter. I didn't understand their relationship until my dad died. Then it became clear.

His death also brought Emma and me a hell of a lot closer.

We walked through the wrought iron gates, rusted like the fallen leaves, and near enough ran straight into Al Looms. He gave a nod of his head as he passed us, but nothing more. He was his usual self: oily with torn shirt and jeans; filthy black hands and face; and long, greasy, greying hair that blew wild in the breeze. He was a short, stocky man, who seemed to just project attitude and menace. That's how Dave and I saw him anyway. He was one of those guys who made you feel uncomfortable just by being in his presence. I often found it odd how I could get on so well with his daughter and yet not be able to say a single word to this guy without feeling self-conscious and stupid.

Al walked over to an old fella who seemed familiar to me, but I could not quite place. David and I stood and watched as Al gave the old man a handful of notes and then, surprisingly, patted him gently on the back.

The old guy was saying, "… My eyes aren't what they used to be, Al. I guess my drivin' days are well behind me."

"Well Elmer, all things must pass I guess. You know, I bought my first car off your son, back in '64."

"Aye, he was a good boy. Rest his soul."

Al noticed us then, still stood staring like a couple of galoots. His frown darkened and he shooed us away like you would a dog.

"Go on. Get! She's over there…" He motioned in the direction of a particular maze of corpse cars. We both headed that way. Quick.

"Man, he's a real piece of work," David said, when we were far enough out of ear shot. "Every time without fail… He just talks to us like we're pieces of shit. I don't know how Em can live with the guy…"

"'Cause he's her dad," I said. "And besides, I wouldn't take it personal – he speaks to everyone like that. The only person he doesn't is Emma."

"… and old Elmie Muxloe, it seems."

"Who?"

"The old guy he was handing all that money over to."

"Yeah, where do I know him from?"

"He's always lived here, Sam – he's, like, part of the landscape."

We followed the maze. Corpse cars piled high around us, crushed, flattened, forgotten. I wondered who once owned them. People would have lived out their lives in these cars, if only for a brief time – they'd go back and forth to work in them, do the weekly shopping, pick up their kids, maybe travel to holiday destinations; people may have been conceived in some of these vehicles, great loves, and affairs, and bitter separations may have played out in these cars; some people may have even died in them. They were an intrinsic part of people's lives, and now they lay crushed and forgotten – mechanical corpses that no one mourned and no one wanted. I thought then how much easier it would be if we all felt the loss of a loved one with the same fleeting sorrow we feel for the loss of a car, or a house, or a bike. We would feel the initial separation, but it would be a trivial and replaceable loss. Life would be so much easier.

We walked on.

We turned a corner and found ourselves in a mechanical cul-de-sac; cars piled high all around with nowhere to turn but back.

"Where the hell is she?" asked David, "Her old man's sent us on a wild goose chase."

The car nearest me was skeletal and exposed. It had no engine, or bonnet, just an open wound where its front had once been. Something made me walk over to it to take a closer look and that's when Emma leapt up with an almighty, "AAAAHHHHH!!!"

Now I admit, it did make me jump, but David, well he near enough ran a mile. He stumbled back and almost lost his footing. Emma howled with laughter.

"You should have seen your faces," she cried. "Dave, I thought you were gonna shit."

David didn't look amused. "I hope you cut yourself getting out of that engine bit and it goes bad septic 'un shit."

"My my, sore much," Emma said, "and… 'bad septic 'un shit' – such command of the English language, Boyle."

"Do one, Looms." He took off his oversized *Blues Brothers* shades.

She went to step out of the *engine bit* and held out her hand, wanting me to help balance her. I let her grab my forearm and she swung her legs over the wheel arch one after the other. Her hand on me felt like an electric charge. Once she was free, she gave me a smile. I looked at her mouth, then she let go.

She walked over to David and held out her arms.

"You want a hug to make up?" she asked.

"No!" he said, the tell-tale signs of another sulk coming on.

Emma just laughed and said, "Your loss, pal."

It most certainly was.

Emma had a boy's school satchel slung over her shoulder, its leather strap crossing her body, cutting between her breasts. I tried not to look. She wore denim shorts, frayed at the cut, and a tatty and faded Bruce Springsteen t-shirt. She looked amazing. She had her hair tied up. She was a brunette, but in the sunshine, it sometimes looked dark red. I know David had a thing for her, but I'd never told him how I felt. I hadn't told anyone.

Emma opened up the satchel and pulled out a pack of playing cards.

"Here you go, Boyle boy, you'll like these," she said, handing the cards over to David. I know for a fact he hated people calling him Boyle boy, but he seemed to let it slide with Emma. He'd always had trouble with bad acne and as such got teased mercilessly at school. His last name served his tormentors well.

He grabbed the cards and began to shuffle them, his eyes wide in wonderment.

"Bleeding hell, where'd you get these?" he asked.

"Found 'em. Find all sorts in these old cars," said Emma. "Once found a glove-box full of bras and knickers, and this other time, I found all these pictures of this naked guy and girl doing it. Found other stuff as well, like toys and clothes, and books 'n such... but I seem to find loads of dirty shit..."

She seemed proud of this, but David wasn't really listening, he was engrossed in the deck. He laughed and held up one of the cards to show me. It was the Eight of Clubs and had a picture of a naked woman in its centre. She was bent over a desk. I looked at Emma, and felt my cheeks flush. She laughed.

"Ahh, you're not shy are you, Crowhurst?" she said.

"No," I said, "give us a look—"

I went over to David and peered over his shoulder as he flicked through each card. They were really graphic. At least, they were in comparison to some of the tit mags I'd seen. These were hardcore.

"Ah man, these are great," said David, "Can I have 'em?"

"Sure," said Emma, "I don't want them, do I?"

"Wow, thanks."

She was watching us closely, studying our expressions as we looked through the cards. "God, boys are stupid," she said finally. "You're all so... *simple*."

David held up a particularly lurid Jack of Hearts and said, "There's nothing stupid about that arse!" Emma just rolled her eyes.

I shrugged, trying to act like I wasn't interested in the pictures and turned away. David carried on; he didn't seem to have any problem with staring at explicitly naked women in front of Emma, but I did. I kicked the dirt and went and stood on a flattened bonnet.

Emma lifted the strap of her satchel up over her head and then laid it down on the ground. I wondered if it was even hers, or just another thing she'd found. I figured the latter.

"So," she said, turning her attention to me, "what have Crowhurst and Boyle got in store for me today? Christ! Crowhurst and Boyle, you sound like bleedin' TV detectives or somethin'."

"Well, Sammy says he's got something to show us, Em..." David didn't look up from his playing cards, "... some derelict building or somethin'... My God, look at that! You can actually see her insides!"

"Nice," said Emma. "So what's this place then, Crowhurst?"

"It's pretty amazing, Em," I said, "you're gonna love it..."

We took the old rail lines out into the country. The sun was already high and beat down mercilessly; a heat more appropriate to July than September. On the TV they'd been calling it an Indian summer, and it was certainly the hottest it had been since late June, no mistake. They'd been saying that these temperatures could well run into October, and on days like this, you could almost believe it. The sky was a deep, majestic blue, broken only by brilliant white clouds that seemed simply to hang, as if painted on. Leaves were turning to their autumn decay – the tracks were laden with them – yet the trees themselves were still fairly green and full, unusually so for this time of year. In years gone by, you'd often feel the fresh nip of autumn in the week or so leading up to school, and the trees would already be falling to skeletal statues. But not this year. This year had felt like one long summer, beginning as far back as April, and it still showed no sign of letting up.

We continued on down the track, the three of us kicking leaves and making small talk. Emma and David were talking about school and how they really didn't want to go back, but my thoughts were elsewhere. I was back at the Electric. It never really escaped my thoughts. Even with everything else that had happened during the morning, it still lingered. The Electric felt like an itch on my mind. I couldn't rationalise it, I just kind of accepted it as yet another mystery connected with that broken-down old cinema. All I knew was that I had to get back there. I had no idea why other than if I didn't, the itch on my mind would just become too maddening to bear.

"Where we going then, Sam?" asked Emma.

"Down to the river again, and then I'll lead us from there."

"The river?" said David. "There's naff-all round there…"

"Shut it, Boyle boy!" I said, immediately wishing I hadn't. My tone had sounded much too harsh, and I especially hadn't meant to use that particular nickname, it just kind of slipped out. Dave looked hurt. He scowled and said, "Piss off!" – real venom in his throat.

He thrust his hands in his pockets and went on down the track, kicking leaves. Emma looked at me, frowning, trying to read the situation. I knew I had to say something to make the peace.

"Dave!" I called, "Look, sorry mate, I didn't mean to… It's just this place, I…"

I couldn't form the words. I had no way of explaining the hold the Electric had over me. It would just seem ridiculous. It was a derelict old cinema, nothing more; they'd think me half-crazy if I started talking about the pull it had on me – that my every thought since its discovery had been shadowed and shaped by it. They'd think I'd finally lost it, and who'd blame them? I was beginning to wonder myself.

David turned and stood waiting for us to catch up.

"You can be a real dickhead sometimes, you know," he said to me.

"I know mate, sorry. I didn't mean it. Look, you guys are gonna love this place, I promise."

"What the hell is it, Sam?" asked Emma.

"To be honest, I'm not even sure myself anymore."

We left the tracks and made our way down a steep hillside towards the river. We could see it in the distance, glistening silver, snaking through the green and undulating peaks and lows of the country. From this vantage point, I tried to pick out the field I had stumbled upon the night before. The one with the old shack at the lower end of the field, but I couldn't see it. I told myself that perhaps I was still too far away to pick out such a small crumbling structure amidst the landscape, or that it was just hidden from view behind trees or what-have-you, but it did concern me. Again, I began to doubt whether any of it had happened at all. I found that I no longer trusted my memory; the events at the Electric were blurred, hazy like a dream. I hoped I could find it again.

The thought suddenly frightened me. What if I couldn't find it? I wasn't so concerned with the shit David and Emma would give me for wasting their time, it was the itch in my mind that really frightened me. Would it worsen if I didn't return to the Electric? I didn't want to find out, because I had a strong feeling I already knew the answer.

Trying desperately to rationalise this weird pull, I wondered if the reason for me wanting to get back there so badly was simply down to the fact that it was a spooky old picture house, and what kid could resist that? Plus it had a poster for a Humphrey Bogart film.

One that doesn't exist, Sammy Boy.

It had to be that simple. Maybe I'd just been building all this up in my head – an overactive imagination juiced into overdrive by the atmospheric creep of a derelict cinema. Hell, any building left to decay for years and years would surely give anyone the spook, right? That had to be it. I also had to consider my borderline obsession with all things *Movies*, but moreover, the connection I had with Bogart and my old man. My dad would have loved that poster.

That was more likely the reason as to why I'd become so attached to the place.

It was the only rational explanation, and yet, as much as I tried to convince myself, I knew it wasn't the right one. There was something more, and I knew it.

There was something that I'd been keeping at bay, behind the itch, something I dared not confess to myself.

I knew it would come to me once I was back at the Electric.

And while that thought pulled me along step by step, it also made me sick with an inexplicable dread.

I saw my first movie at the Trocadero in town, aged four. The film had been Walt Disney's *The Jungle Book*, which must have been on a limited re-release at the time. My mother had taken me, and according to her, while every other kid in the theatre was either yapping or bawling, I was apparently transfixed from the opening frame to the last. Movies never really went away for me from that day forth.

I discovered old horror and science fiction movies on TV soon after – all those wonderful Universal monster flicks, and fifties sci-fi like *Invaders from Mars* (which scared the hell out of me) and *Creature from the Black Lagoon*. I loved that stuff. Then I went the usual route for a kid my age and discovered the worlds created by Spielberg and Lucas, opening up my imagination forevermore.

When I was about eight or nine, I discovered *Jaws*. Or should I say, I discovered there was such a movie, and I wanted to see that film so badly I would have bargained my life on a ticket. You see, in the late seventies, in the days before the video revolution, films were ephemeral. There was one cinema local to us (before my knowledge of the Electric, of course), and that was the aforementioned Trocadero, which was all the way in town, ten miles away. If you missed a film when it came to town, well that was pretty much it, pal. *Jaws* was first released in 1975, when I would have been much too young to see it. After that, well it was pot luck whether it came to town again.

My dad had seen it, however, the summer it was released, and once in a blue moon we'd settle down after dinner and I'd listen, enraptured, as he told all about the film. I began to draw imagined scenes from *Jaws*, just by going on what my dad had described, or by copying any pictures I'd find from the film in books or magazines, often cutting them out and pinning them to my wall.

I seem to remember that I spent a lot of time in my room around that time. I'd escape into comics such as *Savage Sword of Conan, Heavy Metal* and the cash-in magazine that came out in the wake of *Jaws* in '75, *Jaws of Horror*.

Occult warlords, buxom sword-wielding vixens, bloodthirsty barbarians, and of course, killer sharks, were my thing during that time and I devoured every comic I could get my hands on. It seems to me now that my imagination was going through some kind of fertile period; it was opening up, or should I say, being opened up by the likes of Robert E. Howard and Peter Benchley and Steven Spielberg.

I began to draw more and more. At first it was just *Jaws*-inspired stuff, then my sketches began to take on a more fantastical edge – no doubt inspired by the landscapes of *Conan* – and after a time, I began to draw characters and worlds created from my own imaginings – pictures of fantastical worlds, where warriors sailed across dark, raging oceans to battle huge sea creatures beneath brooding and thunderous skies. They were pretty crude, but I kept working at it, and slowly but surely, I began to develop a kind of style of my own. After a time, I showed a few of my drawings to David and he just flipped for them. Before I knew it I was drawing comic panels and bringing them into school the following day to show the other kids.

One panel story got me into a lot of trouble. Eager to impress my small, but devoted, legion of fans, I drew a scene in which a young Princess took off her bra before a battle-scarred Knight – the lack of black lacy bras in the middle-ages didn't seem to trouble this artist. It was, as you can imagine, a huge hit. In fact, it was so huge it became the talk of the playground within about half an hour, and the one copy in existence was soon confiscated by Mrs Pritchard, who gave me a firm talking to about exploitative and lurid material. She told me I was better than that and that I didn't need to lower myself to drawing smut in order to impress my friends. But the thing was, my friends *were* impressed and they wanted more. It was my first banned work, and that was very cool indeed.

For a short while afterwards, breasts became something of a focal point in my work. But I never took those pieces into school again. Whenever David, or another kid from that period, a lad named Nigel Woodings, would come round, they would both go straight to my latest stash of buxom warrior women and scantily-clad princesses.

A lot of my drawings seemed to be set on the high seas, and more often than not, amidst the sword-wielding barbarians and aforementioned female fantasies, there were sharks. They remained a fixture in my imagination. In my drawings they were the size of galleons – which they often tried to devour whole – with teeth the size of telegraph poles. They were pretty ridiculous, but at the time, the bigger and more ferocious the better in my book. It seems to me now that a film I hadn't even seen had fuelled my imagination to the point of creation. If it wasn't for my constant imagining of what that film was like, I probably would have never picked up a pencil to begin with. I found an outlet for my imagination. Even then I understood the power of cinema; how its imagery can hook into our very dreams and shape who we become.

One rainy April afternoon, shortly after my controversial first tit picture, I was in the kitchen with my mother. I must have been about eleven by this time. Mum was reading the local paper while I sat at the table eating a sandwich. Without a word, she placed a page down in front of me. I saw it right away; it was an ad for the Trocadero that read *THIS WEEKEND ONLY*, below which, in huge bold white lettering, was the single word *JAWS*.

Mum and Dad both came; they knew how important this was to me. We went to the Friday night showing. We had to queue outside in the rain, but I didn't care. Dad hummed the famous *Jaws* theme as we headed inside, goofing around like he did. The movie itself: well, it pretty much pinned me to the back of my seat from the get-go. Some parts I even found a little too scary. However, that famous scene where Richard Dreyfuss' character Matt Hooper dives down to investigate the floating wreck of Ben Gardener's boat, and the blue and corpse-less head suddenly pops out from a hole in the hull, well it was my dad who near enough jumped out of his skin, not me – and he'd seen it before! Popcorn flew everywhere and Mum and I burst into laughter. He grabbed me in a headlock and ruffled my hair. Mum told us both to behave then, and Dad and I sat, sunk in our seats, sniggering like two naughty schoolchildren.

It became more than just the night I finally got to see *Jaws* for me. It became a poignant memory of my parents together, and moreover, the moment I return to again and again when thinking of my dad. They say it's the simple things in life you come to cherish, and I guess they're right. That film is forever entwined with my dad.

Soon after seeing *Jaws,* I started going to the pictures with my friends – guess I just hit that age where it just wasn't cool to go and see a film with your parents any longer. Dad and I would have our little Bogart marathons, but I never went to see another film with him at the cinema. A little over two years after we saw *Jaws* as a family, my dad died, and I never watched that film again.

I also stopped drawing altogether.

We passed the river, and although it took me a little while, I finally found the field with the shack. I knew that through the copse lay the Electric, and at that, my stomach lurched.

The crooked shack was a marker, beyond which lay another world.

It certainly seemed like that anyway; the events of the previous night felt like some distant dream, and my memory of what I had seen, and moreover, what I had felt there, now seemed completely untrustworthy. Dreams are deceivers after all; nothing is ever what it seems.

And yet, as dreamlike as the events now appeared, I still felt sure they *had* happened, however vague my memory. The details may have become hazy, but the feeling the place had given me – that strange electrical charge of emotion – still lingered deep within. I figured it was this that was pulling me back there, however thin my memory now appeared to be.

For reasons beyond my understanding, the old Electric cinema had its hooks in my mind and it wouldn't let go.

"That can't be it!" said David. "Please tell me you haven't dragged us all the way out here to show us a rickety old shed?"

"Yeah," I said, deadpan.

"You've gotta be shittin' me, Crowhurst!"

We were halfway across the field, the shack looking as frail and as crooked as I remembered it.

Emma said, "Is this really what you've brought us out here to see, Sam?"

I smiled at her, but didn't say anything. I wasn't entirely sure why I was playing this game, other than I knew I wanted them both to see the Electric as I had seen it – with unexpected eyes.

"What's in the shed then, O mysterious one?" asked Emma, pressing her palms together and bowing to me in prayer.

"Is it a stack of porno mags!?"

"Jesus, Dave! Do you ever think about anything else?" said Emma.

"Not when you're wearing those cut-offs, no. They just drive me cr-r-razy!"

I bit my lip. This bold flirtation was a little out of character for David and it quite surprised me.

Emma responded with, "Go chew on your own dick, Boyle Boy."

"You wanna watch?"

"You wish."

The wind picked up and rustled through the treetops. Along the breeze came the squawk of some kind of bird. Might have been a buzzard. I looked up but couldn't see anything other than a few scudding clouds riding the piercing blue of the Indian summer sky. There probably wasn't another soul around for miles.

As we neared the shack, Emma said, "This isn't it, is it?"

I looked at her and couldn't help but grin, which of course gave me away.

"No, you're quite right, Em, this isn't it."

"So what've we come all the way out here for then?" asked Dave.

"Follow me. It's through the trees."

I led them down the forgotten path. Sunlight splintered through the canopy, throwing thin slices of illumination all around the dim and shadowy copse. Again I glimpsed the Electric's marquee through the trees, but quickly averted my eyes. I didn't want to draw attention to it. Just that single glimpse, however, was enough to send a shot down my spine. Neither David nor Emma noticed the marquee.

My heart pounded as we neared the tree line. The path ran out through an opening between two thick, gnarly old trunks. I turned to David and Emma. "This is it," I said, and took the lead, stooping down to avoid low-hanging branches.

I held my breath as I stepped out into the clearing.

There stood the Electric in all its decaying beauty.

Memories of the previous night refocused in my mind with such blindingly sharp clarity that I gasped. Everything came back in a rushing wave. Suddenly there was such detail to my recollections. I could smell the place, taste it, feel its decay.

The marquee loomed above that dark and eerie lobby entrance and I remembered the fear I had felt looking at the movie posters, and of the strange tramp sat alone in the auditorium, watching an empty screen. I recalled everything about him: his thick ageing beard and the vibrant, spellbinding coat he had worn. But moreover, I remembered his eyes, bright green and glistening otherworldly in the gloom. He hadn't looked real; he had looked like a projection, like something out of a movie from the fifties, one of those they filmed in Glorious Technicolor, only he had been solid and undeniably *there*. He had looked right into my eyes and I had fled. I wondered then if he was still sitting in the auditorium, waiting for a film that never would begin. That now familiar charge shot down my back again and churned my stomach.

So consumed was I with my own memory surge that I momentarily forgot that David and Emma were standing at my side. I looked at them and knew, just from their expressions alone, that the Electric had taken its mysterious hold on them within an instant. Both were dumbfounded, Emma especially. Her mouth hung open and her eyes were wide with questioning wonder. I couldn't help but feel utterly relieved that they both saw it too – not just the building, I mean, but the sheer aura of the place; that strange hold that dug into your mind and wouldn't let go. Nothing before had ever made me feel like that, and I guess, looking back, if Dave and Em had simply seen the

Electric as just a decaying old building, then I believe I may have gone slightly mad. But I knew it had them and nothing for us would ever be the same again.

Emma's first words regarding the Electric were "it's beautiful", and indeed it was. There was beauty in its decay and beauty in its nostalgia, but moreover, there was immense beauty in its *hold*, although it was certainly bittersweet. The fear still lingered, but it was far outweighed by my curiosity and by the sheer pull the place had on me.

"It's quite a find, hey?" I said. They both looked at me, their answers shining in their eyes.

David said, "I can't believe I ever doubted you, Sergeant Slaughter."

"A true soldier should never lack vision, Corporal Bad Ass. You must have faith until the final end."

"What are you two going on about?" said Emma, frowning. "Shut it weirdos, and let's get in there!"

David saluted her. "Right you are, Private Looms."

"A Private! You're joking aren't ya— Big Ass Boyle, or whatever your name is… I'd certainly outrank the pair of you two numbskulls by sheer intelligence alone."

David and I looked at one another. "She's not wrong," I said.

"Speak for yourself, Slaughter."

"Enough!" said Emma. "Sam, I can't believe this place. I've never even heard of an old cinema being out here."

"Nor have I," I said. "First I knew was when I stumbled upon it last night."

"Did you go inside?" she asked.

I thought about the Technicolor tramp. "Yeah, I went in."

"You went in on your own!" said Dave, clearly stunned by the idea. "It would have been getting dark by then, surely?"

"Yeah it was. I went in at sunset."

I had a strong urge to tell them more, to tell them everything, but I didn't. I wasn't sure how they'd take me for one thing, but also, I still wanted them both to experience the place without any preconceived notions. There was the danger as well that if I was to tell them everything, they may not go in at all. David especially.

"Does it still have a screen?" asked Emma.

I looked at them both for a moment, then said, "I think it's best if you see for yourselves."

We all fell silent as we approached the Electric. Once our feet found the cracked concrete of the long-since grand entrance, we all stopped and looked at one another. Something unspoken passed between us; it was nothing any of us could articulate or fully understand, but I guess we were all sensing the same thing – something was very different here.

David looked up at the marquee and at the few letters that remained – the N, the A and M, and the broken in half F. It came to me then that it could well have been the Bogart film, *When the Night Came Fallin'*, that had last played the Electric. Certainly the spacing of the remaining letters would suggest so, not to mention the fact that the film's poster was displayed by the lobby doors, as if it had been the premier attraction.

"How long has this place been empty?" David asked.

"Who knows," I mumbled.

"Been stood out here rotting for decades by the look of it," said Emma.

David gave a puzzled look, then said, "So how come no-one knows about it?"

"Somebody must," said Emma.

I looked at her. "Come on," I said, and walked towards the lobby doors. I glanced at the movie poster, Bogart and his gun, and the dead body floating on a winding brook. I fully expected that electric spike of nausea to rush through me again, but it didn't. I could look at the poster without feeling like I wanted to puke, which somehow felt stranger to me than if I had wanted to. I then begin to question myself, wondering once again if I'd just imagined the entire thing. But then Emma doubled over.

"Oh God! Feel like I'm gonna hurl," she said, bent forward, hands gripping her knees.

Once turned away from the poster however, she went from looking deathly white, eyes streaming, mouth locked tight, to looking fine again almost within an instant. It was quite something to behold; a sudden transformation. Like something from a movie. She stood up and wiped her eyes.

"I don't know what the hell happened…" she said.

"You okay?" I asked.

"Yeah," she said, unsure. "That was seriously weird."

I wanted to console her, tell her it had happened to me also, but David caught my attention. He was standing directly in front of the Bogart poster, gazing at it intently. He didn't appear to be showing any signs of the sickness and overwhelming nausea that both Emma and I had, instead he simply stared, almost transfixed. I went over and put my hand on his shoulder. He flinched. "Christ! What?"

"Nothing," I said, "I was just seeing if you were all right."

"Course I am. Why wouldn't I be?"

"No reason. You like the poster?"

"Sure, it's probably dull as dishwater though – all those old black 'un whites are. You like all that shit don't ya?"

"Yeah," I said. "I used to watch Humphrey Bogart films with my old man."

Any mention of my dad always made David extremely uncomfortable, and this was no exception. We had never really had a full conversation about his death, and whenever it came up, he was always quick to change the subject. But to be fair to David, I was always quite happy about that.

He avoided my eyes and looked back at the poster. "You seen this one?"

"No," I said. I looked at Bogart – profile cast in *noir* shadows, revolver ready to sink a slug into some bad guy – and although it didn't make me feel ill, it did still look strange to me. "In fact," I continued, "I've never even heard of this one."

"There's something weird about that picture," said Emma.

I hadn't noticed until she spoke that she was now standing beside me. She was looking directly at the poster, her own wave of revulsion now entirely passed.

I looked at her and I said, "I felt it too. Last night."

I didn't need to elaborate, she knew exactly what I had meant.

David cut in. "Bogart looks freaky deaky, man."

"He does look strange," said Emma. "I can't put my finger on it. It *does* look like him, but just slightly odd somehow – unnatural almost."

"Maybe it's one of them lookalikes," said David.

"Hey yeah, that would explain why I couldn't find any mention of this film in my Bogart book."

"Well if it's not him," said Emma, "how could they get away with having that large Humphrey Bogart star billing across the top of the poster?"

"I don't know," said David, "maybe they found a lookalike with the same name and those Hollywood bigwigs they just... you know, couldn't believe their luck!"

Emma narrowed her eyes. "How have you made it to this age?" she said. He ignored her.

"There's another poster inside," I said. "For a Harold Lloyd film."

"Did it..." Emma began, but faltered, perhaps unable to fully understand the question she wanted ask. I knew what she meant though.

"Yeah, the same feeling," I said, "but it passed right away. Like now."

"What you two talking about?" asked David.

I looked at Emma and she gave a thin, bitter smile.

"Nothing," I said to David. It went unspoken, but both Emma and I seemed to know that what we had felt would now remain between us. David hadn't experienced anything, and somehow that had immediately created a kind of divide. He only saw the Electric, it seemed, for what it was on the surface: a dilapidated old picture house left out here to rack and ruin, whereas Emma and I were feeling that this place was something more. We both felt it and it had given us a kind of union that hadn't been there before. I couldn't work out if it was my imagination or not, but she seemed to be looking at me a little differently now. Her eyes were intense and I had to look away.

"Anyway, freaks," said David, "we gonna check this place out or what?"

There were faces in the ceiling. I hadn't noticed them in the dying light of the previous evening, but now, in the sunlit height of the day, I could clearly make out the carved phizogs staring down at us. They weren't pretty either, although I guess the craftsmanship had to be admired for such exquisite detail. Sharp and dangerous-looking features leered down into the lobby, owing more to gargoyles than impressions. It was the eyes that struck me the most. Even from down in the lobby I could make out the rich detail in their almost penetrating gazes. There were six faces in all, carved into corners of the coving; some laughed manically, two simply stared darkly, while another, looking down from high above the kiosk, stuck out an impossibly long tongue, its eyes wide in malevolent mirth.

My attention was pulled away by David, who was now round the back of the kiosk searching for anything of interest. He banged an old boot on the counter and shrugged his shoulders at me, then returned to rummaging about back there. Emma was standing near me, exploring the lobby as I had the night before – with bright, wondrous eyes.

She went to walk across to the Harold Lloyd poster, but failed to notice a cracked tile beneath her feet. It caught her off guard – as the floor had done to me the night before, twisting the Crowhurst ankle – and she stumbled. I rushed forward and caught her, one hand wrapping around her waist, the other gripping her arm. She gasped and leaned into me. She looked up and wrinkled her nose, smiling.

"Thanks," she said.

I could think of nothing to say. I was extremely aware of every part of her that I could feel, particularly her right breast, which was squashed up against the back of my hand. I was also well aware that I'd been holding onto her for longer than was necessary, yet still seemed unable to either speak, or more importantly, let go.

"I'm okay, Sam," she said, "you can let me go…"

"Sorry." I released her and stepped back. She smiled at me – again with that intense, almost knowing look that I had no understanding of whatsoever – and went over to look at the Harold Lloyd poster.

Behind me, David had found a flyer of some kind and was stood reading it.

"I haven't heard of any of these films," he said.

I went over to the kiosk and leaned on the counter, immediately felt the thick layer of dust and grime beneath my elbows, and stood straight back up again, wiping the dirt away. David chuckled at me. "You're the film nut, Crowhurst— you heard of any of these?" He handed me the flyer. On faded yellowy paper, the edges torn and crumpled, dense Gothic handwriting read:

The Electric Cinema Proudly Presents

All New Productions!

When the Night Came Fallin'

Starring Humphrey Bogart, Jean Harlow & Victor McLaglen
Directed by Benjamin Christensen

Mad Dogs

Starring Harold Lloyd, John Belushi,
& guest starring Betty Grable
Directed by Harold Lloyd

A Murder Of Crows

Starring Boris Karloff, Bela Lugosi, Lon Chaney,
Theda Bara & guest starring Peter Lorre
Directed by Tod Browning

It was difficult to read, the handwriting spidery and faded, but I took particular care, noting every actor's name. "This is well weird," I said, mostly to myself.

"What?"

"Well, it just doesn't make any sense."

"What do you mean?"

"You read it, didn't you? These names…"

Emma came over and stood next to me. She looked pale and scared. Her eyes glistened with welled tears. I knew the Harold Lloyd poster had worked its bizarre magic.

She said, "What the hell is wrong with this place?"

"I don't know," I said, and I truly didn't. "Look at this." I handed her the flyer. She read it over and then looked at me, and then at David.

"This is impossible," she said. "They must be fake films… you know, like amateur shit with actors dressed up like Bogart, or Lugosi, or whoever."

"They have to be," I said, unconvinced.

"What're you two talking about?" asked David.

We both stared at him.

Emma said, "How dense are you, Dave?"

"What?"

"These stars…" she said, "they could never have made these films together."

"Why not?"

"Jesus! Look!" She held up the flyer and pointed to the credits of *Mad Dogs*. "How could John Belushi have made a film with Harold Lloyd? Or Betty Grable for that matter!"

"I don't know who most of these people are – apart from

Belushi, of course. Oh, and them Dracula and Frankenstein guys."

"So you know Belushi's dead, right?" I asked.

"Yeah sure, the other year…"

"Well, Harold Lloyd was like a silent comedian back in the 1920s," I said.

David frowned, trying to piece together the puzzle. "So when did Harold Lloyd die then?"

"I don't know," I said.

"Christ, Crowhurst, I thought you knew everything!"

"Well I'm pretty sure Harold Lloyd wasn't around making films when Belushi was… and he certainly wouldn't have still looked like that—" I pointed over to the torn *Mad Dogs* poster. "He would have been ancient!"

"Sam," Emma said. "I'm sure Jean Harlow died in the thirties – she was really young. I remember mum showing me a picture of her when I was really little. I loved her hair."

"What's your point?" I asked.

"When was Bogart a big star?"

"The forties, mainly. But he had been making stuff since the twenties, I think."

"So Jean Harlow could've made a film with Bogart then?"

"I guess, but if it'd been early in his career, I doubt he would've got top billing like this."

"Look," said David, "I don't know what the big deal is. Someone's just mocked these things up. Like Em said, they're probably just actors pretending to be them."

"But why?" I said.

"How the hell should I know? Maybe they're just big fans or something… total geeky nerds – like you, Crowhurst!"

I laughed, as did Emma. It relieved a little of the tension, but it was short-lived. A sound came from the top of the grand staircase. We all heard it and looked up into the gloom, towards the auditorium doors. It had been a creaking of some kind, like a dicky floorboard being stepped on, low, but quite audible in the stillness of the cinema.

"There's somebody up there," Emma said.

I went cold. The Technicolor tramp was still here.

"It's probably just the building," said David. "It's an old place…"

Emma looked scared. "It sounded like somebody moving around up there."

"Jesus, Em! I thought you were the smart one!" David looked at us with a sort of pained expression. "What is it with you two today?"

Neither Emma nor I could answer. That divide was growing ever deeper and wider. It felt a little like all our own characteristics had simply gone awry. Emma would normally be the headstrong and logical of us, while David would often shy away from anything even remotely bordering on the dangerous (unless, that is, he felt sure there wasn't a chance of him getting caught, then his true nature would surface). This role reversal seemed to only confirm further that this place was somehow *wrong*. Emma was feeling it too, and because of this, the strangeness had intensified.

Before returning to the Electric, the events of the previous night had felt distant to me; it had been there, but it was like trying to reach for a fading dream. Now, however, everything was clear.

A phrase came to me then:

I can see with better eyes.

I didn't know what it meant; it was nonsensical, but nevertheless, the words framed in my mind like a neon sign – bright with a relevance I had yet to understand.

David came from around the kiosk and marched past us, shaking his head.

"Well, you wimps can stay here if you like," he said, "but I'm going up to check out the cinema."

Emma looked at me and raised her eyebrows in a kind of *I've-gotta-see-this* expression. I gave a sharp, nervous laugh; it sounded hollow and forced to my ears.

David got to the red carpeted staircase and stopped. He stared up at the auditorium doors. Watching him, I suddenly understood that all this cocksure courage had been nothing but an act. He was scared as well, and there was a certain relief in knowing that.

It was also comical to see him standing there, wondering what to do. He turned to us and looked so forlorn and pathetic that both Emma and I burst out laughing.

He got defensive. "What ya laughin' at?"

"Nothing," said Emma. "You get up there, Boyle Boy — us wimps will be right behind you."

He tried to ignore that comment, but I could see it had pissed him off something rotten. If I'd said it he would've jumped down my throat, but as it was Emma he, of course, let it pass.

"Well I think we should all go up," he said. "That way, if there is anyone up there, we'll be able to take him."

"What are you talking about, you psycho!" said Emma.

"You know, in case someone leaps out at us."

Emma laughed, but I didn't.

"Again, I've got to ask Dave – how have you made it this far in life?"

"Oh, you're well funny, Em," he said through gritted teeth. "Now you two comin' or what?" There was desperation in his eyes.

The balance was restored.

The three of us walked up the staircase pretty much side by side, although David tended to hang back a step or two. I became aware of Emma's hand beside my own, close enough to sense. I wanted to take hold of it, but resisted. I was unsure of how Emma would react, but moreover, I just knew David would quite simply piss himself laughing if I was to try anything in his presence.

The auditorium doors were closed, although I was pretty sure I hadn't shut them behind me when I legged it the night before. I felt certain that I'd left one of the double doors ajar, and that I had simply slipped on through, both in and out. The hinges must have dropped because the door had dragged into the carpet, I remembered that. Someone must have shut it after I'd left. The Technicolor tramp, no doubt.

At the top of the staircase I saw that the stairs narrowly split off to the right, leading to an upper level. I wondered how I had failed to notice that before, but then, it had been dark.

David nudged me, "Come on then, Crowhurst, you brought us here. Lead on."

He'd always been good at making people do things he didn't necessarily want to do himself, but I suppose in this instance David was right, I had brought them here, so it was only right that I show them around.

I gripped one of the handles and pulled. The door screeched open, dragging well into the carpet. We all peered in. Balcony seats cut jagged in the gloom, beyond which, across the Electric's once grand auditorium, the ashen grey cinema screen loomed large.

"Smells like your socks in there, Crowhurst," said David, peering over my shoulder.

"Good one," I said, dry as a bone.

I stepped inside and sensed Emma and David following behind. I looked out over the balcony and peered down into the murk, trying to pinpoint the area where I'd seen the tramp the night before. There was no sign of him though. I turned and scanned the balcony seats around me, but there was no one sitting in wait for us. The auditorium was completely empty. I felt a strange mix of relief and, to my surprise, slight disappointment.

"Doesn't seem to be anyone here," I said.

"You sound surprised," said Emma.

I didn't say anything. I wondered why I had kept the

Technicolor tramp from them. Maybe it was because saying it aloud would make it all the more real; it frightened me to admit to myself, but he had just been too damn strange to be real. No one could emanate such vibrancy of colour and presence, surely...

Yet, I felt certain that had been exactly how I had seen him. Like a vivid painting imprinted on reality.

I just wasn't ready to tell Emma and David. It was their questions I was afraid of the most. Or more to the point, the answers I would have to give.

"This must have been quite a cinema back in its heyday," said Emma. "I can just imagine all the ladies dressed in fine jewellery and glamorous frocks and the men all handsome and dashing in their suits and ties. Folk used to really dress up to go out to the pictures back then."

"Back when?" David asked.

"I don't know, back in the forties and fifties, I guess..."

"What makes you think this place was open then?"

"Well, it can't have been too recent, look at the place. Plus, I think we'd have heard about it if it'd been around in the seventies or something."

"Not necessarily."

Emma fell silent. David was right. Just because we'd never heard of the Electric before didn't mean it was this secret place that folk back in town had no clue about it. It was more likely quite well-known, or it had been once upon a time. Some of our parents, maybe even our grandparents, had most probably come here when they were young – maybe I should've mentioned it to my mother after all.

Once a place gets shut down, it is easily forgotten. Especially somewhere like the Electric, stood so far from public view. This triggered a question.

"Why the hell would anyone build a cinema all the way out here?" I asked. "It just doesn't make any sense."

"Maybe it was someone's private cinema," said David. "Like

some rich eccentric or something…"

"It's a big cinema for one person," said Emma.

"Maybe he had a lot of friends. Everybody wants to be your friend if you've got shit loads of money."

"Such a wise old sage you are, Boyle."

"Why, thank you, ma'am."

He bowed to her and she reached out and ruffled his hair.

"Hey!"

"You loved it." She gave him a hell of a smile and I felt a twinge of jealously.

I turned my back on them and walked off along the balcony. I noticed a small dark hole up in the centre of the back wall and realised that through the opening would have once been the projection room. The stairway to the upper level must lead up there. All of a sudden I felt a rush. I had to go and check it out. It was that old *Electric* pull again – the pull that had been consuming me ever since I'd first set foot in the building. I thought of my soul being caught on a fishhook. There was something important in that projection room, something I needed to find. Again, I had no idea how I knew that, I just did.

I could see with better eyes.

I rushed from the auditorium without a word. David shouted after me, but I didn't stop. I saw that the upper level was drenched in sunlight. I ascended the narrow staircase in a leap and a bound. Then I stopped dead.

A corridor ran off to the right, three windows along it, all of them smashed in. Glass decorated the mouldy old carpet, catching the light and teasing my eye. There were two doors along the corridor, both of them shut. Something about them being shut unnerved me. I pictured the Technicolor tramp lying in wait for me behind one of the doors.

"Sam?"

Emma's call made me jump. I turned and saw her staring up at me.

"You all right?" she asked.

"Yeah. There's a couple of rooms up here. Reckon one of them must be the projector room."

David came to her side.

"It's bright up there," he said.

"Yeah, there's windows, but they're all smashed in."

Something occurred to me then, something depressingly obvious. Countless people must have stumbled upon the Electric over the years. This wasn't some secret place we'd found. Some other kids most probably smashed all these windows in – nothing like an old building and a set of windows to bone up on your target practice. Part of me had been thinking I'd discovered some sort of invisible world, a place slipped off map and memory, but this old cinema was more than likely pretty well-known. Every kid in town must know about it, especially older kids. They probably came out here to drink and get high and fool around with each other.

I felt disappointed, if not a little foolish. Many had passed through this place, most probably doing exactly the same as we were doing now, shuffling around its ancient rooms, exploring a past time captured in brick and mortar.

Those shut doors along the corridor no longer seemed so unnerving, and somehow, I felt a twinge of sadness about that. Was there really a mystery here? Whatever it was I felt in this place – whatever that strange hold the Electric seemed to have over me was – it was more likely just all in my head.

Yet.

Emma felt it too. I know she did.

I realised then that since first setting foot in this old cinema the night before, my emotions had grown wildly erratic. One minute I was sensing and seeing with complete clarity the mysterious and strange nature of the place, then suddenly, overwhelming doubt would take root and I'd question everything I'd felt so sure of just moments before. This pendulum of emotions had taken its toll and now I just felt tired. I didn't know what to think or feel any more.

"We going in then?"

It was Emma. She was standing next to me. I hadn't even noticed her come up the stairs.

"Yeah," I said, but my voice was flat and sounded far away.

She looked at me. "You sure you're okay?"

I blinked away my thoughts and looked around. David was standing on the top step, staring at me with strange, quizzical eyes. I turned to Emma. Her eyes were wide, full of concern. Her mouth was open.

"I'm fine – it's nothing. I was just thinking about my dad." I knew this would curb any further questioning, especially from David.

"Oh," is all Emma said. She touched my arm and squeezed, gently. Then she smiled; bittersweet and haunted by understanding. I had to look away.

I moved past her and made my way along the corridor. Glass crunched under my feet. Outside, the breeze had picked up; it rattled at the thin and rotten window frames. Above, clouds had rolled in, obscuring the sun. Treetops off in the copse rustled and leant. Emma and David walked behind me, their own shoes crunching into the glass carpet. I came to the first door and stood motionless, gazing at the handle.

David put his hands over his mouth and nose, muffling his voice. "Earth to Crowhurst, earth to Crowhurst. Is there anybody there?"

I turned and looked at him. Something in my face must have troubled him, because his hands fell from his mouth and he frowned in that kind of *what-the-hell-is-wrong-with-you* way that teenagers seem to have such mastery of.

I didn't like him looking at me like that, so I turned my back on him and gripped the handle. The door was stiff and I had to shove against it to get it open. Daylight fell on the room in a widening arch. It smelt old, as you can imagine, fusty and forgotten. It was also cold in there. My shadow entered the room, twisted and deformed by the jagged shapes it fell upon.

It was the projector I saw first; an ancient looking contraption, bulky and dominant in the centre of the room. My first thought was that it looked more like an old oven than a movie projector. It was huge, thick with dust and cobwebs. Also, to my surprise, I saw there was a spool of film still threaded through the machine.

I looked to the opening in the wall; long ago the flicking light of film would have projected out onto the screen below, filling the Electric with the might of imagination; of romance, adventure, comedy and horror; the myths of our species. The great mirror to our lives. Now the auditorium lay in silent dark, and the projector, a relic from that long gone time, was just left to dust and spiders. I stepped into the room.

There was a poster on the back wall for a film by Erich Von Stroheim. His name was above the title. It was called *This*

Heart's Lagoon and starred Rudolph Valentino and Dolores del Río. The picture had the two stars running hand in hand through a dark and shadowy tunnel. Behind them, at the mouth of this tunnel, several figures were hard on their tail. There was a tagline below the film's title, it read: *Love is a Deadly Game.* The poster didn't give me the same rush of nausea the others had, but straight away I knew something wasn't right about it. It was their faces, Valentino's and del Río's that is. They just looked wrong somehow, just like Humphrey Bogart and Harold Lloyd had done in their respective movie posters. Their faces had a look of some kind; like they'd seen too much, been witness to things beyond the pale.

Even as these thoughts came into my head I knew them to be completely irrational, yet, I guess I was just reacting impulsively to what I saw.

Their eyes looked haunted. There was no other way to explain it.

The thought made me shiver and I turned and walked across the room to the projector. David and Emma came in behind me.

Emma hugged herself and said, "Boy, it's freezing in here."

"Well, the room probably hasn't seen any sunlight for donkey's years," I said.

I was looking at the roll of celluloid. It ran from one spool at the top of the projector, twisting and turning down through a series of complex looking mechanisms – covered in cobwebs – to another spool at the machine's base. I cocked my head to the side and leaned in, trying to make out the image on the frames, but it was too dark to see clearly. I blew dust away and it kicked up into my face. This led to a hard, thick coughing fit that seemed to amuse David immensely. He stood watching me, a big stupid grin on his face. By the time I'd finished, my eyes were watering.

David said, "You all right there, sausage?"

I scowled at him. Emma was across the other side of the

room, looking over a small desk stacked high with papers. She glanced at me and said, "You'll live," then smiled brightly and returned to her snooping.

I coughed away yet more dust from the back of my throat – although it didn't require a repeat of the wrenching fit I'd just displayed – then said, "There's still film in this projector."

They both came over, although David hung back a little.

"Can you see what's on it?" Emma asked. She bent down to take a closer look for herself.

"No, it's too dark in here."

Emma stepped back, wrinkling her nose.

"Hold on," said David, "I think I've got some matches…" He pattered himself down.

"I wouldn't try it if I were you," said Emma.

"What… why?" he said.

"I'm sure I read somewhere that celluloid is highly flammable. Goes up like a rocket."

"What's celluloid when it's at home?"

"Film, Boyle." She pointed to the roll threaded through the machine. "This."

"Oh, right."

David really let things slide with Emma. Although his face did turn a deep shade of red. She didn't seem to notice though; she was busy inspecting the projector. David shuffled his feet, then watched Emma working her way around the machine. I knew he was looking at her body. I took a step forward and blocked his view. He grinned and gave me the finger.

Emma was now round the front of the projector, palms flat against the wall, peering through the opening, down into the auditorium below.

"You can see the whole place," she marvelled, mostly to herself.

Her foot knocked something hidden beneath a fusty green sheet. It sounded metallic. Whatever was under there, it was about three feet tall and circular. Emma saw that I'd noticed as well and gave me a quizzical frown.

"Take a look," I said.

She grinned, then bent down to grab the edge of the dirty old material. In one quick movement she pulled the sheet away, revealing a stack of film cans. The sheet snagged on the top few and the tower toppled, scattering the cans across the floor. One hit my foot. I crouched down and saw there was a label on the lid, handwritten; it read *When the Night Came Fallin'*.

I knelt down and read the label on each film can. All had the same handwritten scrawl across the lid. I came across the Harold Lloyd/John Belushi flick, *Mad Dogs*, and the Karloff and Lugosi horror, *A Murder of Crows*, from the flyer (at least, I assumed it was a horror movie, given its cast). There was also one entitled *Broken People,* and another called *Houses of the Hanged.* None of which I'd heard of (although *Houses of the Hanged* sounded like the kind of movie a fifteen-year-old could get pretty excited about). Nor had I heard of *Beggar's Ash*, *A Second Chance*, or *Ravens' Bower* for that matter.

I also came across *This Heart's Lagoon*, the Erich Von Stroheim film. I glanced up at the poster. Rudolph Valentino and Dolores del Río made my stomach give a quick lurch and I had to force myself to look away.

Emma and David were talking about something or other, but I took little notice. I grabbed for the can marked *When the Night Came Fallin'* and attempted to open the lid. I had to dig my nails under the lip to prise it free. It was stiff and awkward, but finally I managed. The lid came off and my heart sank. It was empty.

"Shit."

David heard me. "What's up, Slaughter?"

"Ah, nothing, it's just..." I trailed off, staring at the empty can.

Emma said, "What about the others?"

I cast the *Night* can aside and reached for another – *Houses of the Hanged*, to be precise. I had the same battle with the lid, but soon had it open. This time there was a roll of film inside, furled up, looking tatty and worn. The quality of these pictures would more than likely be dreadful, if they even played at all. I didn't know much, if anything, about preserving film stock, but I had an idea that these movies were now in a terrible condition.

With delicate fingers, I picked up one end of the celluloid, unrolled it a little, then tilted my head to the side to try and see what lay hidden within its frames. I couldn't see much at first, but then I shifted around on my knees and held it up to a long shaft of sunlight, which now streamed in through the windows out in the corridor.

The light caught the negative and revealed to me a steam train. But it didn't look like any steam train I'd seen before. It looked like a great black insect set upon a rail – that was the first thought that popped into my head anyway. Everything about its design was jagged and sharp. It looked deadly; a mechanical monster tearing on down the tracks. It billowed out huge plumes of smoke and fire from its tall, thin stack, which trailed out along its seemingly endless carriages (I assumed it was fire anyway, it was white on the celluloid). It occurred to me that it looked a little like something I would have once drawn. It had a certain *quality*, often found in the dark and *fantastique*. Nightmarish, you could say.

Each frame revealed more. The train tore through what looked to be a desert. The land was flat and empty, and the ground appeared to be cracked open in a network of deep, black lines. Above the train, the sky brooded with low, dense thunderheads. The old familiar *Electric* dread overwhelmed me once more, and I almost dropped the roll. It wasn't the train that unnerved me so much, it was the land. It made my skin crawl, although I couldn't have told you why exactly. I noticed gooseflesh all the way down my arms.

"What's on it?" asked Emma.

She came around behind me, bent down, resting her hands

on her knees, and leaned in over my shoulder. It felt like a long time before she said anything.

"It's... *wrong*," was all she could manage.

David cut in. "Give us a look—"

He came over and pretty much snatched the roll of film from me.

"Hey! Be careful with that."

"Whadda you care, Crowhurst?"

In that moment, everything changed between the three of us. It was the straw that broke the camel's back, as they say. The divide became irrevocably entrenched. I glanced at Emma. She was staring at David as if he was a stranger to us, and perhaps I did the same. David paid us no mind, he was busy squinting at the roll. He had it so close to his eye it was practically resting on his nose.

"It's just some train," he said, then added, "looks shit."

Emma looked over at me. Her eyes had welled. I tried for a sort of reassuring smile, something that would express to her that I understood, but all I could manage was a kind of dumb-looking grin. She turned away from me and walked across to the doorway. Her shadow threw shapes about the room.

David dropped the roll of film back into the can (with little care, of course), and that's when it happened.

There was a sudden, strong shift in the room; an over-whelming sense that something was in here with us. A presence. We all felt it, even David. We stood motionless, looking to one another like three cornered animals.

There was a loud click and we all turned to the projector. It whirred into life. Light blazed through the machine, striking the celluloid. It began to chatter through the mechanisms. Sound blasted out; a deep, throbbing piece of music that I could feel in the pit of my stomach. Light and image poured from the projector, out across the still theatre, and onto the screen beyond. I couldn't move. You've heard the tired old expression, *I couldn't believe my eyes*, well, I actually couldn't. I didn't trust the reality. It felt like a lie, a trick of some kind. Yet, somewhere deep within, I knew that this *was* indeed happening, and that frightened me very badly. I guess when faced with the strange and uncanny, we never trust our senses – instinct becomes polarised. The rational mind rejects the irrational. It's our defence mechanism.

My pendulum kept on swinging.

I looked at Emma; the side of her face was splashed with flickering light. She looked numb.

"Let's get outta here," shouted David, over the chattering teeth of film.

We fled.

It was Bogart's voice that caused me to stop dead in my tracks. I was passing the auditorium doors, both David and Emma ahead of me, bounding down the stairway. I could see flickering light through the darkened doors, and Bogart's voice, that unmistakable voice, was saying something about a deal gone sour, rotten to the core – pure hard-boiled talk, the kind you'd expect from a Bogart flick. His voice made me think of Dad right away, and I guess it was that which caused me stop.

"Wait!" I shouted. David had by now cleared the stairs and was crossing the lobby. He turned and looked up at me, as did Emma, who had just reached the foot of the stairs herself.

"I have to see," I said.

"You're on your own there, Crowhurst," replied David. "This place ain't right. We need to split."

"But..." I looked at Emma. I could see she was torn. She looked across at David, then up at me. After a moment, she gave me a thin smile, then started back up the stairs.

"Jesus!" cried David, "You two deserve each other."

I said, "What's that supposed to mean?"

"Nothing," he spat. "I'll see ya later." He turned on his heel and headed for the door.

"Dave," I shouted, but he didn't look back.

Emma came to my side. "Let him go," she said. Those words seemed loaded. I watched him slip on out the building, then looked at Emma. Her eyes were tearing. The film's soundtrack, a deep, bombastic score that throbbed and jabbed in manic scales, pulled at my very being. I had to see.

I held out my hand and Emma took it. In any other circumstance I wouldn't have dared such a bold move, but things were different here and we both knew it.

We entered the auditorium hand-in-hand.

A desert, dry and scaly, spread out beneath a brooding, threatening sky.

We stood at the back of the auditorium, staring at the screen, mouths agog – *catching flies*, as my old man used to say. Emma held my hand tightly, but I hardly noticed.

The camera panned across rolling dunes. I pictured the black train from the roll of celluloid up in the projector room. Somehow this looked and *felt* like the same landscape, although I didn't see how that could be.

A figure emerged from the dust. It was Bogart. His white shirt was dirtied and sweaty, and he wore a thick beard. He had a cut lip. His character had certainly been through the mill, it seemed. He looked as if he could have been playing Fred C. Dobbs once again, but this wasn't *Treasure of the Sierra Madre*, this was something else entirely.

It did look like Bogart, but somehow it didn't *feel* like Bogart. More to the point, nothing about the film felt like anything I'd ever experienced before. It had a texture, a tone that was completely alien to me. It made me nauseous to look directly at the screen. Yet, by the same token, I couldn't pull my eyes away. My stomach waltzed. I felt my legs weaken, and would have fallen had I not grasped the back of a seat with my free hand.

Bogart came to a ridge overlooking a great valley. A sparse township lay beneath the thunderous sky. It was the kind of shack town you'd see in westerns, only this town also had great towers jutting up from within the wooden structures – long, thin black steeples that appeared to lick the clouds. I glimpsed what looked to be walkways, running from tower to tower. They were impossibly high. Some were even shrouded in thunderheads.

The film cut back to Bogart. He rubbed his beard. Every crack and line in his face looked like a deep gorge. Briefly, I tried to convince myself that maybe David had been right, maybe this was a lookalike – just some actor *playing* Bogart. Indeed there was something strange and different about him, yet, I knew that that just wasn't the case at all. That *was* Bogart on the screen; whatever my confused state, I knew it to be true.

The action moved from the brooding desert and into a darkened saloon. Jean Harlow, the original blonde bombshell, was stood at the bar, bathed in noir lighting. She was as stunning and as iconic as she had been in the 1930s. I wondered if I was dreaming all this.

Harlow knocked back a shot and looked along the bar toward the saloon doors, which gently creaked in the dying light. A weather-worn figure appeared. Bogart. Like a cowboy from a thousand movies, he pushed the double-doors inwards, stepped through, then let them swing and creak behind him.

I watched the scene unfold in a kind of awestruck daze. I felt numb. I knew I was witnessing something extraordinary, but I was unable to process it properly. I continued to watch the screen, but something about the film wouldn't quite fix in my mind. The story itself seemed pretty standard by all accounts, yet the imagery just wouldn't settle and make sense.

Jean Harlow spoke. "They were meant to leave you for dead."

Her voice was cold and flat; a sure-fire *femme fatale*. Bogart stepped into razor shadow, half dark, half light.

"Sorry to disappoint you, sweetheart," he said in that old, familiar lisp, "but me and the boys had a change of plan."

Bogie crossed the room towards her, his footfalls echoed around the still of the saloon. She poured them each a drink, handing Bogart a glass as he reached the bar. He took it and knocked it back, then exposed his teeth in that characteristic Bogart grimace. They stood side by side, both captured in a beautifully-lit shot. Light poured onto Harlow, while Bogie remained half-eaten by shadows.

I found that I was weeping. I wasn't entirely sure why.

On the screen, Bogie said, "You know, you really should pay

more attention when hiring goons. Salter Harris and I, well, we go *way* back."

A stub-nosed revolver levelled at Bogie's chest. Harlow wore a look that could sink a ship.

"You think you're so smart, hey," she said. "A real tough guy. Well, I'll show you. I'll…"

Bogart grabbed her wrist and brought her arm down hard against the bar. The gun went off, the bullet exploding several bottles behind them. The shot made me jump. The gun fell from her hand and Bogart pulled her to him. She struggled at first, drumming her hands on his chest, but then she submitted. It was pure melodrama. Bogart always seemed to get his dames in this manner – I guess it was because his dames were always dangerous. Double-cross and murder were all part of a Bogart courtship, it seemed. They kissed and the music swelled. That's when I noticed, we were not alone.

The Technicolor tramp was sat in the same spot as before. I couldn't believe I hadn't noticed him right away. His thick, tangled head of hair stood wild in the monochrome light, his beard equally wiry, as if electrically charged. The vibrancy of his dark red coat was undiminished in the shadowy flicker – it practically throbbed. I heard Emma gasp and she near-enough crushed my hand. I didn't need to look at her to know that she had now seen him too.

Old TT was utterly engrossed in the film. When Bogart made some wisecrack to Harlow, the Technicolor tramp shook with laughter. The strangest thing though was that I couldn't hear him. He was rocking back and forth, laughing his head off, but I didn't hear anything other than the film. From this distance, I would have surely heard him, guffawing as he was. I thought perhaps he didn't have any vocal cords – was a mute maybe? But that didn't seem right. As strange as this entire situation was, it was somehow stranger still to see that old tramp laughing wildly and not even hear a squeak. It certainly heightened the sense of *wrongness*.

Emma whispered in the dark, "My God!"

She let go of my hand and stumbled back, her eyes fixed on some corner of the theatre. She crumpled down into a seat behind her, tears lining tracks down her face. I peered into the dark, trying to pinpoint where she was looking. I saw right away. There was a young couple sitting in a row towards the front of the screen. The guy had on a leather jacket and had his arm slung around the girl. His jacket creased the dark, almost shimmering, like an oil slick caught by the sun. The girl was slender and wore a pretty blouse. Her shoulders looked milky white in the gloom, uncommonly so. The flowers on her blouse were as vibrant and as startling as the tramp's winter coat. Her blonde hair was tied up with red ribbons, and these too looked unnaturally bright. I sat down next to Emma.

On the screen, a long black car was rolling into the desert town. Inside, the actor Victor McLaglen, whom I recognised from countless old films my dad used to watch, was sat in the back seat, positively brooding malevolence – undoubtedly the villain of the piece.

McLaglen pulled free a gun from inside his suit jacket and checked the chamber. Six bullets; all, I presumed, meant for Bogart. I wondered if we were watching the last reel. It certainly felt like the story was nearing its climax anyhow.

Emma found my hand again and there we sat, watching this strange, otherworldly film.

Otherworldly.

The word came into my head and took root. That was exactly how it felt. Otherworldly. Once I'd found the word, I knew it to be true. Again, it was irrational and completely improbable, yet I knew that we were indeed peering into another world. This film had been made *somewhere else*. That was Humphrey Bogart, and Jean Harlow, and Victor McLaglen, but they were not of *this* world.

I felt clammy. My t-shirt stuck to me and I kept shifting

in my seat. I suddenly wanted to get out of there very badly. Bogart was crouched down by one of the saloon windows, gun in hand, peering out at the approaching black car. The music wavered on a single, threatening note. It felt like it was cutting into my brain.

I turned to Emma. Beads of sweat had broken out at her brow and were running down her face. Her hair was damp. Her hand was still clamped around mine. She didn't look at me. She stared at the screen with saucer eyes, welled tears glistening like diamonds.

Something moved out in the darkness. I peered past Emma, down along the aisle, trying to focus on the shape. It was a figure, large and bulky. Emma noticed me staring and turned and looked for herself. The sight took her breath. The figure was an old woman, and she was heading straight for us.

She was a big lady, made bigger still by the thick coat she wore. Beneath a crumpled, lopsided hat flowed long slivery hair that fell about her shoulders. Her face was all puffy cheeks and jowls. She was looking right at us. I felt my skin crawl. Emma destroyed my hand.

When the Night Came Fallin' had reached its climactic gunfight. Shots boomed around the theatre. The big lady came and stood over me. I felt pinned to the seat. She looked at the screen, then down at me and smiled. It wasn't threatening or sinister, in fact, it was quite the opposite. It was friendly, kind. I could see that her silver hair possessed that same vibrant quality the other cinemagoers had. As did her coat, which was a rich, deep emerald. She sat down next to me. It took all my willpower to stop myself from screaming.

She watched the shootout; Bogart was filling the black car with lead, McLaglen was shielded around the other side of the vehicle, gun at the ready. The woman turned to me and spoke. At first I thought I couldn't hear because of the sound of gunfire, but then I realised that her voice was like the Technicolor tramp's laugh: it just wasn't there. I looked at her, she was still talking, but I couldn't hear a thing.

Beside me, Emma let go of my hand. She leaned forward and stared at the old lady. The lady noticed and gave Em a big grin and a sly wink, then continued to watch the film. Emma settled back in her seat. She looked bewildered and lost. I figured I wore the very same expression. The look of two people cast adrift in a world that peered into another.

McLaglen took a hit, knocking him across the dirt. Bogart levelled his gun for the kill shot. Jean Harlow placed her little stub-nosed revolver to the back of Bogie's head. A double-cross. Bogart dropped his gun and held up his hands.

"Sorry, Frank," said Harlow, "nothin' personal."

Then, on a close-up of Jean Harlow's sensuous face, the film came to an abrupt stop. The soundtrack popped and cracked, and the screen burned white. End of the reel. There was a sudden and startling quiet.

It happened almost at once. First, the old lady turned and stared at me. Then the Technicolor tramp stood and turned and did likewise, as did the young couple at the front of the theatre. The guy in the leather jacket had hard, sharpened features, and Elvis hair. The girl was extremely pretty, blue eyes unnaturally piercing the dark.

Emma grabbed my hand and whispered into my ear, "We need to go." I didn't need telling twice.

I stood up, pulling Em up with me. The old lady did nothing to stop us, nor did she say anything with her nonexistent voice, she just continued to stare. I couldn't read her expression.

As we backed away down the aisle, the Technicolor tramp caught my attention. He lifted his right arm and pointed up to the projection room. I followed his direction, looking up to the opening in the back wall. It lay in darkness.

We didn't run. I think we were too frightened to run. We backed out of the theatre as slowly and as carefully as we could. My heart was hammering in my chest the whole time and I felt sure the entire room could hear it.

I also felt sure that at any moment, this strange, threadbare audience would suddenly rush us. My imagination went into overdrive depicting the horrific, grotesque acts we would surely become victims to. I'd seen enough George Romero zombie movies to allow a full and hideous account in my mind. None of them came after us though. Not one of them so much as moved. They simply stared.

When we reached to the doors, I chanced one last look at the Technicolor tramp. He was standing beneath the dull, empty screen. He lowered his head and turned away from me, and I felt sure that the gesture was one of disappointment.

I grabbed Emma's hand, and for the second time in as many days, fled from the Electric cinema.

I remember little of running from the Electric. The copse, the shack, the sprawling fields beyond, all nothing but a blur. I didn't become fully conscious of my surroundings until we reached the edge of town. By that time we had ceased running, and lapsed into a kind of aimless gait, complete with kicking gravel underfoot, and arming oneself with a stick and bashing fence posts, flowerbeds and what-have-you. What we didn't do though was speak. Not for the longest time anyway.

We had drifted back into the village by a different route, and soon found ourselves heading towards our school. There was a back way onto the school property behind a cul-de-sac of neat little houses. We turned down there. I walked along the kerb's edge, arms stretched out, as if balancing on a tightrope. I slipped off once or twice.

At the end of the cul-de-sac, we cut down a narrow path that ran between two houses. The path was lined on either side with high wooden fencing; this had been decorated with extremely witty and highly articulate graffiti, such as CLAIRE 4 DOUGY, set within a crudely scrawled love heart; THE SMITHS RULE! – although someone had crossed out RULE and replaced it with the word SHIT – JULIE WARRINGTON IS DOG ROUGH; a PISS OFF written in runny red paint; and G BUCKLE IS A PRICK. I didn't know who any of these people were, although I'd often wondered if the likes of Julie Warrington and G Buckle were even aware of their notoriety. Probably not, as no attempt had ever been made to erase them. At the end of the path – just past my personal favourite inscription, IF U READ THIS, U R A COCK END – there was a gap in the hedgerow that led out onto our playing field. We both slipped on through without a word.

The school stood silent and ominous across the field. Emma, however, was walking in the opposite direction, towards a patch of overgrown ground on the edge of the school's boundaries. It was known to kids and teachers alike as the Triangle, given the area's odd shape. During term time it was supposedly off-limits to pupils, but this "rule" didn't deter many. At break-times you'd often find hordes of kids skulking around its wild foliage and gnarled old trees, smoking like fiends. Oftentimes a teacher would trudge over to inspect the Triangle, but from the area's vantage point, they were often spotted crossing the school's playing field in enough time for kids to either risk it and hide, or simply make a run for it, scattering like marbles. Why this area hadn't been flattened long ago was anybody's guess. Perhaps it just wasn't in the school's budget. Instead they seemed happy to waste teachers' time, pretty much on a daily basis, by having them chase loitering kids through its thick-eted maze. Both David and I had been hounded through the Triangle on numerous occasions, been caught once or twice too, but nothing much came of it.

Emma was ahead of me, the sun shining through her hair, giving it that beautiful reddish tint. It was still pretty hot and I wondered what time it was. I had no idea, although I figured it must be getting on for late afternoon. It had been one hell of a long day, that was for sure. The shooting incident over at David's that morning now felt like it had happened days ago. Weeks even. Everything felt distant. The entire summer felt like I was looking at it through the wrong end of a telescope. The Electric had changed me, and now there was no going back.

Emma led the way into the Triangle. We passed an over-turned shopping trolley which must have been there for some time, as the grass had grown up through it. Emma didn't go in too deep, lingering at the Triangle's edge. She stood for a moment, looking through the tree line to the school beyond, then hunched down onto the ground and lay back. Sunlight, broken by branches, washed over her. I glanced at the rise and fall beneath her Springsteen t-shirt, then quickly looked away.

Out at the school, the sun caught classroom windows and points of light arced in spectrums. It stood silent. It was always strange to see the school so still. It seemed unnatural somehow. I sat myself down across from Emma. She sat up and looked at me. I don't think either of us knew where to start.

Finally, Emma said, "You remember when we came down here that night?"

I did. A group of us, including Emma and David, had come up with the brainwave of camping out in the Triangle overnight. Alibis had been concocted, and bottles of cider and a few beer cans had been sourced. What no one had remembered to bring, though, were any sleeping bags, let alone a tent. And as if our own stupidity could reach any more of a pinnacle, we did this in late October. Man, it was cold.

Still, it had been quite a night regardless. Emma and I had ended up huddled against one another in an effort to keep warm. There had been a moment when I thought we were going to kiss, but I bottled it. I was just too scared. I went off to grab David in a headlock and hated myself almost immediately. The self-loathing took me weeks to get over.

I nodded that I remembered.

"I often think about that night," she said. "I was so surprised you even came out."

I knew what she meant. She was talking about my dad, who'd died suddenly just weeks before.

"I don't know…" I muttered. "I just wanted to be out of the house, I guess."

"Yeah," she said in a low voice. "I get that."

We fell silent. The breeze picked up, whispering through the tall grass. Somewhere overhead, a plane was crossing the sky.

Emma said, "You've never spoken about it, Sam. Not really. You can talk to me, you know… if you want?"

I looked at her, but didn't say anything for a long time. I wondered why we were even talking about this. Finally, I said, "What about today?"

She laughed, but there was no humour in it. It was a nervous, deadened laugh, dry and hoarse.

"Today…" she began. "Today has been, without question, the strangest day of my life."

"You can say that again," I muttered.

"Was it the same for you? Last night?"

I nodded. "… And today."

"You know the funny thing… there's part of me thinking that none of it even happened at all. It's like it's… fading."

"It happened," I said.

She looked at me darkly. "I know it did. It just *feels* like it didn't, somehow. I don't know… I just can't comprehend it. Any of it."

Another silence. I lay back on the grass and looked at the trail of jet stream cutting across the sky.

Emma whispered, "That film…"

I looked at her. Her eyes were wide open. I thought of Bogart crossing the sand dunes of that weird desert land – of Jean Harlow, and Victor McLaglen, and their faces, their texture. Of the shack town jutting great towers lined with walkways. Of the black train from *Houses of the Hanged*, and of the landscape it thundered through.

Emma said, "Was it real?"

"I don't know," I answered.

"Were *they* real? The people in there?"

I sat up again. "Well, they were there. We both saw them."

"We both saw the film as well, but did it feel like anything you'd ever seen before?"

"No," I confessed. "No it didn't."

"You know, in all the ghost stories I've ever read, or heard, they're always transparent."

There it was. She just blurted it out. I was astonished.

"Ghosts?" I said, frowning.

"Well what's your explanation, then?"

My mouth fell open. I tried to speak, but nothing came.

"They weren't normal, Sam," she said. "Their colours – I've never seen anything like it."

"But that doesn't mean anything. And it certainly doesn't mean that they were ghosts."

I winced at my own sharpness. I was in denial. She'd said the word. Out loud. And so had I. A word I dared not even think, let alone say. But now it was out there and I could feel its weight settling on us.

Ghosts.

It surprised and frightened me how readily I was willing to believe. I felt the only thing I could do was try and suppress that belief, though I knew it was a futile game. The pendulum in my mind continued to swing.

"But what if they were?" said Emma.

I shook my head. "I don't know, Em. I guess that would change everything."

She gave me a solemn look. "Everything's already changed, Sam. I don't feel the same as I did this morning, do you? It's like my eyes have been opened – "

I can see with better eyes.

"Don't you see?" she asked.

I looked at her. The sun shone on her face and in her hair, and she looked radiant. I couldn't remember ever seeing her so beautiful.

"I do see," I whispered, then added, "*Ghosts,*" testing the word, allowing the realisation to fully take hold.

The admittance gave me clarity. To say there were ghosts at the Electric seemed to charge me. Suddenly, I felt completely alive. My mind prickled, my every nerve on end. We had glimpsed the supernatural. In fact, more than glimpsed. We had sat with the dead, and it had been nothing short of incredible. I wondered how I hadn't realised this before.

I felt euphoric. It was a rush like I had never known. I laughed; I couldn't help it. Emma frowned at first, but then I could see the corners of her mouth twitching. This made me laugh all the more, and soon enough, she joined me. It was a wonderful release.

However, something else came tugging at my mind. It was sudden and intense. It took me a moment to understand it fully, but when I had it, it fixed firmly and unshakably. It was an urge to draw. I hadn't so much as doodled on a scrap of paper for near enough a year, not since my father's death. But now here it was, that impulse to create, to fantasise in pencil. I ceased laughing and looked down at my right hand. It felt heavy with importance; *pulled* by an overwhelming need to draw. What exactly, I wasn't sure, but I knew that I only had to sit, pencil in hand, and it would come, it would pour out of me. I was certain of this.

I felt a sudden urgency to get home. To my room. To my desk. To a blank sheet of paper. I stood. Emma stared up at me.

"I… I need to go," I said.

"Where?"

"Home."

"You okay?"

"I think I am," I said, and I meant it.

Emma stood up. "Do you ever want go back there?" she asked.

"To the Electric?"

"Yeah."

I knew I had to answer as honestly as I could, for the both of us.

"I think we have to," I added.

"I know," she said, and reached for my hand.

The town looked different somehow. There were kids playing out in the streets, enjoying the last of the day's sun; riding bikes, huddled in groups, sat on walls. Cars drifted by, couples leant into one another, lawnmowers hummed. Music flowed out of open windows and kids laughed and squealed in back gardens. The air was clear, warm, golden. I was seeing it all with complete clarity. Really seeing it.

I usually spent my time following my feet, never really taking the chance to look around, to take in the world I moved through. But now I really looked, and what I saw moved me. It was a strikingly beautiful evening. It throbbed with life – be it human, insect, plant or animal. Here we all were, under the sun. I looked over at Emma, her hand was in mine.

We came to a street corner and stopped. Here we would have to part, as our houses now lay in opposite directions. We stood before one another, both of us looking down at our hands, still interlocked. I couldn't think of anything to say. My mind felt wired, shuddering with ghosts and movies and this late afternoon, which quaked with life. And of course there was still that furious impulse to draw, to create. A force like I had never known. Words wouldn't have been able to do justice to what I wanted to say. At least, not my words. I was fifteen, and the things I was feeling were far beyond my years. Far beyond anything I'd ever thought possible. I wanted to say so much – about the Electric, about this strange and startling clarity I now possessed, and moreover, about how I felt about her, but I couldn't articulate any of it. I had no idea where I would begin, if I was to begin at all; even a simple goodbye was proving difficult.

Finally, I managed, "You going straight home?" Profound, hey.

"Yeah."

"Will your dad be in?"

"Ah-huh."

"You can call me, y'know… if you want to. If you need to."

"Thank you, Sam. I will. If I need to."

And that was pretty much it. We didn't make any arrangements to meet the next day, I guess we just took it as a given. We didn't even say goodbye. What did happen though was I stepped in and kissed her on the cheek. I could hardly believe myself. It just felt natural to do it. She didn't flinch or shove me away; she simply looked at me and smiled. She squeezed my hand, then let it go, and we both headed off in opposite directions. I looked back several times. I only caught her looking back at me once. But that once was good enough for me.

I walked into the house. Framed in the doorway along the hall, I saw my mother sat at the kitchen table. She stubbed out a cigarette into my dad's old ashtray, then called through: "Samuel?"

"Yeah, it's me, Mum."

"Come here a minute."

This is what I'd been avoiding for days. I should've known I'd be collared on sight coming home this early, but I guess my mind had been elsewhere. Completely *elsewhere*. I trudged on down the hall and entered the kitchen. Mum smiled at me, "Hello, stranger."

"Hey."

"I was beginning to wonder whether you still lived here."

I opened the fridge and got out some ham, then busied myself making a sandwich.

Mum continued, "What have you been doing?"

"Nothing," I said, the defences going up.

She looked away. I finished making my pile of sandwiches, threw them on a plate, then made for the door.

"Sam," she said, gently. I stopped and stood in the doorway, plate in hand.

"Sam, where are you?"

"What do you mean, where am I? I'm here of course!"

"No, I mean. Why don't you talk to me anymore? I hardly see you."

I shrugged. "Been busy."

"Where do you go till all hours?"

The Electric flared in my mind. The Technicolor tramp and all his friends, standing in the dark of the cinema. "Its summer, Mum, we're just... *out*."

"Yeah," she said, but sounded sad. "It's right that you enjoy yourself, Sam. Your father was the same."

I wasn't entirely sure what she meant by that.

"I'm gonna go to my room," I said.

She looked at me, managing a thin smile.

"I'm here, you know.... If you..."

"Sure," I said, cutting her off. I headed for my room.

It took me a long time to realise that she had been trying to reach me.

I went into my room, my mouth stuffed with sandwich. I knew right away that Mum had been in here. The window was open for starters – *to give it a good airing,* she would have said in different times. She'd also attempted to stack the pile of books I'd spilled across the floor that morning whilst searching for *The Films of Humphrey Bogart.* She hadn't done much of a job, mind; it was a tower teetering on the verge of collapse. The slightest creak of a floorboard and the books would be back across the floor again. Also, my bed had been stripped and remade in clean sheets. I shut the door behind me and stood, scanning the room for further evidence of invasion. Save for a few dirty cups and plates which had been cleared out, everything else seemed as it was. I pulled off my t-shirt and added it to the mass of dirty washing beside the wardrobe. I then lay on my bed, looking to the window. The curtains were blowing gently in the breeze and sunlight cast across the walls, washing out Molly Ringwald and half of Michael Stipe. I allowed my mind to drift, to settle. I closed my eyes.

The last days of summer rolled along the breeze; the tangled yell of adolescence, the continual drone of mowed lawns, the far-off jingle-jangle of an ice cream van. Sleep came in a wave, and it was dreamless.

It was near dark when I woke. It was also cold. I got up and walked to the window. There was a cylinder of light stretched out across the horizon – a horizon broken by the occasional darkened house; above, the night sky was already shimmering with awakening stars. I closed the window and searched the floor for a top to wear. I found a tatty old woollen jumper and pulled it over my head. I caught my reflection in the mirror above my desk. I stepped closer, examining my face, my eyes. They looked dark, stricken even, but I put that down to having just woken, rather than any legacy of supernatural encounters.

There were several photographs displayed around my mirror, one of which was of my dad and me. We had been on a holiday I no longer remembered, as I would have only been about three or four when it was taken. We were both standing on a beach, the sea glistening behind us. We were both topless, and were both attempting to pose like musclemen. My dad was laughing as he outstretched both his arms, fists raised to the sky, biceps lean and taut. I mimicked the same posture and I attempted to look *mean*. The best I could do however was wrinkle up my nose and bare my teeth. It looked more like I was trying to do an impression of a rabbit. I had no memory of the scene in the photograph, and yet it had become one of my most cherished pictures of my father and me. I guess because I'd come to look at it as an ideal, rather than an actual event.

I looked away, down to my desk. It was cluttered, of course; books, comics, scraps of balled-up paper, and a few drawings which had more than likely sat there untouched for almost a year.

I began to clear it, stacking books and comics in a corner of the floor, throwing the scraps of paper beside the already over-spilling bin, and collecting up the sketches and drawings and placing them on top of my chest of drawers. The desk clear, I rummaged around and found a half-used jotter of clear white paper, then I collected up my pencils from various areas of the room. Finally, I sat at my desk.

I looked at the white sheet of paper for a long time. It had been near enough a year since I'd last sat here. I held the pencil, the lead point hovering over the page. I tried to reawaken the force that had so gripped me back at the Triangle. It lingered still, I felt it, but it had been dulled by my sleep. I worried that my nap had been a huge mistake, that it had destroyed any chance now of creative inspiration. Exhaustion had got the better of me. I closed my eyes and tried to relax my mind, but all I saw was the last time I had been sat at this desk. On the night of the storm.

The sky had been threatening; low, black clouds had coloured the entire day as dull as dusk: an eerie half-light. The air was charged; you could smell that wonderful metallic scent of electricity. It was the first week of October and night came on fast. It was full dark by around six, and with it came the slow brood of distant thunder.

I was in my room when the rain came. It was sudden and fierce, pounding at my bedroom window in moments.

I sat at my desk, idly sketching this Conan-type character I'd come up with, whom I'd named Blackwick. He carried a huge double-headed axe and had a brutal scar about his neck from where he'd once been hanged. He'd lived through this of course – lived to swing his axe in bloody vengeance against his would-be executioners. I had an entire backstory in my head, and harboured dreams of writing and illustrating a comic book of his adventures, knowing or caring little of how derivative my character was.

I soon stopped drawing however, and turned off the light to watch the storm from my desk. Lightning struck. It lit the black rain with its ephemeral whitening charge. Thunder followed soon after. It cracked across the night, as loud as ever I'd heard it. I got up and went over to the window to watch the show.

Lightning flashed as bright as day, sharp and fast – thunder rolled, rattling the window, and the rain pummelled and lashed without letup. I remember thinking that it was like something out of a movie – more like a special effect than an act of nature. It was by far the hardest storm I'd ever witnessed.

There came a knock at my bedroom door, which opened ajar before a chance of invitation. My dad popped his head round and said, "Boy! Is this a good one, or what?"

"I've never seen it like this," I said. "It's like the end of the world or something".

"Mind if we come in?" he asked. "Watch it with you?" He opened the door all the way, revealing he and Mum standing huddled in the hall.

"Sure," I said, and turned back to the storm.

They came to the window, Dad to my side, and Mum behind me, her hands gently resting on my shoulders, and together we watched in awe.

A crooked bolt of blue/white lightning struck the field out beyond our garden. The bolt imprinted on my retinas.

"Storm's right on top of us," said Dad.

Thunder boomed, shaking the house.

Once it had passed, my mother said, "Will we be alright, John?"

"Yeah, we'll be as right as rain, love."

"Very funny," said Mum, dryly.

She squeezed my shoulders, then wrapped her arms around my chest. I leaned back into her.

"I don't think I've seen it like this since I was a lad," marvelled my dad.

"You unplugged the TV, right?" asked Mum.

"Yes."

Another crack of lightning, this one printing the sky with several spidery talons, making me think of jagged lines on some kind of dreadful map. Again it burned in that same eerie blue. Thunder exploded above us.

"Whoa!" cried my dad. "That was a good one!"

There was a tree out in the field which I'd often climbed. A lightning bolt struck that tree and sent shards of white flame shooting out in arcs across the field. The trunk cracked in two and was felled almost at once. It crashed to the earth, branches crunching in its destruction.

"Wow!" I hollered.

Thunder rolled, only not as loud as before. The tree lay smouldering beneath the pelting rain. There was a sense that the storm had reached its inevitable climax – at least over our heads it had.

My dad said, "That was incredible!"

"Sure was," I agreed. "You ever seen anything like that before, Dad?"

"No, Sammy, I haven't."

"Have you, Mum?"

"No, me neither."

We looked out to the broken tree. I recalled the last time I'd climbed it during the summer. It had been blisteringly hot then, and David had wimped out from going right to the top. I'd spent most of my time in the tree breaking off twigs to throw down at his head. Caught him a few times as well, and he'd gone into a sulk about it.

I remember thinking that I couldn't wait to tell him what I'd seen, but I never did. I kept that storm, and the lightning struck tree, to myself, and have done from that day to this.

Mum sighed and said, "I think it's really sad the tree's gone."

"Ah, come on Mum, it was flipping amazing."

She smiled at me. "Well, I suppose it was quite a sight. It's just a good job no-one was out there."

Dad said, "I'll go over to Tom's tomorrow – see if he wants a hand shifting it."

The sky lit again, but there was no lightning bolt, the illumination came from within the clouds, briefly turning them a dark purple colour, as if they were bruised. Thunder followed, but it was far off, and had settled back into a low rumble. The rain abated a little, but continued to fall steadily until the morning. After the excitement had died down, Mum and Dad left me and went off to bed, and I returned to my desk and continued to draw into the night.

That was the last time I saw my father alive.

John Stephen Crowhurst died during the night from what was officially stated as a massive cardiac arrest. My mother explained to me later that he'd woken clutching his chest at around four in the morning. He'd got out of bed, saying to her that he was going to get a glass of water. He never even made it across the room. He collapsed almost at once and Mum raced to his side. She held his hand, but he was already gone. He had been forty-two years old.

Mum in her wisdom had rung for an ambulance, and then sat at the kitchen table waiting for it to arrive, the rain tap-tap-tapping at the windows. At no point did she come and wake me. Not then anyway.

The paramedics recorded the time of death; I guess the coroner was informed, and whatever other official channels these things have to go through, and then I suppose my dad was bagged up and taken away. I slept through the whole thing. Mum often joked about how heavy a sleeper I was, that I would most probably sleep through the end of the world. I guess she wasn't wrong about that.

At seven that morning, Mum finally came through to me. I

woke to find her sat rigid at the bottom of my bed. She looked awful, and I knew right away that something very bad had happened. I don't remember how she told me exactly, but I do remember shuddering and breaking down with a pain I never thought possible. She held me then and we cried together.

How either of us got through the rest of that day I'll never know. I think we just sat around the house, crying regularly, struggling to comprehend what had happened. For a long time, I just couldn't accept it. It didn't make any sense. I kept going over and over what Mum had told me. One minute he'd been sleeping soundly, his life stretched out before him, the next he was lying dead on a bedroom carpet he'd fitted one rainy Saturday three years before. I remembered that, I'd watched him do it, even helped a little.

It was the sheer suddenness that was so brutal. There had been no warning, no hint of ill health, nothing. His heart just gave out and he died, and now, somehow, we had to get on with our lives without him.

Mum made phone calls throughout the day, informing family and friends, every call more difficult than the last. I went and sat in the waterlogged garden. I thought about the storm. It seemed so strange that my final moments with him had been spent watching a tree get struck by lightning. It felt like his death had been marked by some tremendous apocalyptic event: a great tempest that had come and taken him away. It was mythic; a Greek tragedy.

That was how my imagination shaped it anyway. It felt a little easier to make it as fantastical as one of my drawings. If only a little. Putting it down to simple coincidence felt lame.

I remember looking to the felled tree out in the field. My dad would never help Tom Bradley move it. He would never again sit and watch old black and white movies with me. He would never kiss my mother while we were out in public and embarrass me. He would never ask to see my latest drawings, and sit and listen to my ideas for stories and characters and fantastical worlds; his enthusiasm for my imaginings spurring me ever on. He would never again be heard out in the garage hammering and sawing together some new construction.

He would never see me grow up. And I would never be the same again.

The pencil trembled in my hand. I placed it down on the paper and went over to the window. It was full dark now, the sky cloudless and cast in diamonds. The tree in the field had been uprooted and taken away back in early spring. I'd watched as the old farmer, Tom Bradley, and his three sons had wrapped chains around it and dragged it away in pieces with their tractors. I'd cried watching them. It had been the first time I'd done so since Dad's funeral. Now the field lay flat and bare, the earth churned for the harvest.

I returned to my desk. I picked up the pencil, hesitated for the briefest of moments, and then set to work.

I was woken the next morning by someone shaking me roughly by the shoulder. A voice: "Come on… get up, you lump…"

It was Emma.

I rolled over and blinked my eyes into focus. She was sitting on the edge of the bed – *my bed* – looking down at me. Her hair was tied up, strands of it draping down the sides of her lunar face. She had on a white shirt and her trademark cutoff denims. Right away I became very aware of her bare legs mere inches from my hands. Moreover, the shirt was thin, and it was easy to see her flowery patterned bikini top beneath. It was the same one she'd worn earlier that summer when we'd gone swimming in the river. I remembered it well.

"Come on… Up!" she demanded, then left the bed and began to nosey around my room.

"This place is a real tip, y'know."

"Thank you," I said, my mouth dry and hoarse. "And good morning to you too."

She sniffed. "I'm not gonna find anything I don't want to in this debris, am I?"

"Like what?"

"You know… grotty boys' stuff."

"Oh, no, course not."

At least, I hoped not.

While she was occupied, rifling through my clutter, I glanced beneath the sheets to check what I had on and found, to my relief, that I was still fully dressed. I got out of bed.

"You went to sleep in your clothes?" she said.

"Ahem, yeah. Bit of a late night."

"Animal," she scoffed, then returned to flicking through a

Batman comic she'd fleeced from the floor.

It had indeed been a late night. I looked over to my desk. It was abound with paper, all freshly illustrated.

"What time is it?" I asked.

"Little after eight."

"Eight! Bloody hell, Em, what you trying to do to me?"

"What? Don't be such a lazy ass – we've got stuff to do."

My stomach did a little somersault. "The Electric, you mean?"

Emma looked at me and raised her eyebrows. She answered, "Stuff, I mean," providing her voice with the right edge of mystery.

I had set my pencil to the paper, and a rush of imagery webbed my mind, coming on stronger than anything I'd ever known before. The Electric, imagined in its heyday, became so clear to me that it felt as if I'd been there myself – it seemed more memory than imagination.

The first picture I drew was of the outside of the cinema, the marquee all lit in lights, displaying the night's attraction: Humphrey Bogart in *When the Night Came Fallin'*.

I sketched in a fury; a surge of creative abandon. The illustration was rough, yes, yet still felt true. It seemed to have that certain *Electric quality* that I had come to know so well: the same wavering strangeness those old movie posters possessed. My own picture wasn't nearly as intense in this feeling, but it was certainly there. It was there when I drew the picture, and also when I stared at it afterwards.

I'd felt sick when I'd first come upon the Bogart poster back at the Electric, but now this nausea had developed into a kind of tingle, something pleasant and somehow familiar. At least, that's how my drawing felt once I'd finished it anyhow.

I stared at it for a while, then put it to one side. Not wanting to stop, I placed another sheet of paper on the desk, sharpened my pencil, and then set to work again. This drawing was of the lobby, again imagined in its heyday, and this time, I drew people.

They stood in line, waiting to ascend the staircase, tickets in hand. I put the Technicolor tramp in there, and also the others who had made up that strange audience back at the Electric. I caught their likeness with an ease I never thought possible. It was their eyes: the old woman, the pretty girl and the greaser, and old TT himself – I caught their eyes perfectly. It quickly became the most competent drawing I had ever created.

There was a ticket girl at the foot of the stairs, and an usher waiting to guide the cinemagoers to their seats. There were posters hung on the walls. I even created one for *Houses of the Hanged*. It was of the black train bulleting through that strange desert land, a sky full of thunder above.

On finishing the picture, I had a sudden and unexpected sense of complete satisfaction. I'd never had that with one of my drawings before. I suppose I'd never given much thought to the artistic merit of my work. I just drew something and moved on. But with this one, I knew I had created something special, something unique.

I felt utterly elated.

I wondered if this was the feeling all artists constantly strive for – writers and painters, musicians and filmmakers, artists of all kinds – this had to be the drive that propelled them ever onward: the need to create – to tell stories, or project feelings through whichever medium they chose. I knew this euphoria was rare and fleeting, but once felt, never forgotten.

It became very clear that I would spend the rest of my life in creative pursuits. The idea fixed in my mind. It seemed noble to me, but also dangerous somehow. I'd heard of artists sometimes driven mad by their art. I suddenly understood why. I guess the sheer force of this ambition frightened me a little. It seemed immense and unyielding. Still, these were remote, scrambled, late night thoughts. All in all, my elation far outweighed any concern of ambitious folly.

What I did know, galvanised into my very being, was that I would never be deterred from this path now, whatever the cost. It was as sudden, and as simple as that.

I'd never been much inclined to think about my future before, but with the completion of that one picture of the Electric's lobby, my life's work suddenly seemed mapped out. I would be an artist, an illustrator, a creator of imagined worlds. It did occur to me that it had always been there, but I'd never fully embraced it. Before that moment, drawing had just been a pastime, now, suddenly, it was everything.

I felt foolish, and angry at myself for having wasted a year not drawing so much as a doodle. I vowed to make up for lost time.

It was pushing three in the morning when I began my third picture; this one of the audience sat in their seats, watching the Bogart film. I even drew in Emma and me. I placed us up on the balcony.

The sky was a dim blue light by the time I fell into my bed, and again, I slept without dreams.

"Did you draw these?"

She said it in astonishment, her voice paper-thin.

"Yes," I said. "Last night. I was up until dawn."

"They're… they're incredible."

Emma sat down at my desk and hunched over the pictures, inspecting every detail, every face. I watched her. She grew tense, rigid. Colour drained from her cheeks. The phrase, *you look like you've seen a ghost* sprang to mind and I had to stifle a laugh, even though it felt utterly humourless.

"You've drawn their faces," she gasped. "The people from the Electric… you've drawn them."

"Yes."

"And here, in this one…"

She was pointing to my last drawing, the one of the audience.

"That's us!"

"Yes."

She stared at them for a long time, then said, "They make me feel like those posters did back at the cinema." She reconsidered this for a moment, then turned to look at me. "Only… they don't make me feel sick. It's more like…"

"Something familiar," I said. "Like a kind of warm feeling?"

"Yes." She swallowed. "Sam, these drawings really are something else. They're certainly the best things I've ever seen you do." She turned back to my work. "I don't know, maybe it's because I was there with you, and I saw those people too… but I've never had this feeling before," she gave a dry laugh, "not from looking at a drawing anyway. It seems silly." She fell silent for a moment, then said, "They're beautiful, Sam, they really are. In a sad kind of way."

I didn't know what to say.

"Are you going to draw some more?" she asked.

"Yes," I said. "I planned on taking my pad down there today."

She remembered something then, and her eyes widened. "We've got somewhere else to go first – before we head back to the Electric, I mean."

"What? Where?"

"You still got your bike?"

"Yeah, it's in the shed. Where we going?"

She stood up and faced me. She took my hands in hers and smiled. I wanted to kiss her there and then.

"You remember that old guy who was at my dad's yard yesterday morning?"

I thought. "Yeah, Dave pointed him out. He sold his car for scrap."

"Right, that's him. Well, his name is Elmer Muxloe. He lives over in town."

"Yeah, so?"

"Well, last night I told my dad where we'd been all day."

"Really?" I wasn't sure how I felt about that.

"Yeah. Dad knew about the Electric. He used to go there

when he was a kid. He even took my mum a few times when they first started going together. They went to see one of those Hammer horrors that you like… a *Dracula* one I think."

I got impatient and cut her off, "And Muxloe?"

"Sam, Elmer Muxloe was the Electric's projectionist. And I know where he lives."

And so we rode into town. Both of us hunched over the handlebars of our BMXs, our behinds hovering over our seats as we worked the pedals round as hard and as fast as we could. I wore my rucksack. It clung loosely to my back; I could hear pencils being thrown about inside. It made me think of going to school.

Emma's bike was a little more beaten up than mine, which was saying something. I figured it was probably salvaged rather than actually purchased. I'd never asked, but this seemed to be the Looms way. Mine had been what my dad had called "the big present" for my thirteenth birthday. I was getting a little too big for the bike now – when I sat and pedalled, my knees would often catch the handlebars. Plus, it had certainly been through the wars. The frame was a little bent, the spokes had rusted and the chain often came off. I never cleaned it, or much looked after it at all really. Mum used to get on at me about it, but not anymore.

We rode away from the countryside, through narrow streets of neat houses and freshly cut lawns, along the ever widening roads that led into town. Fields gave way to waste grounds and derelict factories. Houses lost their grandeur, became smaller, with peeling paint and overgrown front gardens. Kids that came from this part of town often clashed with kids from our village. Our school was a melting pot of both worlds, and both worlds collided on a daily basis during term time.

We said very little as we rode. I thought about David and wondered why neither of us had suggested calling round for him. I guess we took it as a given that we wouldn't, that he'd somehow lost his privilege to this particular adventure. By doing what…? Not believing in ghosts? The hard truth was that we'd outcast him for being logical, for not even remotely accepting the supernatural. Maybe we'd cut him out because we were so willing to believe ourselves, we just couldn't have anyone else around condemning such a fragile faith. It seemed to me there was a lot of truth in that. The pendulum in my mind swung wildly from accepting the Electric's supernatural suggestions, to questioning the entire phenomena. Being around David would only give rise to my scepticism, and I didn't want that. I wanted to believe. I had to.

By ten o'clock the sun was already sweltering. Before we'd left I'd washed and changed, taking my clothes into the bathroom with me, leaving Emma in my bedroom. Little more than an hour later I was already hot and sticky. Beneath the rucksack, the back of my t-shirt stuck to the skin and my hair was damp at the brow. Emma was the same. Her shirt clung to her bikini top. She kept pulling it away. I suspect she was conscious of my looking. At fifteen there is little mastery in the art of subtlety. My glances must have been obvious and embarrassing. If she noticed (which she did), she took it in good grace and never let on.

We made it across town, to an area I was unfamiliar with. Old brick houses lined around a green. A few kids were kicking a ball about and a young couple lay necking in the shade of a tree. Emma clocked me watching them kiss and I averted my eyes quickly.

I motioned to the houses. "Is this where he lives?"

"Yeah," she said, using her hand to shield her eyes from the glare of the sun.

"You know the number?"

"14."

We rode our bikes further along the road, counting the house numbers as we went. We passed number 10, 12, and then came to 14. Or what we assumed to be 14. It had no number on its paint-peeled door. The place looked empty. The window frames were rotten and lined with mould. The windows themselves were so dirty it was pretty much impossible to peer in. There was even a hole in one of the top windows, covered over from the inside by a piece of flapping cardboard.

"You sure this is the house?" I asked Emma.

"Well, I think so... s'what my dad said anyway."

There was a collective yell from some of the kids out on the green. I glanced over and saw they were knotted together, all laughing and shouting as they each tried to tackle the ball from one another. A car went by. Emma and I stood before that dilapidated old house for a long time. Everything felt very strange again. The ordinary world moved around us, yet seemed very far away, a place we were no longer connected to. I looked at Emma. Her hair was tinged red again by the sun. The breeze picked up and whispered through the trees that lined the green. Emma dropped her bike to the ground and stepped up to the door. She looked round at me before she knocked. I smiled. It felt like a grimace.

Her knock echoed in the hall beyond the door.

The man that came to the door looked a lot older than the man I'd seen back at the car graveyard. I guess I just hadn't taken much notice of him at the time, but the tired and worn face that peered around the door really took me aback. His skin was like dried up boot leather, lined and cracked in cavernous networks. I don't think I'd ever seen such a lived-in face before in my life. He looked like the broken spine of some old book. He wore a thick woolly jumper, despite the heat, that looked to be about as old as he, and a tatty pair of pyjama bottoms. His feet were bare, dirt beneath every nail. Emma took a step back from him.

"Yes?"

His voice was stronger than I'd expected, filled with grit and annoyance. A dreadful realisation struck then – neither of us had any idea what to say. Emma looked at me for some kind of lead, but I had nothing.

"Well?"

He was a hairsbreadth away from slamming the door in our faces, when Emma finally spoke up.

"Mr Muxloe, my name is Emma Looms; I'm Albert Looms' daughter."

"You found the *item* in my car?" He sounded worried.

"No, sir," she said, looking confused, "nothing like that, we've come to ask you about… something else."

"Sounds ominous. Who's this?" He motioned to me.

"My name is Sam Crowhurst, Mr Muxloe. We wanted to ask you…" I faltered, my mouth like sawdust, "…ask about a place you used to work. The Electric cinema."

His face changed at the name. It wasn't fear so much as suspicion – suspicion, and, what, concern, dread? Whatever his thoughts were at that precise moment, it strained his features, deepening the network of lines and crags into dark hollows.

He looked at us, one to another, then said, "I haven't spoken of the Electric to anyone for twenty years or more…"

He let that hang for a moment. I felt sure he was finally going to slam the door in our faces, but instead he said, "You can leave your bikes down the side of the house, I'll go and open the gate."

And with that he stepped back inside and gently closed his front door, leaving Emma and I out on the street.

And so we waited. And waited. Four, five minutes passed – although it seemed a lot longer – and there was no sign of Elmer Muxloe whatsoever. The house stood silent, and uninviting.

"He's not coming back, is he?" I said.

"Give him a chance," said Emma, "he's an old guy." Even as she was saying this, I could see she also had serious doubts about him returning.

"Should we knock again?"

Emma frowned at me. "No, that would be rude. Be patient. He might just be tidying his house up a little, or getting dressed or something."

"Yeah, suppose you're right. Looks like he don't have too many guests round here, hey?" She didn't answer, and we continued to wait in silence.

All in all, it must have been at least ten whole minutes before we heard the latch on the side gate being opened. I'm not sure now if I felt relief or dread at Muxloe's reappearance. Whatever it was, seeing the old projectionist invite us in with a wave of his hand made me extremely nervous.

I had a sudden and strong sense that this could very well be the point of no return. We could turn around now and forget all about the Electric cinema and its ghosts, those either figurative or real, and go back to our childhoods. Or we could stay, and fall deeper down the rabbit hole.

Muxloe, perhaps, would tell us about the strange and mysterious nature of the Electric (at least, a big part of me wished this to be so), and we would learn of things beyond our own fragile understanding of life, and of death. Could we deal with that? How does a person live with knowledge beyond any grasp of the rational? Perhaps we cannot. Perhaps it is a dangerous knowledge to have. The kind of knowledge that could very well drive a person insane. Weren't Poe's characters always driven to madness by their hunger for supernatural cognition? Not just Poe either, all writers of the mysterious seem to warn of such a fate. Tampering with the unknown always has its consequences. Horror tales and ghost stories all tell us this.

Even as these unnerving, and rather unfocused, thoughts rattled around my head, I found myself following Emma through Muxloe's side gate and down through the dark passageway. I grinned to myself as I passed the point of no return. I actually grinned. Maybe because the pendulum had swung again. The shades of belief and non-belief in my mind overlapped and entangled wildly, to the point where it felt like I no longer knew my own self. Perhaps this is the only way we can deal with supernatural encounters, through confusion and doubt. In time, I'd probably convince myself that I hadn't seen anything at all;

that what I'd experienced back at the Electric had just all been in my head. Maybe it has to be that way in order for us to carry on with our lives. The abnormal has to fade.

Muxloe, in all likelihood, would just tell us a few old stories about what the Electric was like back in its heyday, and nothing more, and then we would be on our way. He wasn't going to sit there and expand our minds with supernatural certainties. It was ridiculous to think that he would. He was just some old guy who used to work as a projectionist at a cinema that had long been forgotten by this town. He'd been forgotten too. Perhaps that was the extent of the mystery. Point being, there was no mystery.

I told myself this, but knew that if this were to be the case, I'd feel tragically disappointed. I wanted so badly for all this to be real, and I knew that I was willing to risk everything, even my own marbles, to learn of the world I felt I'd glimpsed back at the Electric.

It took a moment for my eyes to adjust in the passageway. Emma lent her BMX up against the wall and I followed suit. Through the passage, I noticed Muxloe stood rigid out in his garden, watching us. I had to negotiate around Emma's bike. A strap hanging from my rucksack caught on the handlebars and pulled the bike over. The front wheel ran away with itself, catching the back of my leg. Awkwardly I twisted around and somehow untangled myself, then returned the BMX up against the wall. I looked round and saw that Emma was lingering at the end of the passageway. She was watching me. I figured she didn't want to go into Muxloe's garden without me. I could understand that.

I went up to her and took her hand. She looked at me and smiled. It was a strange smile, one I couldn't fully read, but I think it was a kind of appreciation – an appreciation of the fact I had taken her hand, reminding her that, in the simplest way, we were in this together; that she was not alone. She squeezed my hand, then let it go. Then we stepped out into Elmer Muxloe's garden, where the man himself still stood waiting for us.

Emma had been right; it seemed Muxloe had spent that long ten minutes getting dressed. Gone was the tatty old woolly jumper and threadbare pyjamas; they had been replaced by an equally ancient and grotty-looking black shirt, along with a paisley tie, and faded brown corduroys. He'd also put on some shoes. These were the real surprise; they were brand new – shiny black brogues that looked as if they'd just come straight out of the box. He'd even run a comb through his hair. This was Elmer Muxloe trying his hardest in a social situation he was clearly uncomfortable and unfamiliar with. Even his smile was trying too hard.

"Sorry if I seemed curt before," he said. "I don't get too many visitors…"

"That's okay, Mr Muxloe," said Emma, waving away the apology. I murmured and mimicked something similar.

"How old are you two?" he asked.

"We're both fifteen." Emma again. "I'm a little older than Sam, by a couple of months. I'm nearly sixteen." I'm not sure why she felt the need to explain this, but when you're fifteen, things like that seem important. Also, I figured she was just nervous. I certainly was. I couldn't think of anything to say. To use one of my dad's expressions, I just stood there looking like a lemon. I'm still not entirely sure what that means, but you get the picture.

"Fifteen, hey…" mused Muxloe. "Such a wonderful age. You should both cherish it."

Whenever anyone, particularly an adult, expressed sentiment, or became overly emotional, I would just clam up. And true to form, I did just that. I attempted to distract myself by scanning Muxloe's garden. Given his shambolic nature, the garden was suitably overgrown and untidy. Several rusty old bins stood lined up against a crumpling brick wall, all entangled in undergrowth. A large tree stooped low over the majority of the garden, its branches thick and blooming, making much of the area impassable. It seemed very likely that Muxloe hadn't ventured down to the end of his garden for years. Where we were standing was in a relatively tidy area just outside of his back door. Old bricks paved the ground beneath us, sprouting weeds in abundance. There was a window behind me, but the curtains were drawn. However, he had left the backdoor ajar and I could see that it led straight into his kitchen. It looked very old-fashioned (I assumed it hadn't been decorated for decades, if ever), and was cluttered high with plates, newspapers, old car batteries, and other such junk. And that was just what I could see.

"Well," said Muxloe, knifing the silence, "we should go inside if you want to talk."

"We don't want to take up too much of your time," said Emma, more for something to say I suppose.

It was his turn to wave her sentiment away. "It's fine, duck. Come on in."

The kitchen was narrow, made narrower by the clutter. An old paraffin heater stood in the centre of the walkway, blocking off the end of the kitchen. On top of the heater were more newspapers, a couple of well thumbed paperbacks, and randomly, a stack of old bricks. I could make out a large fat spider which had made the bricks her home. I was sure she had friends. Plenty of them in this place. The sink was, of course, piled high with dirty plates; hardened pieces of food remained on many of them.

Muxloe said. "Would you like a drink?"

Emma actually looked scared.

"Oh, that's… that's okay, Mr Muxloe," she spluttered. "We don't want to put you to any trouble."

"It's no trouble." He went over to his refrigerator. He had to move an empty cardboard box out of the way to open it. Once he did though, the smell was immediate. Something had been off in that fridge for a long, long time. I had to take a step back and turn away. Emma's involuntary reaction was to put a hand over her nose and mouth and squeeze her eyes tight shut. It reminded me of the little girl she once was, and if it wasn't for the extraordinary foulness of Elmer Muxloe's refrigerator, it would have made me laugh a lot.

Luckily, Muxloe had his face in said fridge – although I had no idea how he could stand it – and thus was oblivious to our reactions.

"I've got some milk, I think," he was saying, "or some orange juice… oh, no, that's gone."

He took out a bottle of milk, sniffed it, made a face, then threw the bottle into the cardboard box beside the fridge. Surprisingly, it didn't smash, but it made quite a clatter. I took a look and saw that thick, congealed milk had splattered around the inside of the box. I wondered how long he'd leave it there until the smell got unbearable.

I think it was this thought that made me speak up. "It's all right, Mr Muxloe – like we said, we're good for a drink. If we could just talk to you?"

He closed the fridge door and turned to look at me. I realised then that I may have been a little too abrupt, and perhaps, a tad condescending. He looked hurt, which made me feel terrible. He had been trying to play the host; trying to do what he thought was right in a social situation that, clearly, was alien to him, and I had thrown it back in his face. I couldn't hold his gaze and had to look away.

"Come this way then," he said quietly, and led us through to the adjoining room.

It was expectedly murky, incredibly cluttered, and despite the heat, quite chilly in there. The curtains were drawn – as I had seen from outside – and looked as if they had been so for a long time. A stack of crates, filled with cobwebbed beer bottles – all empty, it seemed – were pushed up against the curtains. Light pierced through a slight gap. It cut across the room in a single solid beam, universes of dust caught in its path. It was crammed full with junk. There were boxes and newspapers, old ornaments, engine parts, a taxidermied fox and accompanying rabbit, several lamps – not one of which looked to be in working order – stacks of books, magazines that appeared to go back decades, countless knick-knacks – everything from playing cards to little figurines of strange little winged creatures – and also, to my surprise, a life-size cardboard cut-out of Jean Harlow. That one gave me a jolt.

The place smelt as it looked; of age, and of things forgotten.

Muxloe cleared a stack of unopened letters from a rickety old chair, which he then dragged over to the hearth. He angled it to face the very comfy and extremely worn-looking seat opposite, which I assumed to be where Muxloe sat often.

"Here, miss," he said to Emma, offering her the chair.

"Thank you," she said, and went over to the fireside. I noticed that she brushed the chair down, as discreetly as she could, before she sat.

"And for you, young sir..." Muxloe leant over a stack of boxes, from behind which he pulled out a small red stool. He himself wiped it with the back of his sleeve, then placed it down next to Emma.

"There you go," he said. I muttered a thank you, then shuffled over and sat. It was hard and uncomfortable. Muxloe lowered himself into his seat and leant back. He watched us, but didn't say anything. Again Emma and I found ourselves at a complete loss for words.

I avoided his gaze by looking to the hearth. It was an open fire, dirty with ash and scorched pieces of wood. Stacks of newspapers piled high before it, ready for burning I assumed, and flattened pieces of cardboard lay scattered about here and there. Was this Muxloe's life? Sat here night after night, alone, feeding a fire in a room filled with cluttered memories. I suddenly felt very sad for him.

The room became so still that when Muxloe finally did speak, I flinched.

"There was this kid," he began, out of nowhere. "He used to come along to the matinees every Saturday morning. He was about your age, fifteen or sixteen, something like... Back then we'd show *Zorro, Flash Gordon,* all those old serials... cartoons and what-have-you, before the main feature. There'd be an interval and the ice cream lady would come round and the young'uns would just go nuts. It was a great time."

He fell silent then, caught by his memories. I wondered where he was going with this. To be honest, I couldn't help but feel disappointed. I wanted ghosts and stories of films made by the dead; I didn't want to hear about some kid watching *Zorro* on a Saturday morning and stuffing his face with ice cream.

"So this here kid used to show up every week without fail. He loved *Flash Gordon,* I remember that. And all of those Science Fiction pictures – *Creature from the Black Lagoon, Invaders from Mars* – he was crazy 'bout that stuff. Anyway, he was a bright kid, nice kid – was always asking me about my job. He seemed fascinated by it, which amused me. So I began to show him the projector. We had old 35mm Carbon Arcs back then, two huge machines that stood side by side. They're probably still there..." He gave a strange look then. It was fleeting, but I caught it.

I wanted to tell him the Carbon Arcs were still there, but I resisted interrupting him.

He continued. "Anyway, at first I showed him how to clean the guides by using a toothbrush. An old trick. He took to this, so then I showed him how to load up the spools into the magazines. Before long he was feeding the film through the gates, and jumping the carbon."

Muxloe must have noticed that we both looked totally lost, so he tried to give a little explanation. "The carbon throws light through the celluloid, so's to project it out onto the screen."

"Oh, right," said Emma, attempting to sound like she understood completely.

"Well anyway, this kid picked it up in no time. He was fast and fluid. He mastered reel changes and could line up the soundheads… the whole nine yards. He was great. Of course, I was more than happy to let this eager young man do my job for me. I think I used to pay him in movie posters and lobby cards."

I began to fidget on my stool. I could see Emma was getting restless too, although she was doing far better than me at feigning interest. I tried to suppress a yawn and did a poor job of it.

"I remember the first film he projected entirely by himself," continued Muxloe, "with me overseeing, of course. It was an old Humphrey Bogart picture called *The Treasure of the Sierra Madre…*"

That got my attention, and Elmer Muxloe knew it.

He looked at me and gave a thin smile. "Yes," he said, "your father was the best assistant I ever had."

In that instant, I felt different towards Elmer Muxloe. I became focused, attentive to his every word. Aside from an uncle I very rarely saw, this old man was one of the first people I'd met who'd known my father when he was young.

"What was he like?" I had to ask.

Muxloe didn't say anything for a moment. He just kept on staring at me. Then finally he said, "You look like him."

"I've seen pictures… of when he was a kid. I always thought I looked more like my mum though – s'what everybody usually says anyway."

"It's not just your physical appearance. It's everything about you, Sam. The way you carry yourself, your mannerisms, the inflections in your speech… all like your father. There's no doubting you're his boy, that's for sure."

I couldn't help but smile. It felt wonderful to know this. My mother had often mentioned how alike Dad and I were, but I guess I never really paid much attention. Hearing Elmer Muxloe say it though – a stranger to me until that moment – was like a jigsaw falling into place. It felt good, and it felt right.

"He never told me about working at the Electric." I said.

"Well, it was a long time ago, Sam. Plus, he was only there for a year or so. After that he went off to college and I saw less and less of him."

"Oh."

"Still, he was there when this fella came round one day with a stack of film cans in his arms."

"Sorry? What?" I said. I glanced at Emma. Her eyes were wide open.

"Seymour Janks was his name – strangest man I've ever met. He came with those films you've come here to ask me about."

The room became very still. Muxloe leaned back in his seat and stared at us. I wondered about the things those eyes had seen. I could sense Emma breathing heavily beside me, but I didn't look at her. I couldn't move.

Emma surprised me then by asking a question I thought was a little off track, initially anyway.

"When was the Electric built?"

Muxloe looked at her and rubbed his chin. Emma wanted the whole story, and although I was eager to hear about Seymour Janks and those weird films of his – not to mention my dad – it did make sense. If we were really going to fall down this rabbit hole, we needed to know everything Muxloe knew.

"Depends," said the man himself, after a lengthy silence.

"Depends?" said Emma. "On what?"

"Well, it depends on if you're talking about the actual building that stands there today, or what stood on that ground before it?"

"I don't understand." There was a sharpness to Emma's voice. I figured she was getting annoyed by all these riddles. I was with her on that score.

Muxloe said, "To understand that place I should probably read you an account written by a lanternist over a hundred and fifty years ago. If you want to hear it, I could read it you. But truth be known, I never thought I would speak of these things to anyone – always thought I'd take this knowledge with me to the grave… yet something is telling me I should pass this story on. Maybe it's because I knew your father, Sam, or perhaps… perhaps there are other reasons at play? I don't fully understand why, but something feels very right about you two coming here today…" He fell silent for a moment, then said, "I suppose I have to give these mysteries to you now."

I felt my legs and arms break out in goose flesh.

"We do want to know, Mr Muxloe," said Emma, although I thought her voice sounded shaky, on the borderland of tears.

I cut in. "What's a lanternist?"

"The first projectionists, I suppose. You see, people have been fascinated with moving images long before the invention of cinema. Thousands of years ago the Chinese were putting on shadow plays. They did this by manipulating cut-out figures, much like you would a puppet, and projecting their shadows onto thin pieces of cloth by lighting them from behind. Very simple, but very effective. Already folk were understanding the relationship between how light behaves and the effect it has on the human eye, and were using this… certain kind of magic to tell stories. Lanternists used a similar approach, only their method of displaying moving images were more advanced than simple shadow plays.

"They called them Magic Lanterns, and they were used as far back as the seventeenth century. The lanterns themselves were nothing more than a simple box really, through which light was projected and an image was caught in a kind of sliding compartment – you could pull this and move and enlarge the image as it cast onto a wall or a white sheet; sometimes they even used smoke for a really dramatic effect. They were, by and large, the fundaments of the projectors we have today, only without the mechanics, of course… and the miracle of electricity… and the images were painted onto glass slides, not captured on celluloid. That wouldn't happen until Thomas Edison and the Lumière brothers came along at the end of the 19th Century.

"The lanterists themselves would travel from town to town, village to village, displaying their attractions. They would walk the streets and hawk, rounding up crowds like a carnival barker out on the midway – *roll up, roll up*, that kind of thing.

"Soon enough, the shows developed, and became a grand

form of new theatre, and were almost certainly the forerunner to cinema. They were adopted by magicians and illusionists and the like, and they got increasingly theatrical in their use of sound effects… music, and what-have-you. Also, they became increasingly macabre – depicting phantoms and devils seemingly coming through from the other side to howl and rage at audiences. They became known as phantasmagoria shows, and for many people, they were thought to be real.

"The account I have was written by a Frenchman by the name of Albert Lévesque. He was third-rate magician, a first-rate drinker, and a pitiful gambler… from what I've learned of him anyway. He was also a lanterist, and his account, or at least the fragments I have of his account, are quite extraordinary. I suppose you could also say that he is the reason for the Electric's… how can I put it?… the Electric's certain kind of magic.

"Pass me that box over there, will ya, lad." Muxloe motioned across the room and I saw what he was referring to right away. It was sat on top of a narrow, chest-high bookcase (which was crammed full, of course) and looked like it hadn't moved in a long, long time. I suppose it had once been white, but time and age had dulled it long ago. On the lip of the lid I could make out a single word scrawled in black marker. It read: *Electric*.

I stood up and crossed the room. I had to move a few knick-knacks out of the way to pick it up. Once I did though, I found the box to be heavier than I thought it would be. I had to carry it with both hands.

"Here, lad." Muxloe stretched out his arms and took the box from me, placing it down on his lap. I then sat back on my stool and glanced at Emma. She had a strange look on her face, one I hadn't seen before. Her eyes glistened. She looked nervous, but there was something else as well – wonder maybe, reverence. I wanted to take her hand again, but didn't dare in front of Muxloe.

He opened the lid. The box was full of paper. I tilted my head to the side and tried to read the top page. It appeared to be a letter. I saw that it was addressed to someone named Mr Stokely, but didn't manage to read much further than that.

As Muxloe rifled through the box, a lobby card from the film *Key Largo* fell onto his lap.

Bogart again.

I knew this film; it was another one I'd watched with my dad. The picture showed Edward G. Robinson levelling a gun at Bogie. He stood firm, however – even with a gun pointed at his chest, Bogart took it as if it were all in a day's work.

Everything is connected, I thought.

"Ah, here it is," said Muxloe. From the box he pulled out about half a dozen pieces of yellowy paper. They were hand-written, and terribly faded. I worried that they'd be completely illegible, but Muxloe didn't seem concerned at all. He set these pages on the arm of his seat, then collected up everything else, including the lobby card, and crammed it all back into the box with little care. He then put the lid back on and placed it down on the floor beside him.

"Now then…" he said, settling back in his seat. "It's been a long while since I read this."

He picked up the pages and scanned the opening lines. "This isn't the original," he said. "Gawd knows where that is – long been lost, I suppose. This is a translation I discovered at the Electric in the autumn of 1951; a couple of years after I'd started working there. Who translated it? I've no idea…"

"How do you know it's not the original?" I asked.

Muxloe smiled. "Well, it's not in French for one thing."

"Oh, yeah."

"Also, there's a note at the end. Lemme see…" He shuffled through to the last page. "It says here, 'Translated from French, 1902'… there's no signature."

He then returned to the first page, cleared his throat and began to read. The pages were scattershot, the narrative fragmented. The translator clearly hadn't had very many of Lévesque's original pages, but those he or she had managed to translate astounded me. Muxloe read very slowly and very carefully, his voice low and intoxicating.

It began with a charlatan's séance: a phantasmagoria.

My name is Albert Lévesque, and I made my trade as a lanternist. I first saw this illusion in the winter of 1835. I was but twenty-one years old then and knew from the moment I saw the phantasmagoria that its mysteries had gripped me forevermore.

I had seen this macabre form of magic lantern show at a séance, held in a grim little apartment in the Quartier Pigalle district of Paris. Of course, the séance itself had been nothing more than a hoodwink, but the artistry behind the performance had, quite simply, been nothing short of spellbinding.

A shadowy old man, whose name I later found out may have been Paul de Philipsthal, or possibly just Philidor, was the master of ceremonies at the séance.

He led attendees into a darkened room. The floor was covered in black cloth, upon which was painted a white circle. Philidor, if that was indeed his real name, told his audience not to step over into the circle, no matter what. He then began reading from a book of ancient spells. I was impressed by the theatrics right from the start.

A swirl of fine smoke tendrils hung in the air above the circle, and then, without warning, there was a loud crack and a disembodied head appeared within the smoke; a skull with piercing eyes. It howled in unearthly agony.

A deplorable state of fear overcame the audience at once. One woman fainted outright, while others screamed at the apparition, men and women both, all pushing and shoving one another in their hysteria. It was quite a sight to behold, and I savoured every moment.

And still the séance went on.

More spirits came – a seemingly endless parade of the dead; each more ghastly than the last – goblins and grotesqueries, daemons and devils: every manner of ghoulish manifestation that you could image, and many you couldn't.

Not all were in such eternal agony either, some phantoms danced and laughed in hideous joy. The mirth and clatter terrified the audience beyond all else – some men drew their blades to the spectres, some even fled the room altogether. One lady lay cowering and sobbing, pleading to God for forgiveness.

It was quite a show.

I was struck by how eager the public were to leave their rational minds at the door. In the dark, it seemed people were willing to believe anything.

Muxloe paused here and said, "Seems there's a fair few pages missing after this, because it jumps considerably." He then continued to read.

I had set up my equipment out in the woods at the request of the strange girl from the village. There was something incredibly enchanting about her. She was pretty, there was no doubt. But it troubled me to be giving a performance to just this one person, no matter how handsome she was. I had hoped she would bring others, but she had stated quite firmly that she would be coming alone. Yet the curious thing was that she had also requested twelve chairs – which I had taken from the barn of one of her neighbours, at her advising.

So here I was, in a foreign land, falling for a young girl who wanted nothing from me other than a single performance of my lantern show. She had cast a spell over me, that much was certain. Every curious thing she asked of me, I did without quarrel. This in itself was not in my nature. I felt very out of sorts around her.

I lighted the woods with staffs of fire which I pierced into the ground, making a perimeter around my makeshift theatre. It was certainly a difficult prospect performing the phantasmagoria in such surroundings, but not impossible. My show was not the spectral of the great Paul de Philipsthal, or Etienne-Gaspard Robertson for that matter. I was just an itinerant lanternist and a clumsy one at that. Also, I shall admit my vices greatly hindered my showmanship, the drink being the worst of my sins. Yet somehow I kept travelling and attracting crowds to my shows. I had performed in barns, inns, private houses, even alleyways and gardens, and had crossed many oceans. But I'd never held a performance in a wood before, and certainly never for an audience of one. Still, the girl had allured me; her femininity all too comely to resist.

She came through the woods carrying aloft a lamp, its candle flame casting dancing shadows about her face. It made her look ethereal, like something from my show. She bade me a good evening, but said nothing else. She took her seat before the screen – a white sheet I had tied from tree to tree. I asked her again if anyone else was coming – still puzzled by the amount of chairs – but she ignored this question and simply said for me to begin the show.

So that is what I did. I performed all my trickery; from the ringing of bells to warn of the coming of spirits, to my ventriloquism, where I would throw my voice and howl and screech like a tormented soul. The girl watched, a strange half smile tugging at her mouth.

Then came the apparitions. First, the Death Head, that hideous skull warning of the grim fate of man, then the imps and faery folk – a particular flourish of my own – and then to the daemons of hell. My voice carried well within the enclosure of the trees, and the setting certainly gave the performance an extra dimension. The girl however remained placid, unreadable, only that thin smile of hers gave any hint of emotion. I was used to audiences screaming in terror, so this silence stilted my act somewhat.

I'd just got to the part when the old witch came through from the netherworld, when I heard the first laugh. It was a deep laugh, a gentleman's laugh. I looked at the girl, but she remained as unreadable as ever. The witch hung on the screen, her dialogue forgotten. Another laugh came, then another, and another. I stepped back from my lantern box, leaving the witch, and the act, in limbo. That was when I saw them.

Every one of the eleven remaining chairs were suddenly filled. The people in them guffawed at the screen. They didn't arrive, they appeared. However, as uncanny as that was, their appearance was even more so. Each and every one of them sparked with colour. Their clothes, their skin, their eyes, all seemed impossibly vibrant, as if a great artist had painted them onto the very night.

The girl spoke up then. She told me to continue with the show as her friends were enjoying it. How I didn't run from that place I do not know. Perhaps it was the girl? Her beautiful porcelain face weakening my reason.

So that is just what I did. I continued with my show. At every new spectre that came through my lantern, the audience would howl with ever more laughter. Soon enough, I know not if it were madness or cold hard hysteria, but I was laughing with them.

Muxloe set the pages on the arm of his seat once more, then interlocked his hands and rested them on his belly. He watched us both, reading our expressions. My mouth was dry and I tried to work up some saliva, but the act sounded very noisy to my ears, so I stopped.

Emma asked a question then that I was afraid I already knew the answer to. "Where did all that happen, Mr Muxloe?"

The old projectionist leaned forward and said, "Where the Electric now stands."

I was right, I had known the answer.

"The story goes that Lévesque stayed here," said Muxloe, "and with the girl – who later became his wife – they set up a kind of theatre."

"A theatre?" said Emma.

"Yes, they put on plays and lantern shows and the like… I believe they even built a Camera Obscura around the remains of an old well."

I cut in with a venom that surprised me. "For an audience of what? Spooks?"

I suddenly felt angry, really angry, but was confused as to why exactly. I guess, quite simply, my nerves were in tatters, but I couldn't make sense of that then. Muxloe certainly didn't deserve to take the brunt of my attitude, yet, at that moment, I could have easily laid into him. I had to hold my tongue from going any further.

Muxloe, for his part, gave me a thin smile – which read almost as a grimace – then said, "Yes. Ghosts."

There it was. That word.

The anger drained away in an instant.

Coming from Elmer Muxloe's own lips seemed somehow to confirm everything. It occurred to me then that we had now crossed the threshold. The point of no return had sailed past and neither Emma nor I had even noticed. We were changed now. Our lives marked. Everything we'd grow to be would be tainted by what we'd experienced at the Electric. That fifteenth year would be scorched into the very fabric of me. I knew that then, and I certainly know that now.

Muxloe continued on, oblivious to my epiphany. "The hows and whys are lost on me, Sam. I don't understand it anymore than I understand why the stars are where they're at. All I know is that I worked at the Electric for almost twenty-five years, and in that time, not a week went by when I did not see the *know* of a man."

"The *know*?" I said.

"Yes. The *know* of something is… I suppose… a term for its spectral appearance."

"Its what?"

"Its ghost, Sam. Its ghost."

We all fell silent. The room felt heavy. I desperately needed something to drink. I also felt hungry. I'd hardly eaten in the last few days. I told myself that once we were out of Muxloe's house, we'd go and grab a cheeseburger or something. Somewhere busy, full of noise – full of the ordinary. Somewhere that would take me away from this rabbit hole I'd fallen into, if only briefly. I needed the mundane to anchor me.

My distress must have been visible because Emma grabbed my hand and squeezed. I saw that her face was full of concern for me, and in that moment, I think I truly fell in love with her.

"I'm okay," I whispered, but I knew that I didn't look it.

Muxloe said, "Lévesque's theatre attracted its spectral audience nightly. His wife, who was named Molly, was a sort a medium I suppose. No, not the hokey kind – the kind Lévesque encountered in that room in Paris. No, she was like a kind of channel. You know, like how a radio frequency works, only she picked up the dead, not the hit parade."

It was a bad joke, but I laughed nevertheless.

He continued. "By all accounts she was the key, but Lévesque was the showman. The *know* of many came."

"I've been to the Electric, Mr Muxloe," began Emma, "and there certainly is something very strange about that place, but really… putting on little plays and shows for ghosts… come on."

Her sudden denial surprised me.

"Well, do we not all tell stories, my dear?" said Muxloe.

She looked at him stoically. He continued. "Civilizations were built on stories; our culture is shaped by them, is it not? It is an inherent part of the human condition. We are entertained by them, moved by them, sometimes even changed by them. We are bound by stories of our past; and through countless books, and movies, and songs, we share our wondrous speculations to the meaning of our existence. We mythologize, and embellish. We are driven by this need to tell stories. Do you really think all that goes away when we die?"

She didn't say anything.

Satisfied that he'd made his point, Muxloe continued on with his own story. "It is unknown when Lévesque himself died. One account suggests the 1890s, another claims he lived to around 1910. Whichever is true, Molly certainly outlived him. She had the Electric built in 1921, and Lévesque had been long dead by then. Whichever date, he didn't live to see the meteoric rise of motion pictures.

"The Lumière brothers had the first public showing of a film in Paris 1895, that of a train arriving at a station, which terrified the audience at the time – they thought the train would burst from the screen on its approach. After that it was a gold rush. By the second decade of the twentieth century, Hollywood was already the movie capital of the world – Charlie Chaplin, Mary Pickford and the like, the first movie stars. Molly saw the connection right away – these were lantern shows made real. She put all her efforts, and money I presume, into building a motion picture house on that land out there.

"She hired a man named Reginald Stokely to oversee the cinema's construction, and it took until the spring of 1922 to complete. Once it was finished, however, Stokely stayed on to manage the place, leaving Molly, who was cracking on by then, to simply enjoy her picture palace. The first film shown at the Electric was Chaplin's *The Kid*. Stokely told me years later that that was the night he first saw them. He remembered seeing Molly laughing and crying at the film, surrounded by ghosts, all doing the same. Yet, hers was the only voice Stokely heard, theirs didn't come through, only their image. I suppose you could look at it like… like we're just not on the same frequency."

He fell silent. He leaned his head back and looked to the ceiling, his eyes far away, glazed in memory. It was an uncomfortable silence.

Emma coughed and said, "You say you started working there in the late forties?"

"Yeah, the autumn of 1949," he said. "I'd just got out of the Army. Stokely was an old man by then. Molly, of course, had long been dead. I believe she died in 1927. According to Stokely, she passed away while watching a film called *London After Midnight*, a Lon Chaney picture. He also said that Lévesque had been with her when she died."

I heard the sound of a car going past on the road outside Muxloe's house. It was faint, but I noticed it. It was the sound of normality, the dependable ordinary. It comforted me to know that the world continued on in its mundane rhythms. It was the anchor I needed. My understanding of the world – as limited as that was – had been well and truly turned on its head, but for everyone else out there, it was just another day. I envied that, yet at the same time, the detachment I felt kind of thrilled me.

Here I was, just this average, *didn't-know-his-head-from-his-arse* kid, but I'd glimpsed something wondrous, something more than most experience in an entire lifetime.

Surely I had to embrace it. No matter what.

"How does my dad fit into all this?" I asked.

"I'll get to that," said Muxloe, an unexpected sharpness to his voice. "Stokely opened the Electric to the public in 1924. Before that, Molly had had the cinema to herself – with her friends, of course. But with her personal fortune dwindling, Stokely convinced Molly of the financial gain in opening the Electric, and finally she caved. Perhaps it's not surprising though that in those three years before Molly's death, audience levels were pretty low.

"Things did pick up in the thirties, however, but it never really did big business. I suppose the location was a factor – so out of the way 'un all – but I've no doubt that people could just... *feel* the things in there. I certainly could.

"When I started in '49, the Electric was just about keeping its head above water. It didn't really break even until the mid-fifties, and Molly's trust fund had well and truly dried up by then."

Cautiously, Emma asked, "What did you see... when you started working there?"

"Not too much. Shadows, really... glimpses of things in the corner of the eye, you know... that kind of thing. It was a sense more than anything. It felt... I don't know... heavy, like it was crowded in there."

That sent my skin prickling with gooseflesh again.

"I was there two years before Stokely told me anything of the place's history. I'd found Lévesque's account, or at least the translation, in amongst a pile of old paperwork. Reginald caught me reading it at his desk and... well, that was when it all came out. He looked relieved to be telling me, truth be known, like he was unburdening himself of it.

"After that, I started seeing things more and more – like my eyes suddenly attuned to it."

I can see with better eyes, I thought.

"Reginald Stokely died about three or four months after he told me all this. His son ran it for a while after that, but he was about as much use as a trained chimp. I took the reins of the Electric in the mid-fifties; the height of all that giant radioactive monster stuff your dad loved so much. It certainly brought in the crowds, I'll give it that. Kids mostly. I guess the 1950s were the apex of teenage cinema, and because the Electric was so tucked out of the way, it became a kind of Mecca for them... and, well, your dad was one of them, Sam."

"Who was Seymour Janks?" I asked.

"Janks…" mused Muxloe, rubbing his chin. "Seymour Janks came to the Electric in the winter of 1961. Your dad was there alone, sitting out under the marquee, waiting for me to arrive, when Janks made his appearance. It had snowed heavy that year and I'd had difficulty getting to work, so was running late.

"Janks came walking out from the trees; a tall, gaunt-looking gentleman whose suit, hair, and skin pallor all seemed to blend in with the surrounding snow. He was stark white from weathered head to shiny shoe… thin as a rail. He was by far the strangest looking fella I've ever laid eyes on.

"Your dad told me that when he'd come striding out of the trees, he was smiling, and cradling a stack of film cans in his arms. He walked straight up to your father and said, 'You like Humphrey Bogart films, don't ya, kid? Well, I've got one here, and it's a real good one. You wanna see it?'"

"*When the Night Came Fallin'*," I said.

"That's right. How do you know that?"

"We saw it, or at least part of it… at the Electric."

"When?"

"Yesterday."

He fell silent for a moment, watching us closely. Finally, he said, "Seems as if you've both got a few stories to tell me also."

"We have," I said, "but I'd like to know about my dad first."

"Well, there's not much more to tell really, Sam. I arrived just as Janks was handing the cans over to your father. I trudged through the snow, and by the time I reached the marquee, Janks had melted back into the white trees.

"Your dad was sitting there shivering; he had his arms wrapped around the stack of cans in his lap. I saw the film's title, and the name of its star, handwritten across the lid. I knew right away that no such Bogart film existed. I asked John who the man was, but your dad didn't answer at first. His eyes were wide open, and when he looked up at me, I saw they were rimmed with tears.

"Finally, he found his voice and told me. He said that the

man in the white suit had given him a picture to watch, and had said that if he liked it, he would return, bringing with him more films."

"Your dad and I lined up the first reel right away. We had two hours before the afternoon matinee... it was a Thursday if I remember rightly, so business was slow anyhow. We only opened Thursdays through to Sundays back then. John fed the film through the machine, and within moments that magic light was beaming out across the theatre, and I knew right away that there was something very different about that film. It was the score that got me at first – there was something in that music. A tone... a sound I couldn't make sense of. It set me on edge, although I wouldn't have been able to tell you why exactly.

"Your dad raced down to the auditorium, and I followed. And there we sat... neither of us saying a word, watching this... otherworldly film."

Muxloe's eyes glazed over with the memory. "*Otherworldly...*" he said, his voice a rasp. It was the word that had taken root in my mind also, and Muxloe was right, there was no better word to describe *When the Night Came Fallin'*. Everything about that film felt otherworldly, every texture in every frame, every sound, every word, every action, coming through from another place. It was Bogart, but it wasn't Bogart. It was Jean Harlow, yet it wasn't.

It was the *know* of them.

I looked at Muxloe. He was still locked in the past, his eyes brimming, his face haggard and weary to the core. He looked impossibly old.

"My son died in 1971," he said. Emma glanced at me, frowning. "Hardest thing a parent can do is bury his offspring. His mother had been gone nine years when Harvey died... a small mercy, I suppose. Least she didn't have to see it... live through it."

This sudden change of subject threw me completely. I had

to look away from the restrained anguish on Muxloe's face. I found it hideous to look at, frightening even. It made me think of my mother's face on the long, horrific day after my father's death. I looked to the hearth and saw a spider scuttling up and between the stacks of newspapers. I tried to concentrate on that.

"He sold cars, nothing fancy, but I was proud as hell," continued Muxloe. "He died of an asthma attack. Just like that... gone. He was twenty-four years old."

I now wanted to get out of there as fast as possible. The spider tucked itself into a slight opening between the heavy folds of pages. If I didn't know it was there, it would've been nigh-on impossible to see.

"I ran Janks' films day and night, one after another, for weeks and weeks. The know of many came... but not my son... not my son."

Muxloe lent forward. The movement caught my attention. He was looking straight at me. He said, "You may not find who you're looking for at the Electric, Sam. I want you to know that."

I didn't say anything. I couldn't.

"I think it's time you both left," he said. "I'm very tired."

"But..." Emma protested.

"Go."

We both stood up. Muxloe remained seated and picked up the box containing Lévesque's letters. This he handed to me. As I took it, he looked at me and said, "These mysteries are yours now."

I still have that box.

Half an hour later Emma and I were sitting on a wall eating cheeseburgers. It felt good to finally be getting some food inside me, and I wolfed mine down in no time. We were on a busy street in the town – cars passing, people milling, kids yelling. The sun was on my back. This was what I needed. The dependable ordinary.

Across the street, a little further down from us, stood the Trocadero, the picture house where I'd seen *Jaws* with my mum and dad – the last time we'd gone to the cinema together as a family. I thought once again about my dad near enough jumping out of his skin at part of the film, and him grabbing me in a headlock and ruffling up my hair because I'd laughed at him. I thought of Mum telling us both to behave, and us sniggering into our hands like little kids. He had sometimes been a hard man to reach, but at that moment I'd felt very close to him.

I wondered if he'd thought about *When the Night Came Fallin'* as he sat with me in that darkened theatre. If he remembered Seymour Janks and, as Muxloe described, the *know* of many at the Electric. I wondered if he told anyone about it after he went off to college, or if he ever went back there later in life.

Did he ever tell my mother?

My mind throbbed with questions, and not just about my father. It seemed Elmer Muxloe still had a great deal to tell us, especially concerning Seymour Janks and those films of his. If he hadn't brought up his son, we would no doubt have heard a lot more.

I looked to the Trocadero. On the marquee it said *Weird Science* was showing, a film I wasn't to see until the following year on VHS. Emma finished her cheeseburger, and then jumped off the wall to throw her crumpled up napkin into a nearby bin. She came back, wiped her hands on her shorts, and then leaned on her bike.

"What do you wanna do now? she asked.

"What do you want to do?"

She shrugged her shoulders, then fell silent. I looked back to the Trocadero. I remembered us lined up outside in the rain waiting to go in, Dad humming the *Jaws* theme and nudging me saying, *not long now, kid.*

If only he'd known what he was saying.

If only I'd known.

Emma pulled me back to the now. She said, "We've got to go back there."

I knew she meant the Electric, not Elmer Muxloe's. I had a sudden image of my dad as a young man, sat in the auditorium with the Technicolor tramp, watching Humphrey Bogart in that weird, desert land. I pictured the black train on the rail, thunderheads brooding above. Then I pictured my dad in one of the carriages.

I looked at Emma. "I know," I said. "Let's go."

I remembered something as we were riding over to the Electric, something that didn't mean much to me at the time, but suddenly seemed to make a lot more sense.

I'd come home from school one afternoon to find my dad sprawled out on the sofa watching *The Harder They Fall*, a Bogart flick set in the world of boxing. It was a *noir* world, a Bogart world, filled with shady promoters, down-on-their-luck fighters, and rigged championships. It was also the final picture Bogart made before he died.

It was rare to find my dad at home so early, yet I can't remember asking him why he wasn't at work. I just sat in the chair across from him and started to watch the film. He asked me how school was going and if I'd drawn anything that week. Small talk, nothing out of the ordinary. I muttered vague answers, then changed the subject and asked him about the film. He started to fill me in, telling me that Bogart was a washed-up sportswriter, dragged into the world of fixed fights.

I said, "He looks pretty old in this one, Dad."

"Yeah. He died a year after it was made."

"Oh," I said. "Was this his last film then?"

He sat up, and the look he gave me was so strange, so pained, that I made some excuse about homework and got out of that room as fast as I could.

Over dinner that night, he never said one word to me.

We stopped riding once we reached the shack, and pushed our bikes the rest of the way. Emma had been very quiet on the way over. Whenever I tried to say something, she'd be short with me. I wondered if I'd done something wrong and upset her in some way, but I didn't know what it could've been. Mind you, I suppose she had every reason to be a little curt. We were involved in something beyond any kind of rational thought, so if she wasn't exactly in a talkative mood, then I guess that was pretty understandable.

It had taken a little under an hour to ride back from town to the Electric, and by now it was mid-afternoon. The sun was sweltering, and I wondered how much longer this Indian summer could last for. Autumn was only around the corner after all.

This struck me with a sudden sense of melancholy.

Summer's end.

Our final one together before the last year of school.

I wondered where we'd all be in a year's time. We'd have to get jobs, or apply to colleges (depending on grades, of course. Something I didn't hold much hope for – for myself, or David for that matter). We'd be spat out into the world and would, more than likely, all go our separate ways. I suddenly felt bad for having ditched Dave, then remembered that he'd run out on us, and that made me feel even worse. In fact, it made me feel angry.

These thoughts were rattling around my head when I suddenly remembered staying up and drawing into the night. That wonderful sense of *completeness* rushed back to me, and all my bitter feelings blew away in an instant. It all slotted into place. *I* slotted into place.

I'd felt this focus before, albeit fleetingly, back when I'd been drawing before Dad had died, but it had never been so strong. Nowhere near. The Electric had brought it back to me, and intensified it. I had drawn the *know* of many, and it fuelled me with such a great sense of ambition, I just knew that it would never again leave me. I would draw, whether people paid me to or not. It would be my life's work.

Knowing that with such certainty at fifteen was extremely overwhelming, yet at the same time, I knew that it would be all the anchor I would ever need.

Before we entered the copse, I looked back, past the shack and across the field, out to the sheer blue horizon and its saffron sun. At that moment, I knew exactly who I was, and exactly what I wanted to be.

It was lovely and cool inside the copse. Emma led the way, following the track to the clearing. Again, I glimpsed the Electric through the trees and immediately broke out in gooseflesh. It was beginning to become something of a habit.

Even though it had been less than twenty-four hours since we were last here, it seemed a lot longer. In fact, it felt like days had passed.

Out in the clearing, Emma and I stood and stared at the Electric. The place looked different somehow, although I knew nothing had changed with the building itself. It was how I *saw* it that felt different. There was familiarity for one thing. The Electric was no longer new to me. I knew its history, its secrets. I knew the names of the people who had built it, and died in it. But more than any of that, I knew my father had come here, long ago, when he'd not been that much older than me. I felt that connection. It gave me a deeper sense of purpose for being there.

Emma dropped her bike to the ground and took a step forward.

"Do you hear something?" she asked.

I listened for a moment, but could hear nothing but the rustling of trees. She glanced over her shoulder at me. "Do you hear it?"

"No," I said.

"*Listen*," she said.

I dropped my bike next to hers, then went over and stood beside her. I heard birdsong coming from the copse, and the far-off drone of a plane crossing the sky, but that was all.

"What is it?" I said.

"It's…" she began, but her attention was caught up in whatever she was hearing. She titled her head to the side, listening intently. Finally, she turned to me and said, "There's a film playing inside the Electric."

There was indeed a film playing at the Electric, and the *know* of many were there to watch it.

The film itself was *A Murder of Crows,* and starred the glitterati of fright pictures: Karloff, Lugosi, Lon Chaney, Sr, and the unmistakable Peter Lorre.

I knew Lorre from Bogart movies. They'd made a few together, including *Casablanca* and *The Maltese Falcon*, two of the most celebrated films in Bogart's canon. Here, however, Lorre crept around moonwashed graveyards, scattershot with crooked tombstones, and trudged down cobwebbed catacombs, lighted by lanterns. This was Gothic horror land. His shifty, sinister drawl and bug-eyed stare made him pitch perfect for such murderous and macabre plots, and he certainly played it up to the hilt in this one.

The audience for this carnival of horrors were ghosts. Far more than before. Three of the rows near the front of the screen were pretty much filled entirely. Sparks of colour ignited the dark from each and every one of them; their collective bulk creating a kind of hazy moiré.

A few rows back, sat alone in his usual seat, was the Technicolor tramp. He glanced round and gave me a nod. I couldn't bring myself to return the greeting though. I thought about Albert Lévesque's phantasmagoria show.

On the screen, Peter Lorre was showing Boris Karloff a collection of jars and bottles, which cluttered up a few dusty old shelves in a lantern-lit cellar.

"They're known by many names," said Lorre. "Fire-drakes, freits, powries, gringes... many, many names."

"And more still besides, Mr Mavelock," said Karloff, his

distinctive lisp instantly recognisable. "Scrags, shellycoats, fetches, spoorns, old-shocks, swathes, scar-bugs, nickies, chit-tifaces, and clabbernappers… I could go on."

"You know your spooks, Mr D'Lack."

"I've made them my life's work, Mr Mavelock."

Karloff leaned in and inspected one of the bottles. Inside was a vaporous substance that, immediately on inspection, shifted and formed into that of a figure, or at least the vague shape of one. Then it solidified, becoming the tiny manifestation of a woman.

The film cut to a close-up of her trapped inside the bottle. She had long black hair and pallid, almost incandescent skin. Her eyes were dark and intense. I was struck by her right away.

"That's Gracile," said Lorre's character, Mr Mavelock. "She was one of the first I captured. She was murdered by the hands of a jealous lover more than a century ago. Beautiful, isn't she?"

"Quite," said Karloff.

Voices coming through from another world.

It really wasn't very difficult to believe. Not anymore.

A Murder of Crows had that same weird texture the Bogart film had. Just as Bogie had felt in *When the Night Came Fallin'*, so too did Karloff and Lorre. It looked like them, but it didn't *feel* like them. There was a quality that was entirely alien to me. An *Electric quality*. Yet, what surprised me was that it didn't seem to affect me badly anymore. My mind had adjusted some-how, like it had with the movie posters. There was no nausea, no fear even. I just seemed to accept it.

I looked over at Emma. Flickering light cast across her face; her eyes glistened. We were standing just inside the theatre, by the doors. We hadn't moved since entering. I took her hand and caught her attention.

"You wanna sit down?" I asked.

"Do you?"

"Yes," I said. "I'd like to see this film."

The film was a phantasmagoria show. It had a hallucinogenic quality. Much of the plot made little to no sense, but it didn't seem to matter. The imagery was so spellbinding that I hardly noticed the film's lack of narrative. It was a kaleidoscope of the strange and uncanny. By far, the most surreal movie I'd ever experienced. (Up to that point, anyhow. There were stranger still to come.)

What I could make out of the film's plot centred around Lorre's character, Mr Mavelock. He was a collector of ghosts.

For reasons I wasn't too clear on, he had the ability to capture and bottle the spirits of the dead, and then sell his prizes to the wealthy and dangerous.

Enter Karloff's wonderfully creepy Mr D'Lack. A man out for revenge.

Emma and I had walked in on the scene in which Karloff was attempting to buy the most malevolent ghost he could. He planned to release this *phantom*, as he called it, into the house of his enemy, a certain Crichton Snarks, played by Bela Lugosi. (Karloff and Lugosi seemed to be pitted against one another in every movie they made together.)

As the scene unfolded, however, Karloff got distracted in the pursuit of his revenge by the beautiful and vampiric bottled ghost of Gracile, and on impulse, haggled out a price for her with Lorre. Gracile was played by Theda Bara, who, I later discovered, was a silent movie star. In fact, she was one of the biggest stars of the era, alongside Chaplin and Mary Pickford. She was also cited as being the first sex symbol of the medium. She was sensual, and mysterious, and wore extremely risqué costumes (in those early days of cinema, before the production code, films often pushed boundaries). In *A Murder of Crows*, she certainly lived up to her legend. She was a *femme fatale*, alluring and dangerous, and I was smitten with her right away.

I became very conscious of staring at Bara whenever she was on screen. I felt sure Emma knew what I was thinking, and I found myself getting a little embarrassed.

On the screen, Karloff too was smitten, and cradled the bottled Theda Bara against his chest like a talisman.

"You should watch yourself with that one, Mr D'Lack" said Peter Lorre. "Gracile's not what she seems."

Karloff turned, caught in shadows.

"I haven't finished," he said, ignoring Lorre's warning. "Show me the most harrowed spirit you have."

Peter Lorre's bug-eyes widened, making him look like a kind of living gargoyle. "I could show you *The Wretch*, but I'm warning you Mr D'Lack, you unleash that thing on someone, be prepared for hell on earth."

Karloff stepped towards him, his frame towering over Lorre. He said, "Show me."

Lorre led him to a particular jar on the bottom shelf. Unlike the other jars and bottles, it wasn't on display; it was set back, wrapped in shadows. Lorre bent down and grabbed it. Karloff's eyes were captured in a brief close-up.

Lorre placed the jar on a higher shelf and stepped back, allowing Karloff to inspect the supposed *Wretch* trapped inside.

Again, a manifestation swirled and formed into being. This time it was a man, hideous and disfigured; his shape crooked and bent into a strange and unnatural posture. This was indeed a *Wretch*; a pitiful, tormented creature, twisted by deformity and, I imagined, much more besides.

The actor playing this phantom, as Karloff had referred to it, was Lon Chaney: the man of a thousand faces, as he was known in life.

Chaney had been a master of pantomime, specialising in the grotesque and deformed. He created and applied his own make-up, and transformed himself with each new film into a hideous array of villains and monsters; a legacy that was a rogues' galley of the strange and the disturbing.

At fifteen I hadn't seen any of his films, but I'd seen plenty of pictures of his various creations in the few books I had on old horror films – stills from *The Phantom of the Opera* and *The Hunchback of Notre Dame* often being the most frequently pictorialised. I had seen his son, Lon Chaney, Jr, seemingly countless times in *The Wolfman* and its many sequels – and in school when we'd watched *Of Mice and Men*, where Chaney, Jr had played Lennie – but I'd never seen his father on film until that moment. Quite fitting, I thought, that I should first witness this macabre master onscreen by seeing the *know* of him.

The scene ended on a two shot of Karloff's face staring at the grotesquery in the jar. He smiled, and *The Wretch* smiled back at him.

Emma and I sat and watched the entire film. She never once let go of my hand.

Karloff unleashed *The Wretch* upon Lugosi, and Chaney, free from his glass prison and returned to life-sized form, led a merry dance around him. There was something of the trickster in Chaney's performance. He didn't speak, but laughed and jeered his way through the film like a kind of hideous jester; a pantomime horror whose presence was felt even when he wasn't on screen. Chaney pinned me back to the chair. He was astounding.

Karloff also released Theda Bara from her bottle. This time for himself. But true to Lorre's word, she was not what she seemed. She was a succubus, a temptress and deceiver. She could have been Lilith, or Grendel's mother, or a witch woman from the *Conan* stories I used to read. Bara's character Gracile was a sorceress, and ultimately, she was Karloff's ruin.

In one phantasmagorical sequence, Bara levitated over a bedridden Karloff. He lay in a delirium of madness and fever. Through some kind of psychic jiggery-pokery, Bara fed a cascade of images into Karloff's already overwrought mind. It was at this part of the picture that the narrative began to break down. From then on, the film became a kind of hallucinogenic ride.

The pictures seemed to drill into me, filling my mind with

their strange, *otherworldly* substance. Much of it was difficult to make out, yet even the more obscure imagery still resonated. It all had that *Electric quality*.

There were great rivers filled with black boats, skies full of moons, night roads that stretched out under vast scintillations of stars, and great mountains from which towers jutted high into clouds; images that made little sense other than their sheer poetry and beauty.

There was also the desert, and the black train.

I found, to my surprise, that I was crying, and I tried to wipe the tears away as discreetly as I could. I don't think Emma noticed.

That sequence affected me so much that the remainder of the film went by in a blur. Karloff, sent insane by Bara's malevolent spirit, finally confronted Bela Lugosi with murder in mind. Lugosi, driven to despair by his own resident demon, rose to the battle, and both men killed each other in a somewhat anticlimactic final reel.

The film did have an epilogue, however, that returned to Peter Lorre and his collection of ghosts. He placed two jars on a shelf side by side. The camera tracked into them and the vapour swirled and formed into that of Karloff and Lugosi, both men imprisoned in death and tormented by their proximity to one another.

Perhaps a somewhat obvious ending, but still, it was satisfying.

I read each and every credit at the end of the film. It had been directed by Tod Browning. Browning had made many films with Lon Chaney during the silent era, but was perhaps better known for having directed *Dracula* with Bela Lugosi in 1931, and the infamous movie *Freaks* the following year.

The credit that astonished me more than any other however was the one that immediately followed Browning's. It read: *written by Edgar Allan Poe.*

The screen went black, and the audience rose in unison.

Emma and I remained in our seats as *they* began to file out of the theatre. I attempted to avoid eye contact, but found it impossible. Each and every one of them looked at us as they passed, perhaps as curious and perplexed as we were.

I saw the large lady from before, the one with the lopsided hat and long silvery hair. For some reason, her hair made me think of a bright moon reflected in a river. It was translucent, and seemed to move about her chubby face as if picked up by a breeze. There was no breeze, however; there was only stillness and silence now inside the Electric. There was no sound of shuffling feet, no mutterings or discussion of any kind, even though I did notice many of them talking to one another. We just couldn't hear it, though.

The large old lady gave us both a smile. I don't know if Emma smiled back, but I certainly didn't.

The faces that passed us all had that heightened vibrancy. Colours seemed to spark and bleed into a tapestry of light. Some were difficult to see clearly, their features so washed out by brilliance.

My old friend the Technicolor tramp was the last to leave. He gave me another nod, and this time, I managed to nod back. He smiled, then left, and Emma and I were suddenly all alone.

Then there came a sudden rush within me. I turned to Emma and said, "I need to draw that film."

She looked at me and said, "I know."

I set up in the lobby. In my haste to get started, I tipped the contents of my rucksack across the floor and grabbed what I needed. After this, I took a large piece of broken tile and laid it before me to use as a kind of rest, then I sat cross-legged and hunched over my paper.

Through all this, I hardly paid Emma any mind. She stood at the foot of the staircase watching me. Her expression was difficult to read, but I think it was one of concern, or perhaps grim fascination.

I sharpened one of my pencils, then set to work.

Emma shuffled around the lobby, at a loss as to what to do. I found her movements distracting, and had to bite my tongue from telling her so.

Finally, she said, "I'm going to take a look around."

"Okay," I said, relieved. I didn't even look up at her.

I heard her ascend the stairs and cross the floor above. I figured she was heading for the projection room. It struck me how relaxed we were; both happy to wander, and to be alone. I knew *they* had left though, I could feel it, and felt sure Emma could to. I didn't doubt that they'd be back, but for now, the Electric was nothing more than a dilapidated old cinema, its ghosts gone to ground.

I sketched furiously. I felt out of myself; my mind thoughtless. I allowed my subconscious to guide the pencil. I didn't want to get in the way of that by having any notion of what I was doing. I totally shut myself down. It was like drawing from a dream. I stared only at the nib. If I did glance at my work, it was for the briefest of moments, and even then I didn't allow myself to take in what I was doing. This trance state came easily to me, although I couldn't say how I did it exactly. It just seemed to turn on as soon as I put the pencil to the paper – the same as it had been in my bedroom the night before.

How long I sat on the floor drawing, I have no idea, but as immediate as that surge of creative hurly-burly came, so too did it leave. It cut off, and I blinked my eyes into the clear and present.

Even then I didn't look closely at what I had done. I took the paper and stood up, my legs stiff and aching. I walked over to the Harold Lloyd poster, *Mad Dogs*, and placed my own picture on top of it, sliding the edges beneath the frame as best I could until it held. Then I stepped back and stared at my work.

It was rough, to say the least. Yet it had the same quality as my other pictures. That *Electric quality*.

I had drawn the inside of the theatre. A shaft of light cut across the darkness, spilling out onto the screen. Below, rows of darkened figures sat watching *The Wretch*, Chaney's malevolent trickster, dancing a jig inside his bottle.

It was crude, obviously rushed, but I'd somehow managed to get across the *essence* of watching *A Murder of Crows*. Even the audience, which I'd sketched in very little detail – nothing more than shapes, really – still rang true. I'd only used pencil, therefore there was no colour, but the nature with which I'd drawn these cinemagoers, all huddled up, my lines crossing, creating a kind of mass bulk, made me think of the haze; the bleeding of brightness which *they* all possessed.

I stood enraptured with my work. Yet I felt no egotism in this, simply because, even though I knew I had physically drawn the picture, it didn't feel like I could take all the credit. I knew I was channelling something with this stuff. It wasn't entirely all me in the drawing. It was also the Electric.

I noticed two figures sat several rows back from the main knot. Again, there was no detail, they were nothing more than shapes, yet they *felt* different. The lines were sharper, for one thing; they didn't merge into one another. Somehow, I knew they were real. Even without any detail, their forms were drawn with more care, as opposed to the frenetic scrawl of the others. I knew they were meant to be Emma and me.

I stepped forward, bending a little to take a closer look, and that's when I sensed that there was somebody standing behind me.

I couldn't bring myself to turn around. I knew that it wasn't Emma. It was the *know* of someone. It was a ghost.

The word sliced into my mind and quivered there, dressed up in neon, singing and dancing. *Ghost. Ghost. Ghost.* I felt clammy; my t-shirt clung to the skin. I couldn't move. The only sound I could hear was my own breathing. It sounded very loud to my ears; an amplified rasp that rattled around my head. I wondered if I was going to faint. Sweat ran down my face. I did think about bolting for the door, but only for the briefest of moments. Still, the alternative of actually turning around seemed equally impossible. Instead, I somehow managed to take a step to the side, as if to allow whoever was there a look at my picture.

Then the shape came and stood next to me.

It was a man. I could tell by his frame in my peripheral vision. I focused on a long, spidery crack in the wall. It struck me that this was by far the closest proximity I'd been to one of them. All it would take would be for me to reach out a little and I'd be able to touch him. Could I touch him? Perhaps my hand would go right through his body, like it did in the movies. I noticed the shape bend forward and stare at my drawing. That was when I finally managed to turn my head, and take a look at him.

He was a lean man – tall, refined, with deep black hair and a pencil-thin moustache. His nose was crooked, yet this did nothing to diminish his handsomeness; if anything, it only added to it. He wore a black suit. It had tails. The shirt was white – beaming white. A bow tie hung loose around the neck. To me, he looked like an old-time magician. He stared at my picture like it was some great piece of art. I suddenly felt very self conscious about my work. I noticed his shoes, black and shiny.

He turned to look at me.

The word came into my head again.

Ghost.

It did its merry little jig.

The man spoke. I didn't hear his voice, but I read his lips. He said, "It's good."

He gave me a smile, and in that moment, I felt elated. It was the first critical response I'd had from anyone outside of my friends and family.

And it had come from a dead man.

Fitting, I thought.

I managed a meek "Thank you," and he gave me a nod of his head as if to say, *that's quite all right.* I couldn't help but smile back.

Suddenly, I heard Emma running across the floor above. She shouted my name, over and over again. She was in one hell of a hurry.

The magician heard as well and tilted his head up to the ceiling.

"Sam, where are you?" she cried.

I didn't answer.

She came running down the staircase, still calling my name. She was beginning to panic now. I could hear it in her voice.

The magician – I could think of him as nothing else now – looked back at me and arched one eyebrow. It was almost comical.

Then he was gone.

There were no bells and whistles, no fading into transparency like you see in the films, he was just simply not there anymore.

Vanished, like a true magician.

Emma saw me as she came down the main staircase. She stopped in her tracks and shouted, "Why didn't you answer me?"

I couldn't answer.

"Come on," she said, "you've got to see what I've found."

"What is it?"

"I think…" she trailed off.

"Em?"

"They're drawings, Sam. Like yours. Only, I think they're by your dad."

We walked along the corridor of broken windows, glass crunching underfoot. I fully expected Emma to lead me into the projection room, but instead she walked right on by, toward the door at the end of the corridor. It had been left slightly ajar, by Emma I presumed, and through the gap I noticed a stack of boxes. I could even make out the inscription written on the side of each one: *The Electric*.

Outside, the sky was still a cloudless blue wall, broken only by a white sun that kicked out fiercely, seemingly without mercy. The humidity was so close, the air so stifling, that I wondered, in a moment of whimsy, if the summer would blaze away forever. It felt like it had no end.

We reached the door, and Emma pushed it open. The hinges creaked, sounding uncommonly loud in the stillness. It was a small room, cluttered to the hilt with boxes and papers and what-have-you. There was a desk, or at least, there was a desk somewhere beneath all the clutter, behind which stood an ancient looking filing cabinet that had browned with age. The room had once been wallpapered – judging by its strikingly old-fashioned Art Deco design, it could have been papered back when the place had been built – only now it hung in shreds and tatters. It was a time capsule.

However, little of this caught my immediate attention, for across the room, on the far wall, was an open door that led straight outside. I saw there was a rusty wrought iron staircase attached to the back of the building. I assumed this led up to the roof. This was what fascinated me most of all.

"Was that door already open?" I asked Emma.

She said, "No, I opened it. It was pitch black in here, and really fusty and horrible. I had to let some air in."

I walked around the desk and noticed the drawings right away.

"I made some space for you," Emma said, and she had. Much of the desk's debris had been pushed back, and my father's work had been laid out front and centre. I hung back.

"This must have been Reginald Stokely's office," I said, "back in the day."

"Yeah, I suppose it was."

"You know where those steps lead to?"

"I've poked my head out. Goes up to the roof."

"Thought so," I said, then fell silent. I stood motionless. My clothes stuck to me. My mouth was a sawdust factory. One glance at the drawings had racked me with loss, and I wasn't sure if I could bring myself to look again. Ghosts were one thing, but any kind of legacy of my dad seemed to be another thing entirely. I also worried about crying in front of Emma. I wasn't sure I could take that kind of humiliation.

There was something else as well.

My dad's drawings looked like they had been drawn by my own hand. Our styles were indistinguishable. We both had that *Electric quality*.

Emma stepped toward me. "Sam," she said, "it's okay. You should look at them. They're quite amazing."

She took my hand and squeezed it. It seemed to be our thing.

I looked at her, and so strong was the urge to kiss her, that it propelled me over to my dad's pictures, if only to avoid the humiliating spectacle of me lunging for her mouth.

There were three drawings in all, two of which were little more than sketches really, but the third was something else entirely. It was incredibly detailed – dense and rich, and far beyond my own abilities. The sketches, however, were fairly crude, but as familiar to me as if I'd drawn them myself.

The first was of Humphrey Bogart, gun levelled at his hip in the classic stance, while the other was more abstract. It was of a windmill cut against a hailstorm sky, and there were bodies strung up between each sail. I couldn't look at that one for very long.

The third picture appeared to be of Albert Lévesque's phantasmagoria show. The one he performed that night for Molly and her *friends*, on the very ground the Electric now stood.

The centrepiece of the picture was a giant skull, hanging in midair, surrounded by swirls of smoke. Dark woods lay beyond it. In the foreground, Lévesque was stood operating his lantern box. He looked horrified, and perhaps had good reason to, because the audience for his supposedly terrifying show were all falling about laughing. A few had even fallen right off their chairs and were sprawled out on the ground. I noticed Molly, or what I thought to be Molly, sat at the back of the chair set, watching her friends as they rolled around. She was smiling.

The detail with which my father had drawn each and every face was extraordinary. I was awestruck. Yet, what astonished me more than anything else was that I recognised one of the faces – that of Albert Lévesque himself.

He was the man I'd just met down in the lobby.

There was a tiny signature in the right hand corner of each picture. It simply read, *Crowhurst*. It was the trigger that sprung the well. I turned my back to Emma and tried to control the rush of tears, but it was futile. They came and they came in a great surge, and I was helpless to their onslaught.

I felt Emma's hand gently rest on my shoulder. I had to stop myself from shaking her off. From somewhere far away, I heard her say, "It's okay, Sam… It's okay." But it wasn't, too much had happened, and I couldn't make sense of any of it. I was also embarrassed; angry with myself for breaking down in front of her.

"Sam," she said. "Please turn around."

That request was too much for me. I couldn't let her see me in such a state, so I did the only thing I could think of in the given circumstance, I fled across the room and out onto the iron staircase. I didn't look back.

My footfalls reverberated all the way to the roof.

I immediately regretted it of course.

I stopped crying by the time I reached the roof, and all that remained was anger and shame. My face seemed to burn with it. I felt mortified. At that moment, I would've been quite happy for the ground to open up and swallow me whole. I would've gone with a smile.

I didn't see how I could ever look Emma in the face again. I'd ruined everything. Of that much, I was certain.

The iron staircase had led me up to what was a flat roof. A crumbling brick wall, only several courses high, enclosed it. One part of the wall had toppled entirely, leaving a scattering of bricks in its wake. Many more bricks, I felt sure, must have fallen to the ground below. The roof itself was cracked and broken up in places. It certainly didn't look safe, that was for sure, but it didn't stop me. I paced, trying to figure out what to do, what to say to Emma. A few lengths of rotten old timber lay about here and there. I kicked one or two of these, and the scraping sound they made caused a quarrel of sparrows to take flight from the treetops beyond. I gazed up and watched them mark the sky, but then something else caught my attention. From out of the tree line below ran a gravel track that led right up to the back of the building. If we'd had taken the time to explore the outside of the Electric, as we had the inside, we would, of course, have stumbled on it before now. But we hadn't, and seeing that track made me realise there was a lot more to discover about the old cinema, and its grounds. Even more curious was that there were yellow markings in spray paint at several points along the track. The paint looked fresh.

I was puzzling this over when I heard Emma coming up the iron staircase behind me. I kept my back to her.

The sun was edging down the sky, but the stifling heat remained. I wanted a cold shower. I felt grimy and horrible. In fact, it'd been days since I last felt clean. I wondered how bad I smelt.

I heard Emma walk up behind me. I felt the hairs on my neck prickle.

She stopped short of me, and just stood there. I suspected she was angry with me. I could feel her eyes boring into the back of my head. Gooseflesh broke out along my legs and arms.

Suddenly I knew it wasn't Emma behind me.

It was the *know* of someone.

This realisation caused an involuntary reaction that propelled me forward in a wild, stumbling lurch. I felt sure it could have been worthy of the very finest of slapstick comedians. It was spectacular in its clumsiness. My feet didn't stand a chance;

they just couldn't keep up with my trajectory. My arms flailed about like a drowning man. I must have been quite a sight to behold. I came down on my right foot, and it went from under me, twisting violently.

The *Crowhurst Ankle* strikes again!

I think I yelped as I went down. My right knee thumped hard against the roof, and I felt skin tear open on both hands. I hit the deck in a crumpled heap. I rolled about like an upturned beetle, holding my knee, feeling very sorry for myself. Finally, I managed to sit myself upright and scan the roof.

There was no one there.

At least, not anymore.

Whoever it was, though, they must have had a hell of a good laugh at my expense. I looked at my hands. I picked out grit and dirt from the blood. Twice in relatively quick succession someone had come and stood behind me. It made me angry. "Yeah, really funny, numbskull," I spat to the empty roof. "My sides are splitting." Witless sarcasm seemed to be my best line of defence when humiliated.

"Who are you talking to?"

The phrase *I nearly jumped out of my skin* applies here. I think I may have even yelped again.

Emma was stood at the top of the iron staircase looking at me in total puzzlement.

"Is somebody up here with you?" she said.

My nape prickled once more. "No," I said. "They've gone."

She came onto the roof and walked over to me. "You saw them?"

"No, I didn't see them. They were stood behind me and I tried to get away… and, well, I fell right over… like a complete tool."

She knelt down beside me, looking down at my hands, and general pitifulness. "You are a tool all right," she said through a smile. "You all right?" she added.

"Yeah, I'll live. Went over on my ankle. It kills."

"Can you walk?"

"I don't know, I haven't tried yet," I said, laying it on a little thick.

I looked at her. The lowering sun caught her hair and brought out the beautiful deep red again. "I'm sorry," I said.

"For what?"

"For running out on you down there. I was just being stupid."

"Sam, it's understandable. If it'd been a drawing by my mum, I would have reacted in exactly the same way. It's okay to feel sad, and hurt… even rejected. I've felt all those things, and more besides. It doesn't seem to get any easier, it's just…"

She trailed off.

"It's what?" I asked.

"It's just that you learn to live with it, that's all. It's like a shadow that follows you around. It's always there; it's just that sometimes it's sharp, and sometimes it's dull. Like a blade." She put her hand on my forearm. "You don't have to pretend around me, Sam. I know what you've been through."

I felt tears brimming again. I wiped them away with the back of my wrist.

Then I kissed her.

It was awkward and clumsy, and our positions in no way accommodated such an act, but still, I went for it. I tilted my head up and pressed my lips against hers – perhaps a little too hard at first. Still, she didn't pull away. In fact, she cupped a hand around my face and she kissed me back, equally as hard, which, to be honest, astonished me. I fell back against the roof. She followed me down, never once leaving my mouth, and draped herself over me. There was little grace in this manoeuvre, teeth clashed and noses were crushed, but it didn't seem to matter. Once I was laid on my back and she was pressed against me, then I believe the first real kissing of my life truly began.

We were up there for a long time. I went under her shirt and over the bra, but that was as far as it went. For the most part, we just buzzed off the exhilaration that comes with a first kiss. My hands were sore, my knee and my ankle throbbed, but I didn't let any of that stop me. I kissed Emma so deeply that I wondered, on that halcyon day of adolescence, if I would ever kiss anyone like that again. I did of course, but not until I was much older.

After a time, we simply lay there, wrapped in each other. I turned my head to the sun. It was creeping down behind tree-tops. Dusk was approaching, the borderland between day and full dark. It occurred to me that the Electric itself was a border-land, a neither-here-nor-there place; a kind of way station for the dead.

Suddenly, Emma sat bolt upright and exclaimed a breath-less, "*Oh my God!*"

"What?" I said. "What is it?"

She turned to me. I sat up a little, resting on my elbows, trying to look cool and nonchalant. I wasn't in the least bit comfortable.

"Remember when we got to Muxloe's and he asked us about his car?"

"No," I said, without giving the matter much thought.

"You do," Emma said, annoyed. "When he first came to the door, he asked if we'd come about the item in his car."

"So?"

"So… he sold the car to my dad for scrap. Remember?"

"Yeah," I said, slowly catching on.

"There's something in that car, Sam. Something that con-cerns the Electric. I'm sure of it."

"You think your dad would've crushed it yet?"

She thought for a moment, then said, "Come on. We've gotta go."

A gibbous moon hung low over the fields. Emma rode ahead of me. I pedalled hard, even though my ankle still throbbed. A scattering of stars had begun their grand reveal across the deep blue twilight. To the west, the sun slipped beneath the world, leaving blood on the horizon. I wanted to kiss Em some more, but knew the time had passed. The Electric and its mysteries eclipsed all else, whether I liked it or not.

As we rode, a memory came back to me. It was of the time we watched *The Texas Chainsaw Massacre* round at Dave's house – the first time Emma hung out with us.

Back then, David and I would rent a video out every Saturday without fail. Often times, if we were particularly taken with a given film, we would watch it twice in one day. It was usually horrors that were given repeat viewings. At thirteen, it seemed David and I had a bloodlust that just could not be quenched.

We would meet at our local video shop in the morning, spend a considerable amount of time choosing a tape, then, once we'd finally decided on something, we would race back, usually to Dave's, and stick the video straight on. Afterwards we'd get something to eat – usually a raid on Dave's mum's biscuit tin – analyse all the "best deaths", then re-watch it in the afternoon. A few films in particular – *Halloween, The Evil Dead, A Nightmare on Elm Street* – were given three viewings in one day. This was quite an accolade. In fact, I seem to remember *The Evil Dead* being rented out several times over the course of one summer.

In those early days of video, a film's certification held little sway over us. Ray Ellis, a local entrepreneur in the video revolution, would happily rent any film, of any certification, to anyone of any age. And every kid in our village knew it. At school, if you hadn't seen *The Evil Dead*, or *Zombie Flesh Eaters*, or *The Last House on the Left*, then you were a loser.

The Texas Chainsaw Massacre, however, wasn't rented from Ray Ellis' Video Emporium; it came by way of Emma. At school one day, Em overheard David and me discussing George A. Romero's *Dawn of the Dead*. She cut in and started to wax lyrical about the social commentary running through the film, something which David and I had been totally oblivious to. We were suitably impressed with Emma. Not only did she know the film inside out, providing us with an insight on consumerism and the foibles of modern society – and a lot of other stuff we couldn't make head nor tail of – but she was also, as David so tactlessly put it, "a girl". She gave him a bit of shit for that.

We spent our entire lunch hour sitting around in the Triangle talking about films. Emma had seen everything. She seemed to own everything as well. Or, at least, her dad did. She told us that he had a huge collection of "pirated" videos, most of which were horror films and, as she termed them, "blueys". David took a special interest in these. I can't remember how the subject of *The Texas Chainsaw Massacre* came up, but at that time, neither David nor I had seen it. The film itself was infamous, and for this very reason, it had been catapulted to the very top of every kid's must-see list. And Emma had her own copy.

Without us even prompting her, she said, "I could come round Saturday and bring over *Texas Chainsaw*, if you want…"

Well.

David's mouth hung agape. I guess mine did too. The idea of a girl – a female person – hanging out with us, outside of school no less, to watch horror movies all day, was perhaps more than our tiny little minds could comprehend.

Emma looked at us, and said, "You both look like that dude in *Scanners* before his head blew up."

Saturday morning came and Emma was a no show. David and I tried to conceal our disappointment, but it was clear we were both utterly devastated. We waited in silence for what seemed like an age, brooding, munching our way through the biscuit tin, and drinking far too much Coke. I felt sick after a while.

Around noon, David put on a video; I think just to drown out the silence. It was a *Mad Max* rip-off called *The New Barbarians*, which did absolutely nothing to alleviate the gloom. It was bad.

However, Emma finally did turn up mid-afternoon, armed with a stack of videos. David and I swanned round her like a couple of imbeciles, but she soon put us in our place. Emma had a way of disarming you, but also, she had a sharp tongue, and right away she would tell us when we were being "complete tools", as she so wisely put it.

Her horde of videos consisted of a dazzling array of low budget gore-fests, with incredible titles – *Faces of Death*, *I Spit on your Grave*, *Cannibals' Ferox*, *Holocaust*, and *The Burning*. All good, meaty stuff for a teenage mind. But it was *The Texas Chainsaw Massacre* that Dave and I wanted to see above all else.

David drew the curtains against the sun and shoved the tape into the player. Now, maybe it was down to being at an impressionable age, but that film scared the shit out of me like no other. I'd seen gorier films, perhaps films that'd made me jump more, but there was something else going on in *Texas Chainsaw* – something very bad bubbling away beneath the surface. The entire film made me feel dirty. It went right to the line. The film's director, Tobe Hooper, really tapped into something – something which most films do not, if any. It remains for me still perhaps the most psychological horror ever made. Everything about it, the shrill sound design, the heat, the screaming – poor Marilyn Burns must scream non-stop for half of that movie – the chickens, and the bones, and the skin; all of it compresses into the brain. The part where the nightmares are. And that's just what the film was: one long nightmare. When I finally saw it again years later, I was struck by how much humour there was in the film. I didn't pick up on any of that when I first saw it though. Moreover, that first viewing was made even worse by having to conceal my terror in front of Emma. She watched it like it was an episode of *Scooby-Doo*. I don't think David fared much better than me either, although he did laugh a few times, but I think that was more nerves than an actual understanding of the film's macabre humour.

When it ended on that unforgettable shot of Leatherface swinging his chainsaw about wildly, his frame cut against the red fire of a Texan sun, nobody moved. We sat in complete silence for a long time, even Emma.

It seems to me now, looking back, that the feeling *The Texas Chainsaw Massacre* left me with, was the closest I ever came to feeling that *Electric quality* outside of the films of that haunted place.

Finally, Emma said, "What did you think?"

"Yeah, it was all right," said David, clearly trying his damnedest to play down the complete assault he'd just received.

"Do you want to watch it again?" she asked.

Neither of us did. The next time I watched it, I was in my thirties.

It was full dark by the time we reached Albert Looms' Car Breakers. We walked our bikes along the old railway lines, then cut down the slope. The gates were all locked up of course, but there were plenty of gaps in the fence. The old thing was riddled with them. I looked up at the moon; it hung high over the tracks, shrouded in black and sliver clouds that scudded across its face. It looked like a painting.

Emma led the way to a small, jagged hole in the bottom of the fence. I hardly noticed it at first. It didn't look big enough to get a dog through, let alone us.

"That looks really tight, Em," I said. "Be well easy to snag yourself going through."

"We can slide under on our bellies," she said. "I've done it loads of times."

"...Suppose..." I said, completely unconvinced. I couldn't understand why she'd chosen this particular gap, when surely there were larger openings further along the fence. Still, I was already covered in blood and filth anyway; a few more scrapes and dirt hardly seemed to matter anymore. Plus, and perhaps more to the point, I didn't want to make a big deal out of it in front of Emma.

She leaned her bike up against the fence, and I followed suit.

"Ladies first," I said.

"Go on then," she said.

Emma did go first. She disappeared through the gap like she was being sucked through. I, however, crawled under with all the grace a gangly, uncoordinated, fifteen year-old buffoon could muster. I came away with a torn t-shirt, and a scrape down my right arm and lower back. I wasn't amused. Emma was though.

I looked out across the breakers. Crumpled cars stood in the moonshine, stacked in row after mangled row. Every one of them was somebody's past, trashed and forgotten; a metal graveyard of discarded affluence. Their dark and gnarled headlights seemed to look right at us. The night did indeed make them corpse cars. I immediately wanted to draw them, characterise their front grilles and smashed-in headlights with menacing, hungry expressions.

Emma walked off in the direction of her dad's office, and I shut away the idea for another day.

There was a rickety old outhouse to the side of Al Looms' office (which itself was little more than a shack) that Emma stepped into and started to rummage around in.

"What you looking for?" I asked, but she didn't answer.

After much clattering and banging about, Emma reappeared with a bulky yellow torch in her hand. She pointed it at me and turned it on. The light sliced across the night and hurt my eyes. I spun round and tried to blink away the afterimage. It took some doing.

"Nice one," I said.

"Don't mention it," she said, and walked off into the maze of corpse cars.

I had to run to catch her up.

I had begun to get the impression that Emma was being a bit funny with me. Since arriving at Looms', some of her remarks, and general sort of flippancy, seemed more in the manner of how she was with David, than me. Everything – everything directed at me, anyway – struck me as being one big joke to her. The girl I had kissed up on the Electric's roof suddenly seemed completely out of reach. I felt confused, and a little hurt.

Surrounded by moonwashed corpse cars, all headlights leering at us as we passed, I said, "Hey, how will we know which car is Muxloe's?"

"All new arrivals get parked over this way," she said. "And as only two cars have come in this week, I think we'll be alright."

I grabbed her forearm and said, "Hey…"

She stopped and turned around, pulling her arm from my grip. "What?"

"What's wrong?"

"Nothing. Why?"

I struggled to find an answer to that.

"What?" she said. Her sharpness stung me.

"It's just…" I began. "… On the roof. It was great."

Her face softened a little.

"Yeah," she said, "it was. But please don't be funny about it, Sam."

"I'm being funny?"

"Yeah, don't get all soppy on me – we've got a lot to do."

That wounded me. I think she could see it as well.

Don't get all soppy on me.

The line left a scorch mark on my brain. I felt emasculated, dejected, and totally and utterly befuddled.

"Come on," she said, and walked off.

I hung back for a moment. Above, the moon slipped behind a black veil of cloud. The corpse cars all looked at me. I could have sworn they were grinning.

Don't get all soppy on me.

I got moving.

I kicked the dirt – dragging my heels, as my mother would say – and meandered through the maze. I felt immensely tired all of a sudden. Too much had happened, very little of which made much sense. I no longer felt fixed to a reality of any kind; everything seemed so unstable now. The world appeared to be cloaked, illusory, full of misdirection. Like a movie. If the mysteries of the Electric were anything to go by, then what else was out there? Were there phantasmagoria shows behind everything, behind all our thinly-veiled realities? The thought made me shiver.

And then there was Emma. A mystery of a different kind, but no less bewildering. I felt bruised by her. At fifteen, any complexity in human emotion would just confuse the hell out of me. I began to wonder if I'd said, or done, something wrong, but I couldn't think what. I was totally mystified by her.

I turned a corner of stacked cars and found myself in a clearing of sorts. There were engine parts, and tyres, and skeletal chassis strewn about here and there. The ground was churned up from the endless assault of Looms' machinery, leaving behind long, snaking quagmires that looked as if they would swallow up small children. I saw Emma across the clearing. She had found the new arrivals – two cars parked beneath a slice of moon, seemingly awaiting their trial and execution – and was busy searching the first vehicle. Her torchlight cut up the night.

She was in the wrong car though. I recognised Muxloe's old banger right away. I recalled the old projectionist handing his keys over to Em's dad the previous morning, just before Looms had shooed Dave and I away as if we were stray dogs. I walked over to the new arrivals, being careful to avoid the grooves of mud and oil in the earth. Some were so deep and wide I had to leap over them.

"It's not in that one," I said as I reached the cars. I knew my tone was sharp, and I didn't care.

Emma's head appeared in one of the back windows. "What?" she said, then ducked down again to continue her search.

"That's not Elmer Muxloe's car," I said.

"How do you know?" I heard her say, her voice muffled. She was shuffling around in the back seat, kneeling on all fours, searching the dark footwells and door pockets. Emma sliced up the black interior of that abandoned old vehicle with piercing torchlight, and I knew as soon as I saw it that I wanted to draw it. I could feel my right hand twitching. Something about it put me in mind of *Close Encounters of the Third Kind*; a sharp and narrow quizzical light probing the dark. There was something quite menacing about it, yet at the same time, it was kind of beautiful.

"I saw him bring it in yesterday," I said, "when we came over to get you."

"Oh," she said, and stopped. She knelt on the back seat, and sighed. Her position was awkward. She had her back to me, and her head was shoved up against the car's roof, causing her shoulders to hunch. She must have stayed like that for about thirty seconds, which struck me as very odd. Then, for some even stranger reason, she decided to back her way out of the car. It wasn't a very dignified manoeuvre to say the least. Her behind greeted me as she stumbled out of the vehicle. It was uncharacteristically clumsy for her, and I had to stifle a laugh. I could hear her huffing in frustration, and just knew that this little escapade would not improve her mood in the slightest.

Once she was out, she turned to me and said, "Get a good look?"

I decided to play her game. "Yeah," I said. "Thanks."

"*You…*!" She punched me in the arm. I saw that she was smiling.

"Oh, that's it!" I grabbed her round the waist, then proceeded to tickle her to death. She laughed and squealed, and struggled against me.

"Get off me!" she cried, "I'll drop the torch!"

Pleas only made things worse for her. I wouldn't let up. I growled, pretending to be monstrous. She laughed like crazy.

"Please…" she shrieked, "Please, I submit… I submit…"

Finally, I let go of her, and we both stood laughing, trying to catch our breaths.

"Git," she said after awhile.

"Scratter," I gave back.

She smiled at me, dressed in moon shadows. It's strange the things that sometimes pierce the memory – that wedge in there and never dislodge. Emma stood by those dark and forgotten cars, smiling, dipped in silver, is an image that I've never gotten out of my mind. I've drawn it many times, but my artistry has never come close to recreating how I saw her that night.

I guess I've never forgotten her.

We searched Elmer Muxloe's car. I did the back seats this time, and Emma searched the front. We came up with nothing. It was Emma who suggested we try the boot. I thought it was locked at first, but it turned out it was just really stiff. I had to wrench it open. Emma shone the torch into the boot, and there, in amongst piles of newspapers, oil cans, beer cans and, randomly, tins of soup, was a roll of film. It lay spooled up on a browned newspaper. I picked it up as carefully as I possibly could, and held it out before me in both hands. Judging by its size, I couldn't imagine the film would run for very long. There didn't seem to be much of it. But still, no matter the length, I knew that if it came from the Electric, then whatever was on it would more than likely possess its certain *qualities* and, therefore, it was a hell of a find.

"Can you see what's on it?" asked Emma, shining the torch into my hands.

"I don't know," I said. "I don't really want to unravel it out here."

"Yeah," she agreed.

Just then, the moon was swallowed up by black clouds, snatching its silver light from the breakers. Even the breeze seemed to die away. Both Emma and I looked around us. Dark headlights grinned.

"You hear that?" said Emma.

"No," I said.

"Listen…"

I did, and what I heard was laughter coming from across the metal graveyard.

There was a group of kids over by the car crusher. One of them was David.

I was astonished to see him. Not because him being there was so unexpected – although it was – it was who he was hanging out with that was so puzzling. David was stood watching the front grille of an already flattened car be kicked to pieces by Mark Drake – or, as he was known to everyone at our school, Mean Stare Mandrake.

He was the kind of kid you gave as wide a berth as you possibly could. You *certainly* didn't hang out with him at a local breakers yard, at night, surrounded by metal objects. That was sheer lunacy. The guy was a psychopath. I'd once seen him repeatedly punch a boy *up* three flights of stairs. That is to say, Drake pounded on this poor lad, as he innocently tried to reach the top floor for a class. The blows had been relentless, one fist after another. I heard afterwards that all the lad had done was glance at Mandrake as they passed on the stairs. A fatal mistake. Mark Drake didn't like anyone looking at him. Yet the irony was that Mark Drake stared at everyone – all us lads anyway – with such menace that you'd be left wondering what the hell you'd done to offend him. It was no great mystery though; it seemed merely existing was reason enough for Drake to mark you out for death.

This staring had, of course, earned him the moniker Mean Stare Mandrake – quite why *Man* had been placed before Drake I had no idea. I suppose it just rolled off the tongue better than Mean Stare Drake. Nicknames are like that. They mythologise, even dumb-sounding ones like his.

Mandrake's strategy was to pinpoint someone, seemingly

at random, and make their day a living nightmare. Simple as that really. Often times, you'd turn around at school and see Mandrake stood perfectly still within the rush of bodies, his eyes fixed right on you. It was unnerving to say the least. Sometimes this led to a beating right away, sometimes it didn't – although *not* receiving a beating was sometimes worse, as you'd be left a nervous wreck for days on end wondering when the inevitable would happen.

The other unnerving thing about Mean Stare Mandrake was that he hardly ever spoke. He would stalk in silence, and his beatings were given out in this same cold, emotionless manner. This in itself was seriously creepy. I'd heard from David that Drake had modelled his entire persona on Michael Myers, the masked killer from the *Halloween* movies, and whether or not that was true, he certainly gave a *tour-de-force* performance in terrorising us kids. His very presence was enough to put the frighteners on any one of us mere mortals. He was beyond being just a school bully; there really was something not right about him, that was for sure.

Everybody, it seemed, had a Mean Stare Mandrake story. My own involved a stalk and attack scenario that was indeed worthy of a slasher film. For three consecutive afternoons, I'd noticed Mandrake watching me as I walked home from school. He seemed to just appear, either on a street corner or a playing field, or most effectively, down a narrow alleyway, and simply stared right at me. Dave claimed I was a "Dead Man Walking", and I had to agree with him. I knew it was coming. I'd been marked for death.

The attack came on the third afternoon, just as my nerves were in tatters. I'd been walking home with David, and another lad named Ben, when Mandrake struck as if from nowhere. No words were spoken, other than my own pathetic pleadings, nor did it last for very long. The thing with Mandrake was, he never really went for the face, instead he concentrated all his efforts on destroying your upper body. I remember my right arm ended up bruised quite badly. David and Ben hung back and watched as I got *Mandraked* – as it was often known. Neither of them said a word. After a good few minutes of relentless punches, Mandrake's expression changed from one of mild contempt, to outright boredom. He gave me one last jab to the arm for good measure, then crossed over the road without a word and went on his way. The following afternoon, David got Mandraked.

And now here David was, hanging out with the nutcase. It was utterly bewildering. A lot had happened since David had run out on us back at the Electric – a hell of a lot – and seeing him, standing around, sniggering like an imbecile as Mandrake tore a wing mirror off a rusty old corpse car, suddenly filled me with a great sense of loss. I wondered if there was any way back for us. I had little doubt that we would remain friends, but it would be different now, less intense. The days of us watching videos together and riding our bikes across the countryside were ebbing away. Or perhaps they were already gone. This was, after all, our final weekend of our final summer, before our final year of school. We were standing on the threshold of childhood's end, whether we knew it or not.

There were two other kids hanging out with David and his new mentor, one I recognised, and one I didn't. Kurt was the name of the one I did know; a gangly kid with perhaps worse acne than David, while the other member of Mandrake's car trashing outfit – the one I didn't recognise – was a girl. She looked a lot older than the rest of us, by a couple of years at least, and just looking at her made me nervous. She wore extremely tight jeans and a low, *low* cut top; her hair was permed, peroxide blonde, and her make-up seemed to feature all the colours of the rainbow. Dangling down into her quite spectacular cleavage was a shiny silver cross, and from her ears hung accompanying crosses. These were black. She was a material girl living in a material world.

There were countless Madonna clones in the mid-eighties,

but this one girl really sticks out for me. Just looking at her seemed to scramble my circuits. I immediately felt self-conscious in front of Emma, and tried to look at this girl as little as possible.

Emma and I were crouched behind the rusty shell of an old van, peering through its skeletal frame at the mindless destruction playing out before us. Mandrake was now skimming hubcaps at the car crusher. The film we'd found in Muxloe's car was safely stashed away in my bag, its secrets gnawing at my mind. I felt very tired, and wondered how late it was. I knew I would be in for it with my mum when I got in, but that didn't concern me too much.

Emma looked angry. Really angry. I knew then that she was going to go out there and say something. Butterflies awoke in my stomach. This had the potential to get very bad indeed. Especially for me. At least, that's how I saw it.

Emma stood up. "Oi!"

Her voice carried across the copse cars, met Mandrake's ears, and sent him spinning round to Mean Stare us. I stood up, reluctantly, and tried not to meet his gaze. David peered into the night. "Em?" he said. He looked guilty as charged. "Sam?"

"Yeah, it's us, Dave," Emma said. "What the hell are you doing?"

That's when the Madonna girl piped up. "What's it to you?"

Emma looked momentarily stunned by this, but then said, "My dad owns this place, and you're all trespassing."

"Ooh, I'm scared," said the girl.

Mandrake, true to character, didn't say a word. He didn't even move. He was just a slab wall topped off with two horrible little eyes. I suppose it would've been funny if I wasn't so petrified of him. Kurt, on the other hand, walked over to us. He stopped just short of the skeletal van we were stood behind. "Come on out," he said with a grin. "We can sort this out."

I didn't like the sound of that at all.

Emma walked around the van, and I followed her lead.

"So…" Kurt began. "You're Looms' daughter then, eh?"

"I am," said Emma, with pride.

"Lot of my old man's cars have ended their days here, y'know."

"Really?" she said, completely uninterested. She walked past Kurt and headed straight for David. I hung back a little. Mandrake was still Mandraking me.

"What are you doing here, David?" Emma asked.

"We're just minding our own business…" said the Madonna girl. "Like *you* should."

Emma shot her a stare worthy of the Mandrake. "I'm talking to him," she said, pointing a finger at David. The girl fell silent. I could tell Dave just wanted to get the hell out of there. I didn't blame him either; I was absolutely with him on that score. Not only did I have Mandrake's death stare to contend with, but also, Kurt had decided he'd use me as a leaning post. He rested his elbow on my shoulder, as if we were the best of pals, and then began to blow into my face. I didn't say or do anything. I felt utterly pathetic.

Emma was oblivious to all this, thankfully; it seemed she just wanted to take her anger out on David. "Well, Boyle…?" she said.

"It's nothing," David muttered. "We were just hanging out."

Emma lowered her voice. "Did you really have to bring *them* here?"

David looked to the ground.

"Look, missy," said the girl. "It's no big deal. Just get over yourself. We weren't doin' anyone any harm. Like he said, we were just hanging, that's all. It's not the crime of the century…"

Emma looked about ready to claw her eyes out, but then the girl added, "Mind you, I do apologise for my knucklehead of a brother – I know he's a tool, but…"

"Do one, Claire," said the Mandrake.

I was astonished. I glanced over at Dave; he caught my eye

and gave me a look that seemed to say, *I know, nuts right*.

Even Emma looked stunned. "Mark Drake is your brother?" she said, eyebrows raised.

"Yeah," said Claire Drake. "Tragic, isn't it… We think he was either adopted, or somebody dropped him on his head when he was a baby." She thought about that for a moment longer, then added, "Or, he's just an actual moron."

"Piss off!" Mandrake said, with surprisingly little venom. He looked utterly deflated. The trademark Mean Stare was gone, replaced by a long, surly face that could have rivalled even one of David's full-on sulks.

Kurt started to laugh, and then, amazingly, Emma did the same.

"Shut up," cried the once-mighty Mandrake, but it did no good. Even his sister was sniggering.

"Oh, come on, Mark," said Claire, "you are a bit *special*, aren't you?"

"No."

"You are, Mark. Even Mum says. I mean, look at you – doin' that death stare thing all the time. What are you? – A complete gimp or what… I've seen shits more terrifying than you." She shook her head. "Jesus, what am I doing here? I could be out tonight with Scott Bradley – if he wasn't such a complete bellend as well. Instead I'm here with Mean Stare Moron and the junkyard kids. When are you gonna wake up Mark, no one gives a shit about this whole *Friday the 13th* thing you think you've got going on. You need to stop watching that crap."

And that was it, the myth was destroyed. In just a few short moments, Mark Drake had been belittled so much by his own sister, that any power he once held over us was gone forever. Of course, he would've still been more than capable of pummelling me into the ground, but without the fear, he was nothing. He was just like the rest of us – a dumb kid who didn't know his arse from his elbow.

Mark Drake was perhaps my first lesson in the lies many of us wear in order to hide our true selves from the world. He projected himself in a guise of his own making; perhaps knowing, perhaps not, that staring out kids and then beating them black and blue would make him notorious around our school. His modus operandi for hardly saying a word was his masterstroke. Being laconic gave him his power. But he'd made a fatal mistake in having his older sister hang out with him. His two worlds collided; Claire, of course, knew an altogether different Mark Drake from the one we knew. To her, he was just her dipshit little brother; she clearly thought of him as an absolute joke. And she was right, he was. The staring, the whole silent stalker thing – it was hilarious. She knew it, and now we knew it. And Mark Drake *knew* that we knew it. His whole Michael Myers/Jason Voorhees thing was over. Once school started up again, this little episode would no doubt be round its populace in a bullet.

Kurt left my side and I relaxed a little. This entire situation had not gone how I envisioned at all. I thought I would've been eating the graveyard dirt by now, but instead, I was laughing with everybody else. At Mark Drake no less. It was surreal.

Kurt went over and put his arm around Mark. "There there," he said, patting Drake on the head.

A curious thing happened then. As I was watching this further humiliation, Mark Drake glanced at me, but instead of fixing his notorious stare, he just looked away again.

Claire came over to where I was standing. "So, what's your name then?"

"Sam," I said. "And that's Emma."

Em looked over at the mention of her name.

Claire said, "She your girlfriend?"

I felt my face turn the colour of beetroot.

It all made me feel like a kid again. That is to say, the Electric, and the films of that haunted place – their lingering *quality* – left me for a while. It was short-lived, but to be concerned with numbskull bullies, and teenage girls, and whether David and I were still friends, was strangely wonderful. I suddenly felt absolutely in the moment. Claire fixed me in that place. The nervousness I felt in even looking at her, let alone answering questions about Emma – who was stood scowling not twelve feet away from us – struck me as so funny that I had to stop myself from laughing in her face. After everything I'd been through in the last few days, all the mysterious and incredible sights I'd seen, to come back to worrying about Mean Stare Mandrake, and how looking at his sister made me ache – even if her peroxide perm did look ridiculous – not to mention the anxiety I felt when it came to Emma, seemed like some grand cosmic joke. But a good joke nonetheless. It all felt real; fixed in a reality I could understand. These lame teenage problems anchored me. They were the dependable ordinary.

I mumbled something about Emma and I just being friends, and tried to change the subject. "So… you're Claire, right?"

"Yeah. You go to Mark's school?"

"Ah-huh."

"Poor you."

I grinned, lowering my gaze. The fabric of her top was quite flimsy and I could easily make out that she was wearing a black lacy bra beneath. The silver cross rested on the rise of her right breast. I had to avert my eyes quick-sharp. She probably knew exactly what I was looking at though. Thankfully, David came over and gave me good reason for distraction.

"Alright, Slaughter," he said.

"Right you are, Corporal."

He smiled at this, and suddenly I knew we were going to be okay.

"Oh, so you guys are mates then…" said Claire.

"Sure are," said David.

Yes, we were going to be just fine.

I didn't know too much about Kurt. I wasn't even sure of his last name, although I think it might have been Haywood, or Haystock; something like that. I'd seen him round school, but he wasn't someone I'd had any dealings with. He was known to be as hard as nails, although he did tend to keep himself to himself. He wasn't like Mandrake; he didn't make a habit of going around terrorising and beating up other kids. I'd only seen him in a fight once, and that had been in the Triangle with some cocky lad in the year above us. Kurt made a real mess of him; bloodied up his nose and cut his eye open. Head wounds tend to bleed quite profusely, and this one had been like a Monty Python sketch. Blood squirted out everywhere. I think Kurt had been suspended for that. I also knew that school for Kurt was strictly a part time gig. He would often go to class in the morning, get himself marked in on the register, then skedaddle off somewhere, missing every lesson of the day, before returning for final register in the afternoon. He seemed to get away with this for a hell of a long time as well, before all his teachers cottoned on of course. He may have been suspended for that also, although I'm not entirely sure. It doesn't seem like much of a punishment for a kid whose main objective was to go to school as little as possible anyway.

Mandrake may have been an everyday terror, but Kurt truly was someone you steered clear of. And now here I was, in the car graveyard with the two most notorious kids in school.

Kurt came over to where I was standing with Mandrake's sister, and looked me up and down. He said, "What films do you like?"

I knew right away that this seemingly random question was nothing more than a test. Kurt simply wanted to gauge where I was coming from. Kids would often do this: try and suss out whether they could hang with someone based purely on what that person was into. One wrong answer could outcast you forever. I once saw one kid confess that he was into Duran Duran and Culture Club. That was the end for him. If he'd have said, say, Iron Maiden or Motorhead, his future may have been assured, but instead he made the fatal mistake of being honest.

"Into all kinds of films," I began. "Me and Dave get videos out every Saturday. Horrors mainly."

"Oh yeah," said Kurt. "What horrors?"

Another test.

"Dunno. Seen loads. *Texas Chainsaw Massacre* was a good one."

I mentioned *Texas* knowing full well it would impress, given its infamy. It was *the* horror film to watch, and those that had seen it, wore it like a badge of honour.

"Ah yeah," said Kurt, "that film is well wicked."

"Sure is," I said. "I watched it with Dave and Em. It was Emma's own copy."

"Really?" Kurt said, mightily impressed now.

Emma came over at the sound of her name and stood next to David.

"What's up?" she asked.

"Just telling Kurt 'bout us watching *Texas Chainsaw* that time."

Kurt jumped on my words, "You got a copy?"

I saw a flash of annoyance in Emma's face, but then she said, "Yeah, well, it's my dad's actually. He's got loads of films."

"Can you lend us some?" said Kurt.

"Not sure," said Emma. "I'd have to ask me dad."

I knew she had no intention of asking her dad.

"Nice one," said Kurt.

Claire cut in, "I hate them kinds of films. That's all the shit Mark watches, and look how he turned out."

Mark scowled at this. Claire and Kurt turned to look at him, and both burst out laughing. I had to stifle a laugh myself.

Their mirth was suddenly cut short however. A loud and venomous shout cut across the metal graveyard. "Oi!" came the yell. "What ya doin' in 'ere..."

We all froze. I didn't have to turn to see who it was. I knew that voice all too well. I looked at Emma. Her eyes widened. It was almost comical. "Christ!" she said. "My dad. Get outta here!"

All six of us bolted.

Kurt was laughing as we ran. It was quite infectious, too. Once he started, both Claire and David joined in; all three giggling like maniacs. I guess they felt a kind of giddy excitement in being chased. I was a little surprised David was laughing, given that he knew the wrath of Albert Looms only too well, but I guess he was just caught up in the moment. Emma was not laughing, however. She was running ahead of us all.

I could hear her father shouting from deep within the maze of cars. "Get out!" he bellowed. "Go on, run! Catch you in here again, I'll give you what for…"

I glanced back, but couldn't see him. He was a disembodied voice calling out from the hollow shells of dead cars. It was quite eerie.

Emma, being the first to reach a gap in the fence, slithered under in a heartbeat. Mandrake was next, then his sister. Once Claire was through, David moved to go, but Kurt shoved him back and went on ahead. Behind us, perhaps fifty yards across the night, the bulk of Albert Looms seemingly materialised before a tower of cars. David gasped.

Looms just stood there, watching us, cast in silver and black moon shadow. I had the urge to draw him right away.

"Let's go," David said to me, and without waiting a moment longer, he scrambled under the fence.

I, however, continued to stare at Albert Looms, unable to move. Looms took a step forward and his face caught moonlight. To my astonishment, I saw that he was smiling. It was a sly, knowing grin, not unfriendly in the slightest.

He said, "Look after her, Crowhurst, or you'll have me to answer to."

I had no idea what to say. Instead, I just gave him a nod, and then slipped on under the fence.

I met the others up on the tracks. As I approached them, I noticed the moon through the trees; it was being swallowed up by scudding clouds again. They looked thick and black, and I wondered if it might rain. It was a lot darker out here; the trees saw to that. The old rail line ran off into complete blackness in either direction. Also, the wind had picked up considerably, bending the treetops, and scattering leaves along the lines. For the first time in what seemed like eons, it felt chilly, and I wondered if the summer was finally coming to its end. I looked at Emma; her face was nothing but a dark smudge. Only her eyes registered. I glanced at the others. All their faces were shrouded by the night. David had my bike, and was leaning on the handlebars. Em's bike was laid across the tracks.

"He catch you?" Kurt asked.

"No," I said. "I got out before he could get me."

I looked at Emma. She looked away.

David said, "I though he'd got you for sure, man. He saw us, didn't he?"

"Maybe, I don't know," I told him. "It's pretty dark, and there was quite a distance between us."

"Aw, I dunno, Sam... I think he nailed us."

Kurt cut in, "Can you bum chums stop fretting. What's he gonna do?"

We fell silent.

Mark Drake was stood further on down the track, kicking ballast. He spoke up. "We going or what?" I think he directed this question at his sister primarily, although I couldn't be sure.

"Whoa, whoa there little horsey," said Kurt.

Claire said, "You don't need my permission, Mark. You can go home if you want."

"You not coming?" said the Mandrake, sounding genuinely concerned.

"No," said Claire, narrowing her eyes. "Why, do you need me to hold your hand or somethin'?"

Kurt snorted.

"Do one, Claire."

And with that, the Mandrake stormed off down the tracks.

The Arboretum was a small public park on the outskirts of our village. It had a pond – which I had once walked across when it froze over one year – a playing field, a BMX track – which Dave and I had often frequented – and within its heart, a playground. This had swings, a slide, monkey bars, and a merry-go-round that looked as if it had been there for a hundred years. After dark, it became a haven for teenagers.

And it was here we found ourselves, long after we should have been home. I was going to get merry hell when I got in, but I just didn't care. Not then anyway.

After Mandrake's sudden departure, we had walked on down the tracks somewhat aimlessly. Claire and Kurt seemed to just tag along, which made it impossible to talk to David about the Electric. Instead, we muttered half-hearted musings on the impending school year, and whether or not George Lucas would ever make another *Star Wars* film. This had been a topic brought up by Kurt. He seemed to be quite the film fan. Claire rolled her eyes at the discussion, and Emma had remained quiet, but I enjoyed talking about such trivialities. It took me out of what was really going on.

No one had suggested we go to the Arboretum, we just seemed to drift there, instinctively heading straight for the playground. Emma and I threw our bikes down and went and sat on the swings. David had a brief play on the monkey bars, but then came to sit on one of the swings nearest Emma. Kurt and Claire went over to the merry-go-round.

I sat, gently swinging, looking up at a dark scrim of clouds roll across the face of the moon. I thought about my dad, and how he had brought me to this very playground when I was a boy. I looked over at Claire and Kurt and saw that they were kissing.

Emma said, "I guess she isn't too bothered about that Scott Bradley guy she mentioned…"

"No," I agreed.

David glanced over to the merry-go-round. "Lucky git," he muttered.

"You like her?" Emma asked.

"Yeah," said David. "She's well fit."

Emma rolled her eyes.

Quickly interjecting before one of them asked me what I thought of Claire, I said, "Dave, what were you doing hanging out with them… with *Mandrake*?"

"I was down the shops with Rhys and Ben," he began, "and they went in well early, so I was just kicking around the green on my own, and Kurt and Mandrake turned up. I was bricking it. I thought they were gonna batter me, but then Claire showed up and started talking to me. Mark gave me the *Mean Stare*, but she soon sorted him out. She gave him a right load of shit – it was great. I kinda just tagged along after that."

"Why did you go to my dad's place?" asked Emma.

"It was their idea. I couldn't say anything – they would've just ripped the piss… or worse."

Emma understood this and let it lie.

"Why did you run?" David asked her. "From your dad, I mean. Surely *you're* allowed to hang out there?"

"I don't know. I just…" she faltered, ran her fingers through her hair, then picked up the thread of her thoughts. "I just didn't want him to think I was bringing back every kid in town to smash up cars. I didn't want to disappoint him."

It was on the tip of my tongue to tell her that he knew, that he'd seen us good and proper, but I resisted. I just didn't want to get into it, and Looms hadn't seemed pissed at all, more amused if anything, which still perplexed me.

"Oh, right," said David. "Makes sense, I suppose." He

sounded a little guilty.

He fell silent. We all did.

David pushed off the ground and swung. I was just content to be still. The night and its silence were soothing.

Finally, David slowed, and dragged his feet across the concrete to stop himself. Kurt and Claire momentarily stopped necking and looked over to see what the noise was, then returned to each others tonsils.

David said, "You two went back there, didn't you?"

I looked at Emma. She was miles away – off staring into space, as my dad would've said.

I answered David. "Yeah, we've been back to the Electric. Found out a lot of stuff, too – you know Elmer Muxloe?"

"Sure, we saw him at Corpse Cars yesterday," said David. "I had to tell *you* who he was."

"Yeah well, turns out he used to be the projectionist there…"

"Really?"

"Yeah… and we went to see him this morning. He told us all sorts of stuff. That place is for real, man."

"What place is for real?"

It was Kurt. He came striding over, looking mightily pleased with himself. Claire was beside him, holding his hand.

David blurted out, "The Electric." I could have strangled him.

"What, the old cinema?" said Claire.

"You know about it?" I said, astonished.

"Yeah," she said. "Used to go down there when I was younger. There was a load of us. We used to drink cider and smash the windows in. I thought they'd pulled it down…"

"What? No…" I said. "It's still standing. Just."

It rattled me that Claire had been to the Electric, which was ridiculous, I knew. It was a derelict old cinema on the outskirts of a small town; stands to reason it would be common knowledge. Still, I felt saddened that the Electric wasn't *our* secret place – that its mysteries weren't just meant for Emma and me.

Yet.

"You ever *see* anything there?" I asked, choosing my words carefully.

I noticed Emma turn and look at me, but I kept my eyes fixed on Claire.

"Like what," she said, "a film?" She frowned at me.

Kurt said, "The place has been shut for years, dipshit. You dense or what?"

I ignored him.

Claire said, "It was a pretty spooky place, I suppose."

I looked at her. "Spooky?"

"Yeah, you know, old places like that are always well creepy."

"Yeah," I said. "I guess they are."

After that, the night just seemed to peter out. It was late, and I knew I was going to be in for it when I got home. I was also exhausted. Claire and Kurt continued to lock jaws, and it became increasingly uncomfortable viewing. Once his hands started wandering I knew it was time to leave.

We called over to them and said, "See ya," but only Claire acknowledged us. Kurt was busy.

The three of us went our separate ways by the BMX track. David on foot, Emma and I on our bikes. Before parting, David said, "I'd be up for going to the Electric tomorrow." I had mixed feelings about this, but still agreed to it. Emma did the same. Then David walked off across the mounds and dips of the BMX track and disappeared from sight.

As we watched him go, I said to Emma, "Been quite a day…"

"Sure has," she said.

"You okay?"

"Yeah. Just can't stop thinking about that place."

"Yeah," I agreed.

After that, I couldn't think of anything else to say. The silence pressed against us and I just wanted to go.

Finally, Emma said, "See you then," and rode off, which made me feel infinitely worse.

I rode home through darkened streets. I could no longer find the moon. The night sky was a low slate of metallic cloud. The air felt heavy, charged. I could smell the electricity, almost taste it. There was quite a storm coming. Of that there was now little doubt. There hadn't been a big storm since the night my father died, so the thought of another made me feel very anxious indeed. In fact, there was so much going on in my head, I wished I could just unplug it, disconnect the mass. My stomach felt as if it were being ground up with nerves.

I wondered if I should have accompanied Emma home. I felt annoyed with myself for not having done so. She'd been funny with me ever since our time on the Electric's rooftop, and I felt at a complete loss with her. Perhaps she thought we'd made a mistake, and now she didn't want anything to do with me. I felt sick with worry about that.

And then there was the Electric itself, which gnawed at my mind relentlessly. There was so much to think about concerning that place; I just couldn't get a grip on any of it. All that happened to us there had become a tangled mess in my head; I couldn't form any chronological sense of it. There was nothing to anchor me; it was just a web of images and feelings. I felt a dull throb in my temples every time I tried to think on the Electric, so I gave up on it. Although it pained me, it was far easier to think about Emma. She was a slightly more manageable mystery.

Once home, I unlatched the side gate as quietly as I could, and put my bike down the side of the house. I then walked back round to the front door. I hesitated on the step for a moment. The sky was velveteen. I put the key into the lock, slow and silently, then opened the door.

"Samuel."

I closed my eyes.

"Where on earth have you been?"

My mother was sitting bolt upright in my dad's old chair by the telly. The television wasn't on. She was just sitting there, waiting.

"Well…?" she pressed.

"I… I lost track of time. I'm sorry."

"You lost track of time? Sam, it's pitch black out there, you must've known it was getting late."

I shrugged my shoulders.

"Sam!"

"What?"

"This has got to stop."

"What has?"

"You… this attitude."

"I haven't got an attitude."

"No?"

"No."

She sighed. "Sam, you're back at school on Monday. You need to buck your ideas up and focus."

That jolted me. With everything that had happened, I'd completely lost track of what day it was. I realised that it was Saturday. I looked at the clock on the wall. It read eleven thirty. No wonder mum was angry. The latest I was allowed out until during the summer was ten. I couldn't believe I only had one more day left before school began. The thought opened up a chasm of depression.

"I will," I said, half-heartedly.

"You will what?"

"I'll get focused and buck my ideas up."

"Good," she said. "Make sure you do."

She sat back in my dad's chair. She looked tired, and old. She'd definitely aged considerably in the last year. Thinking she was done, I turned to leave the room.

"Sam," she said, all the bite gone from her voice. "You're still my boy…"

"Of course, Mum."

Her eyes welled up. "I don't know who you are anymore. I just can't seem to reach you. Your dad always could, but…"

She fell silent. I couldn't think of anything to say. I just wanted out of there.

Finally, she said. "I know this past year has been incredibly hard on you, Sam… but I am here, you know. I'm always here for you."

"I know, Mum. I've just got some things going on, is all – I'll figure it out. It'll be fine."

A tear spilled over her eye. She wiped it away quickly, hoping I wouldn't notice. Then she stood and turned her back to me.

"Go get some sleep, Sam," she said, and walked off into the kitchen.

"Okay, night," I said, but she didn't answer.

In my room, I made sure Muxloe's roll of film was still safely tucked into my bag, then got undressed in the dark. I left my underpants on and lay on the bed. I cried then. It thought about the day Tom Bradley and his sons removed the lightning-struck tree from out in the field. And I thought about the Electric.

I don't remember how long I cried for before I fell asleep. But when I finally did drift off, it was dreamless.

I awoke early and took a long shower. I must have stood under it for fifteen minutes or more. I only got out then because my mum banged on the door and shouted, "What are you doing in there?"

There was a moment while I was in shower that I actually considered not going back to the Electric. It was fleeting, but nevertheless, it was something I thought about. Part of me could have quite happily spent that last day of summer sprawled out on the sofa, vegetating in front of the television. It even crossed my mind that perhaps Dave and I could get a video out, and all pile round his house.

The pull of the dependable ordinary.

Of course, I dismissed these ideas as soon as they came. I knew there was no running from this now. We were going to the Electric. There was little doubt about that.

We had to.

I had to.

After I dressed, I grabbed my rucksack – again making sure the roll of film was still in there – then went down to the kitchen and began to fix breakfast. I heard my mother stomp into the bathroom above and turn on the shower. I took some bacon out of the fridge and put several rashers in the pan. I spread butter on bread and made tea. By the time mum came downstairs, there was orange juice, a pot of tea and two bacon sandwiches waiting for her. I'd even lined an array of condiments out on the table.

She had a towel around her head and had on her dressing gown. I stood proud by the kitchen table, but at first she didn't seem to notice. She made a beeline straight for the kitchen sink and scowled at the bacon-charred pan.

"Sam, if you're going to make breakfast, can you at least rinse the pots off before you put them in the sink."

"But..." I protested. "I made us both breakfast,"

"Huh?" Mum looked over and saw the table. "You made bacon for me as well?"

"Yeah," I said, as proud as could be.

"Oh Sam, that's lovely. Thank you." She came over and kissed me on the cheek. "I can't remember the last time you made me breakfast."

She sat down and began to reach for the sauce. I sat across from her and got tucked into my own sandwich. Mum smiled at me, then poured herself a cup of tea.

"This is really nice of you, Sam."

"S'okay," I said, my mouth full of sandwich.

I wolfed mine down as fast as I could, then gulped an entire glass of orange juice in one.

"I'll just wash up before I go, Mum."

"Oh, I'll do that. Don't worry. You get off and have a nice day."

A nice day.

"Thanks Mum."

I got up and went to take my plate over to the sink, but Mum stopped me. She held my arm and said, "Thank you, Sam."

As small a gesture as me making her a bacon sandwich was, things did begin to change between us after that morning. It took a long while, but eventually we did find our way back to one another.

My dad saw to that.

I rode straight to the Electric. Whatever was going on with both Emma and David – particularly Emma – just seemed too much to deal with that morning. Plus, I wanted to get there, not have to faff about calling on people and waiting for them to get their acts together. Tomorrow school would begin; I needed to make the most of the time I had left.

The morning was dark and stifling. There was still the heavy scent of electricity in the air. I was surprised the storm had held off through the night, but knew it couldn't hold out much longer. West of the fields, great brooding thunderheads were moving in. Seeing them caused anxiety to rise up again. I felt short of breath, but still pedalled harder. I needed to get to the Electric. I felt almost hungry for it. I knew the storm would come once I was there, and oddly, that felt right, regardless of how anxious it made me. There was something cinematic about it – something which satisfied my imagination. I could already picture myself drawing a great electrical storm, raging over the abandoned ruins of the old Electric cinema.

Everything is connected, I thought, and pedalled on.

As I approached the Electric, doubt began to creep in. It was dark out here; the sky so low and heavy it felt as if I were entombed in a cloud cave. Also, the air was oppressive; it smelt metallic, amped up and ready. Anxiety intensified. My right hand began to shake. My drawing hand. I abandoned my bike on the grass and walked up to the old marquee. The wind picked up and pressed against me. I looked to the building's name above the marquee – THE ELECTRIC. It was set against the black sky. I thought how impressive it would look lit up neon in this dense half-light. My right hand was shaking quite badly and I had to grip it by the wrist to try and steady it. A rumble, low and guttural, cut across the sky. I had to laugh. It felt like I had stepped into a movie – that I had become the protagonist of a haunted house picture filled with all the clichés of the genre. That storm-laden sky just seemed *too* fitting.

It was, perhaps, a mistake to have come here alone. How much more mystery and wonder could one mind take? Perhaps I'd had my fill for an entire lifetime, and now I was just pushing it too far. I certainly didn't feel strong. And yet, the *need* to step inside that old cinema was so great, I just knew it would be futile to resist. So I didn't.

The restless sky rumbled another threat, and I headed inside.

The Technicolor tramp was standing in the lobby, staring at my drawing. He was so vibrant, so brilliant cut against the darkness, that he put me in mind of one of those old Disney movies where they mixed live action with animation. He stood out from reality, just like a cartoon. Except he wasn't a drawing composited onto celluloid. He was a ghost, breaking through to his old world.

He turned his head and looked at me. I stood stone still. He pointed a thumb in the direction of my drawing and gave me an approving nod. A small gesture, but nevertheless, something about it made me feel immense. I suddenly realised what it was I'd been doing. My drawings – my recent batch of *Electric*-inspired drawings – weren't meant for the living. They were pictures for the dead. *They* were my work's true audience. And here was the Technicolor tramp admiring my work. It spoke to him, resonated with his kind. I acknowledged old TT by mouthing the word *Thanks*. He took this in good grace and bowed his head, then turned back to my picture.

At that moment, I felt complete. This must be what all artists are constantly striving for, I thought. The pursuit of an ephemeral self-worth; a meaning to life through art. It is glimpsed, but never kept, only hungered for through the next project, and the project after that, and the one after that; a never-ending search for that one true moment; a moment that makes everything worthwhile – a moment I was having now, and could already feel slipping away.

Just then, an overture struck up from inside the theatre. A film was about to begin; the daily matinee for the dead. The Technicolor tramp glanced at me, smiled, then headed on up the staircase, as giddy as a child.

Outside, the rain had begun to fall.

The silver light, flickering with imagery, cast upon the Electric's tatty old screen. The film opened on a beach. It was in black and white; desolate and cold. The camera panned from the sea to a seemingly endless stretch of sand. Row upon row of strange black boxes lined the beach. Looking at it made my head spin; like all my wiring had got tangled up and was short-circuiting.

The film cut. A title card appeared. Simple white-on-black text, accompanied by a score that pulsed and jabbed in a disjointed and disturbing arrangement. It read: HOUSES OF THE HANGED.

This film had already jolted my imagination, imprinted its strangeness on me, just by looking at a few frames of the celluloid on which it was captured. Now it was playing out before me, and the effect was immediate.

I sat in the first seat I came to – before my legs gave out – and searched the dark for the Technicolor tramp. He was sat in his usual row toward the front of the screen. There was just me and him in the theatre. For now.

On the screen, we returned to the beach in a grand panoramic shot. The lines of black boxes, which made the sands look like the brittle back of some kind of sleeping monster, were now populated with milling people. Their attire looked Victorian; all stovepipe hats and tea gowns, and they appeared to be moving from one box to the other, peering inside; although it was difficult to tell for sure in such a wide shot.

Then the film cut suddenly, and the image that burst upon the screen pinned me back to my seat.

It was the black train; the mechanical insect of the rail, pushing its impossible speed through wastelands. I watched in awe and horror.

The scaly, unearthly desert stood indifferent to the blazing machine as it tore along the rail. The sky above was as dark and threatening as the one outside the Electric. I felt there was something hallucinatory about the scene; it was like a dreamscape too vivid to stand.

All of a sudden, however, the film began to run backwards – the black train sucked into the desert from whence it came. The sheer *Electricness* of the scene was expelled in an instant and the image became almost comical.

At first I thought the projector had broken down or something, but then a child's voice said, off-screen, "Where's it going?" and I realised it was part of the film.

It cut back to the beach. A young boy was looking into one of the boxes, via a viewfinder. A man was standing beside him. He was tall and thin, and dressed in a brilliant white suit. His hair was equally white, and he was incredibly pale.

I knew who he was right away.

"It is the train that goes into the night lands, my boy," said Seymour Janks.

"Edison's Kinetoscope," said Seymour Janks. He was standing proud before a forming crowd. The black sea behind him. The sky like a fossil. The monochromic use of deep blacks and stark whites gave the image an almost ethereal quality. It was a beautifully photographed film.

"In the race toward moving pictures," Janks continued, "Thomas Edison was ahead of the game. His kinetoscope was built in 1891, and was quickly installed in penny arcades and fairgrounds around the globe. Folk would use the peep-holes in these devices to view the wonder of motion pictures for the first time. The kinetoscope was curious because it enabled a customer to not just watch the film within, but also manipulate it – they were built with a switch, or handle, that you could use to run the film back and forth; so you could either watch the reel again, or simply delight in the hitherto unknown mystery of reverse motion. Yet Edison's Kinetoscope was a solitary device. It gave room for an audience of only one, so when the Lumière brothers demonstrated moving pictures to a Paris audience in 1895, the shared experience of cinema was invented.

"Edison's Kinetoscope had more in relation to television – a more singular, private viewing experience – than the social marvel of the movie house. And yet... and yet, ladies and gentlemen, it was through the Kinetoscope that I first discovered my... particular talent."

The film then cut to the gallery of images that lay within the Kinetoscopes themselves. This part of the film was in colour. That *Electric* kind of colour – sparking with brilliance and impossible vibrancy. From this point on, *Houses of the Hanged* lost any form of narrative structure. It became an expression of film in its purist form – the wordless image, edited to manipulate and astound. And that's just what it did.

Any preternatural, or indeed supernatural feelings I had felt at the Electric up to that point, were intensified tenfold by the montage that played out before me. Every shot seemed to stamp itself onto my mind until, after a while, all I could see was a delay of afterimages, all blurring and meshing into one another. Like an echo chamber of visions.

The black train featured heavily throughout, intercut with one bizarre image after another. It was like a series of dreams, strung together with frenetic precision. The score returned to its jolting, lurching arrangement – a brood of shrill strings and deep, throbbing cellos.

The rush of images came, flickering in mesmeric rhythm:

A black ship sailing a raging sea; a skyline of smokestacks belching plumes of fire; a snowstorm from which a fire eater emerged, swallowing an emerald flame, and dragging behind him a dead wolf; a beautiful woman lay upon a bed of bodies; a roomful of mirrors reflecting a lightning-lit sky; a carnival barker stood out on the midway, tipping his hat to a crowd of ownerless shadows; a red moon rising above a dark shoulder of hills; and a wall made of eyes.

The surrealism of the sequence was completely disorientating. After a while the shots bled into one another, and I was no longer able to decipher what it was I was actually looking at. Also, the pace of the editing quickened, and I just sank lower and lower in my seat. At one point, I realised that I had begun to cry. I allowed the tears to fall down my face.

I suppose if these images had been shot on a Hollywood soundstage, with special effects and all that hoopla, I wouldn't have paid the sequence much mind – I'd seen far more extreme imagery in some of the video nasties Dave and I rented on Saturday afternoons – but I knew I wasn't looking at something shot out in California. This was an *Electric* film. A Seymour Janks film. I was looking at places and people I wasn't meant to see.

Just like my own drawings, *Houses of the Hanged* was not meant for the living. It was a movie made by ghosts. For ghosts.

The film returned to the beach, and to stark black and white. Janks now led a march across the sands. Each and every individual, even the children, had a rope tied around their middle, and was dragging the Kinetoscopes. Their trails stretched out behind them like deep scratch marks.

I felt dizzy from the assault of imagery I'd just been subjected to. I raised my right hand and stared at it. It was shaking quite badly. Cinema light, that moony spill, flickered upon my skin, and I watched it dance.

Then, without warning, the film sputtered and ran out, and I was suddenly plunged into the darkness. It took a long while for my eyes to adjust.

From beyond the walls of the Electric, I heard the storm raging outside. It was loud, and I wondered how, even with the film playing, I hadn't noticed it sooner. I guess *Houses of the Hanged* took command of all my senses.

I heard a crack of thunder, so loud it seemed more like a sound effect; heightening a sense of the natural.

Then a voice said, "So, how'd you like my film?"

Seymour Janks was sitting in the row behind me.

I wondered how long Janks had been sat behind me. Had he been there all along? I hadn't sensed him, but then, *Houses of the Hanged* did have me spellbound. I doubt much of anything would have registered while that film was playing. After all, I hadn't even noticed the storm.

Yet, now Janks did have my attention, his presence positively rattled through me. His very being seemed to change molecules in the room. I didn't dare look round, but I could make out the thin white shape in my peripheral vision. He was leaning over the back of the seat to my left, close enough to whisper in my ear.

I glanced in the direction of the Technicolor tramp and saw that he was gone. I was alone with Janks, and the impulse to get the hell out of there was immediate.

"Say, kid," said Janks, "Saw your drawin' – you've got real talent..."

I still didn't respond. I could hardly breathe, let alone speak. I looked to the theatre doors. I could hear the storm echoing down in the lobby. I wanted to make a run for it, but just couldn't move.

I thought about Janks' voice. It had a certain rhythm to it; a patter that was tough and decidedly old-fashioned. He sounded like he'd stepped right out of a James Cagney or Humphrey Bogart movie. A 1930s gangster; the kind Warner Bros. used to make their bread and butter out of. The white suit just seemed to top this image off as well. Yet the real puzzler was that I'd heard him at all.

I thought back to the evening I first stumbled upon the Electric, when I'd been lying by the river and heard a woman's laugh carry along the breeze. I'd forgotten about it until that moment, but on recollecting, I knew it had been the laugh of the *know* of someone. Of this I was certain, yet I hadn't heard another's voice since; their frequency being far beyond my register. And yet, here I was, listening to the Cagneyesque spitballing of Seymour Janks.

"Edgar G. Ulmer directed parts of that picture. Along with Michael Reeves, the Halperin brothers, and even Edward D. Wood Jr. A real ragtag band of sharp shooters. Which is probably why the flick makes no sense. There was no *one* driving vision, see – not to mention an actual script. I took a real kicking as producer on that one, but, whaddya gonna do, eh… Say, you don't talk much. I thought you'd be a real smart guy, given your pictures 'un all."

I turned to look at him. His face was pale and gaunt. He had thick, wiry eyebrows that matched his hair (and his suit), and skin that looked as brittle and weathered as a dry desert. He looked about a thousand years old.

"I want to watch the storm," I said.

"Sure, kid," he said. "Let's skedaddle."

The storm was a real house-rattler – or in this case, a cinemarattler – and it was as dark as dusk down in the lobby. As I descended the stairs, a shock of lightning lit the Electric in one brilliant, ephemeral charge. It left a negative afterimage on my eyes. Thunder followed almost immediately. The storm was right on top of us.

I could sense the thin white man behind me, but I didn't look round. Instead I walked right across the lobby and came to stand before the cinema's entrance. I watched the rain lash down outside. Lightning lit the world once more, and I thought back to the night my father died. Which was inevitable, I knew, yet it didn't hurt as much as I'd anticipated. It was a bittersweet sorrow, not the all-encompassing turning knife I usually felt. For the first time in a long time, it felt good to think about him.

The wind rattled through the Electric. Window frames banged and clattered, and the whole building seemed to creak and groan under the strain of the storm. I felt cold for the first time in months. Summer was being snuffed out.

I felt a very profound sense of time; of how it scurries on so subtly that, unless you really look, you hardly notice it passing at all. I was really looking though. The season was changing before my very eyes. Autumn lay beyond this storm, and my final year of school. Beyond that, the world waited for me. My childhood was ebbing away faster than I'd realised. I know it seems funny for a fifteen year-old to be struck by nostalgia and loss, but at that moment, I felt those things very strongly.

Janks leaned on the wall across from me. He looked out at the storm and whistled through his teeth. "Jeez Louise, that's a humdinger."

I looked at him and said, "Tell me about your films, Mr Janks."

"Whaddya wanna know, kid?"

That stumped me. I had so many questions I didn't know where to begin. I looked back at the storm. Janks waited patiently for me to say something. It seemed he wasn't going to let his story go that easily.

Finally, I said, "The films that play here... they're full of ghosts, aren't they?"

"All films are full of ghosts, kid," he said. He walked over to the kiosk and leaned against it. Another shock of lightning lit the world. "Cinema is a haunted house," he continued. "An image is captured onto celluloid, trapped within frames, and immortalised. You watch a film made a hundred years ago, 'un all you're seein' are ghosts; the representation, caught in shadow and light, of someone who once was. I'll tell ya, *the* art form of the twentieth century is indeed one big spook house."

He was stalling and it angered me. "But these films, Mr Janks, they're *different*, right?"

He gave a thin smile. "I'll tell you a ghost story, if that's what you want..."

So I stood and listened as Seymour Janks began to spin his tale, and the storm raged over the Electric.

"In 1899," Janks began, "I was makin' pictures for The American Mutoscope and Biograph Company out of New York. I was there a good five or six years before D.W. Griffith. Anyhow, my boss, William Kennedy Dickson, was an inventor for Edison – he really pioneered the technology for capturing moving images onto film. He bolted on Edison and set up the Biograph in 1895. They created the flip book Mutoscope, which was a rival to Edison's Kinetoscope – which you saw in *Houses of the Hanged.* It was like the Kinetoscope; it was a peep show machine for an audience of one, but the Mutoscope was cheaper and simpler to use than Edison's contraption.

"We were the first company in the United States devoted to the making and exhibiting of film. And boy, it was a blast! We made what we called "actualities" – documentaries, really. Basically, we shot one or two minute films consisting of an actual place or person, or event. We did make the occasional narrative, usually a one-scene comedy that played out without any editing, but I didn't work on many of those.

"Our studio was on the roof of 841 Broadway in Manhattan, the Carhart building, and we made reel after reel. It was a golden age. I was a cameraman there, but back then, we pretty much mucked in on every aspect of filmmaking. We were creating an entirely new art form. There are very few people in history that have ever experienced that. Think on it, kid. People forget, there was an entire film industry for nearly twenty years before Hollywood. I never made it out there, mind. I'd *moved on* by then."

Janks talked fast and I had trouble keeping up. He had a rhythm and pattern that was almost musical. I didn't understand a lot of what he was saying, but I got the gist. I also knew what he meant by *moved on* and it made me shiver.

"In 1900 I was sent out on location to upstate New York," continued Janks, "to a small town on the outskirts of Woodstock.

The reason being, there had been reports of a ghost being sighted by many of the locals, and a few of us at Biograph got it in our heads that we wanted to capture the entity on film. And you know what, to our utter astonishment, we saw and filmed the ghost on our second night in town."

"What did it look like?" I said.

"I'll get to that, kid. The townsfolk said that the sightings had mostly been up on the Grove, a local beauty spot over-looking a river – usually a promenade for courting couples. We found that a surprising number of folk claimed to have encoun-tered the spectre. So, we set our camera up in the area the spirit was said to have been seen, and waited. And sure enough, the ghost came.

"Now one of the chaps I was with was a guy named Johnnie Scanlan. He was our director. He was from Brooklyn and afraid of nothin'. Bold as brass he walks up to the ghost and asks it its business. All the time we're filmin'. Ghost doesn't respond, so Scanlan backhands it round the back of the head. This drew a somewhat surprising reaction, because then, the ghost reached beneath its white veil and pulled out a revolver."

I stared at Janks as if he were insane.

He continued. "Well, Scanlan fell upon the ghost and a tus-sle ensued. It ended with Scanlan in possession of the gun and the ghost having it away on his toes."

I said, "The ghost was just a guy dressed up, wasn't it?"

"Bingo." He let that hang for a moment, then continued. "You see, at one time, the act of dressing up as a ghost and scaring the bejesus outta folk was quite a craze, particularly in Victorian England, but the US had its fair share of have-a-go-horrors as well. The ghost impersonator we came across turned out to be a young man named Christopher Burrows. He was the son of some town official. He narrowly escaped jail time for firearms offences because of his little stunt with Scanlan. There's nothin' as queer as folk, hey, kid?"

A sense of dread began to seep into me as Janks told his

bizarre tale. I suddenly felt very sure that what he was about to tell me was that the mysteries of the Electric were nothing but fakery. Pure hokum. Just like Burrows' ghost. I could already feel the threat of crushing disappointment, embarrassment, and a strange sense of failure. Not to mention loss. I already knew that if this were to be the case, my drawing would instantly cease yet again, and that terrified me. Also, I was getting tired of riddles. I needed answers.

A thought occurred to me. "What was on the film… when you watched it back?"

Janks looked at me and gave his thin smile. "You're a real smart kid. Yeah, the footage was developed when we got back to New York, and the reel played out almost like a macabre comedy – the ghost pullin' the gun 'un all, and the scuffle – it was like it was a scenario rather than somethin' that actually happened."

"But there was something else on the film, right?" I said.

"You're really pullin' out the bingos today, kid. Yeah, sure, there was somethin' else. A whole lot of somethin' else."

"Were they laughing?"

"Yeah, they were laughin'. Three actual ghosts, left of the frame, laughing their asses off."

"The film pretty much put the frighteners on everyone who saw it," said Janks, "and the Biograph were gonna shelve it. Johnnie Scanlan had other ideas, mind. He wasn't gonna allow his film to get buried, see. Unbeknownst to our bosses, Scanlan and I slapped a crude title on the flick, *Ghost with a Gun,* and went out to Atlantic City one weekend. Scanlan knew some hood out there who owned a penny arcade on the boardwalk and figured we could debut our little film far from prying eyes.

"We ran the film through a Mutoscope, made up a sign that read somethin' like, *See the Supernatural Sensation, "Ghost with a Gun"! Witness REAL Ghosts!* – that kind of thing, and charged folk two bits a pop."

I cut in, "What happened when people saw it?"

"Pandemonium, kid. Flick went through the roof. Scanlan and I watched as word got round and a line formed down along the boardwalk. A great many watched the film and then went 'un joined the back of the line again. A few fled after watching it – a few others never even made it to the end of the film. A couple of times a fight broke out, and one fella even wept after watching it and marched off down the boardwalk crossing himself. It affected different folk in different ways. Some had no reaction at all… like they couldn't even see the ghosts – like they were blind to it."

I thought of David, and said, "Some people have better eyes than others, I guess."

"You're not wrong, kid. Anyhey, I suppose you could say we had a sensation on our hands and we knew we had to get back to the Biograph and try and persuade them to release *Ghost with a Gun* nationally. Only… only we made a dumb move.

We went back to New York and left the print in Atlantic City, blinded by the big bucks it would be making in our absence."

"There was only one print?" I said, stunned.

"Things were different back then, kid. We never did any prints because we thought the flick was being canned, and besides, Scanlan assured me his man in Atlantic City was on the level. Well, by the time we got back to New York, word came down the wire that the Mutoscope had caught fire and just like that... the film was gone. Or at least, we thought it was... Scanlan's man said it nearly burnt his joint down and tried to blame us for the fire. He demanded we pay for the all damage. Scanlan told him where to get off. Yet, even though Scanlan was afraid of nothin' 'un nobody, he never went back to Atlantic City again."

I said, "What did you do then?"

"Well, I knew something remarkable had happened, to say the least. I continued to work at the Biograph, but the idea of capturing ghosts on film became the focus of my mind. Scanlan however, always quite a drinker, seemed to sabotage his own career, and he was soon out on his ear. He went back to Brooklyn, where he disappeared into oblivion. All the films he directed were lost and his contribution to those early days of film has been completely forgotten. His name slipped from the history books. As did mine, truth be told.

"Anyhey, about a year or so after *Ghost with a Gun*, I received a telegram from a lady who'd somehow heard about our film. She asked, in a very straightforward manner, if I could come and film her ghosts. Her name was Mrs Molly Lévesque, the architect of this temple of film. I was outta New York in a bullet."

Outside, the storm appeared to be easing off a little. The rolling thunder sounded distant now, and the lightning lit the land more and more infrequently. The rain was no longer as ferocious either; it was now just a steady patter. Seymour Janks fell quiet, as if his motormouth had finally run out of steam. I felt a strange sense of calm; the realisation of which I found some-what amusing. After all, I was talking to a dead guy.

After a while I picked up the conversation. "You came here and filmed Lévesque's ghosts?"

"Yes," he said, but didn't appear to want to say any more.

I pushed. "What happened?"

"I found that this place was like some kind of supernatural way station. The footage I got was just... nothin' short of spell-binding. I came here in 1905, when the Electric was nothing but a shack, puttin' on magic lantern shows and plays, and was here when Albert Lévesque died, right through to when Molly and Stokely first started making plans to build the cinema – A palace that would show entertainment for the dead, is how she put it. I *moved on* in 1919, but before I went, I'd already had the idea to make narrative films with ghosts as the players."

Janks walked over to me. I took an involuntarily step back.

He said, "You wanna know about the pictures this place shows, kid?

His manner had changed and I suddenly became nervous of him. He stood before me, and I struggled to hold his gaze.

"Whataya wanna know?" he said, his bite somewhat antago-nistic – or at least it seemed that way to me. "You want film trivia? You wanna know how, originally, we were gonna have John Garfield and Francis Farmer in *This Heart's Lagoon* before Valentino and del Río came on board... and that it turned out a weaker film because of it. How David O. Selznick helped me get Clara Bow for *A Second Chance,* or that Dickens wrote the most beautiful screenplay... still yet unmade. We're waitin' for David Lean to *move on* so that he can direct. How about the time Buster Keaton and I stalled on a grand remake of *Sherlock Jr,* or maybe you'd prefer I tell you about the time Canada Lee and I had a lil' bust up during the filmin' of *Ravens' Bower.* I've produced dozens of pictures, kid. Some had their fair share of nightmares, some went just swell. That's just the way it is in the picture business. It ain't no walk in the park. Not ever."

My mind brimmed with questions I wanted to ask, but I just couldn't get the words out. My thought pattern wouldn't align. There was still so much I didn't understand, so much I needed to know. I was also confused by Janks' darkened mood.

While struggling to make sense of my thoughts, I noticed that once again my right hand was shaking very badly. I grabbed it at the wrist with my left hand and tried to steady it. Then I said, "The desert… with the train… where is that?" The question had been itching at my mind for days.

Janks looked at me and gave his thin smile.

He said, "You don't ever want to go there, kid."

That made me shiver.

I was about to ask another question when I suddenly heard voices coming from outside the Electric. I looked out to the rain and saw two figures approaching. I turned back to Seymour Janks, but he was gone.

Moments later, Emma and David came stumbling into the old cinema looking like two drowned rats.

Like drowned rats. A turn of phrase my dad would've used, I'm sure.

Emma's hair was matted to her head, and her jacket and jeans were completely sodden. David was similarly *drowned*; only he wore a baseball cap that dripped at the brim. "We've been looking everywhere for you," he said, the telltale signs of a full-blown sulk evident in his voice.

Emma stared at me, then said, "You came here without me."

It wasn't a question. It was a statement, and I knew by her tone that she was hurt. I didn't know what to say. Until that moment, I had no concept that my coming to the Electric alone would upset Emma. I was still trying to make sense of my encounter with Seymour Janks, and seeing Em clearly wounded and betrayed by my selfishness was not something I could deal with, so I simply shrugged my shoulders and said, "Yeah."

She looked hurt and angry, and I felt low and stupid.

"We went round to yours," said David, "and your mum thought you'd gone to call for us. So we went back to my house to see if we'd missed you. Then we went to Em's. You gave us the runaround, man."

Emma said, "She's probably worried that you got caught out in the storm."

That gave me a jolt. I thought of my mother all alone at the kitchen table, watching the rain and the lightning, and remembering. I felt lousy.

All I could think to say was, "Looks like you guys did get caught out in it."

"You tryin' to be funny?" snapped David.

"No... I..."

"Yeah, we got caught in it," Emma said. "We sheltered though… in that shack out in the field."

"Fat lotta good it did us…" Dave said.

"Why?" I said. "What happened?"

Emma went over to the kiosk, pulled her matted hair back into a ponytail, then took off her jacket and laid it on the counter. She was wearing a red sweater. Whenever I think of her now, I often picture her dressed this way, coming in from the storm.

She said, "When we couldn't find you we figured we'd come over here. We went like the clappers to try and beat the storm. The sky was pitch black, and… well, we didn't get far past the village before it broke. We were drenched in seconds. Somehow we made it to the shack."

"Why didn't you turn back?" I asked her.

She looked at me, then said quietly, "I couldn't," and I understood exactly what she meant.

"I wanted to go back," Dave butted in, "but she wouldn't."

Emma continued, ignoring him. "We stood in that old shack for a long time, and watched the lightning over the brow of the hill. It was quite something."

She fell silent for a moment, and wiped her face with the sleeve of her sweater. I noticed that she was shivering a little. "You saw what that shack was like…" she said. "Who knows how long it'd been out there. I'm sure it was only the cobwebs and filth that was holdin' it up. It took such a pounding from the wind and the rain that, well… it just toppled over. We bolted out the door just in time to see it hurtle down the field and smash into pieces."

David cut in, "It was wicked, man. There was a massive boom of thunder as well. It was like somethin' out a film."

"The shack's gone," I said, half to myself.

"It's a pile of firewood now, Sammy," said David.

I thought back to the night I discovered the Electric. The shack was the marker; a beginning point to the strange adventure

I had found myself in. That rickety old place had been where I'd first laid eyes on the Bogart poster – or at least part of it – and where I'd stood watching the sun bleed across the horizon, before venturing into the tree line that would lead me to the Electric. Hearing of the shack's destruction struck me with an unusual sadness. It was almost like a sense of loss, which was ridiculous I knew, but still, it was potent. That yearning feeling for what had passed returned to me. It was a nostalgia I could make no clear sense of. Yet I was acutely aware that something was indeed ending, or perhaps had ended already. Although what it was exactly, I did not know. At least, not then anyway.

"What have you been doing here, Sam?" Emma asked.

The question dragged me back into focus. I said, "I've been watching a movie."

The rain stopped. I walked over to the Electric's once-grand entrance and peered out. The sky was opening up, allowing sunlight to poke through. The trees glistened in this new spectrum of light. The ground was waterlogged. Also, the wind had dropped and there was an eerie stillness to the world. It seemed such a melancholic calm after the savagery of the storm.

I heard David come and stand behind me. "We need to make tracks," he said, "before it starts chucking it down again."

"It's not going to rain anymore," I said. "Not today."

"Yeah, well, I'm soaking. I think we should go."

"Don't you want to hear about the film I watched?"

"Not really. It'll just be more of your weird bullshit again."

I turned to him. "Why did you come here, Dave? Is it just because of Emma?"

"No!" he spat. "I came back to see what all the fuss was about. Which, by the looks of things, is just a big sack of nothing. You've been well weird the last few days, Sam. I mean, what's up with you? I know your dad died, but…"

That's as far as he got. I rushed him. He tried to fend me off, but he wasn't quick enough and I soon had him in a headlock;

his baseball cap knocked from his head – headlocks were a big thing when we were young. He kicked and punched and trashed about, but I had him, good and proper. I squeezed as tightly as I could.

"Stop it!" shouted Emma, but I ignored her.

David tried to grab at my face, but I got hold of his wrist and twisted it. He yelped. He then tried to bite at my torso, which quite surprised me, but I applied more pressure to his neck and he soon quit. We must have looked ridiculous.

"Enough!"

There was so much venom in Emma's voice that I glanced over. She looked furious. I shoved David away and he went stumbling over the broken tiles. He somehow managed to regain his balance, however, and shouted across the lobby, "You prick!" It was a fitting end to such an infantile act.

We stood apart, trying to catch our breath. My anger ebbed away, and all that remained was how wretched I felt. I'd handled things very badly and had absolutely no idea how to resolve it, any of it. I figured my friendship, with both David and Emma, was more likely lost. Gone with the season.

I looked at Emma. "I should bang your heads together," she said. "You're a pair of numbskulls."

I turned away from her gaze, and when I did, I caught sight of something in the corner of my eye.

There was a figure stood watching us from the top of the staircase.

At first, I thought it was Janks, but then I sensed that something about this particular figure was different. I glanced over at Emma and caught her eye. I gave her a subtle tilt of the head in the direction of the staircase. I then looked over at David, but was surprised to find that he was already staring at whoever was up there.

Finally, I looked for myself.

Standing before the auditorium doors, dressed in a

crumpled and ill-fitting tuxedo, was Elmer Muxloe. I gasped in amazement.

He said, "What's all that ruckus down there? Keep it down will you, I'm about to start the next show."

"Mr Muxloe," Emma said, as equally stunned as I was. "What… what are you doing here?"

"Why, my dear," he said, deadpan, "I work here!"

David chimed in. "But this place has been shut for years."

"For the likes of you maybe," retorted Muxloe. "Now, are you all attending today's matinee performance of *Mad Dogs*, or are you not?"

I looked over at David. He looked more bewildered than unnerved.

"Well?" demanded the old projectionist.

"Yes," I said, suddenly finding my voice. "We would really like to stay for the matinee."

"Excellent!" he said. "It's gonna be a packed-out show today."

And with that, Elmer Muxloe scurried up to the third floor, to his beloved projection room.

David said, "What does he mean, it's gonna be *packed*?"

I didn't know how to answer that. Instead, I said to Emma, "You want to?"

She didn't respond right away, but then gave me a small smile that made me fall in love with her all over again. It was all the answer I needed.

As I led the way up the staircase, the sound of the opening moments of *Mad Dogs* suddenly filled the Electric. It was rag-time music; a jubilant banjo and brass orchestra, underscored with a lively boogie-woogie piano line. It stirred the soul. I looked over at my friends. They both smiled back at me. There was uncertainty in those smiles, but still, it made me feel good. It felt like we were together again.

At the top of the stairs, I found Emma's hand. She gave me that smile again. David was standing beside Emma, trying to peer into the silvery dark of the auditorium.

I said, "Okay then, let's go to the movies."
I led them through the doors.
Inside, the cinema was full of ghosts.

Row after row was a pulsating tapestry of colour; ribbons of bending and shifting lights. It took a while for my eyes to adjust. At first, I couldn't separate where one *know* ended and another began. But then, the shapes finally formed in my mind and I began to make sense of what I was seeing.

Pretty much every seat in the cinema was taken. Many faces turned and stared as we entered, but they soon dismissed us and returned to watching the film. Emma was squeezing my hand very tightly, but I hardly noticed. What did register, however, was that David was stood in a kind of horrified awe. I recognised the expression right away and had to smile to myself.

He was finally seeing the ghosts of the Electric cinema.

I looked out across the wave of spectral colour and tried to imagine how it would've been if I'd seen so much in one immediate unveiling. There'd just been the Technicolor tramp on my first experience (and his presence had sent me running); if I'd walked into this right away, my mind might've snapped and never healed. I looked over at David and saw that he was weeping.

Afraid that he might bolt on us at any moment, I decided I needed to find the nearest available seats and get us sat down. I led Emma up the aisle a little and found five empty seats at the end of an otherwise full row. I waved at David and he came ambling over with all the life of a George Romero zombie. An antiquated gentleman in a colourful dickie bow and derby hat stared at me from along the row. He smiled in a very friendly and cheerful manner, and with a wave of his hand, he invited us to take the empty seats. He even tipped his hat.

I jostled David along the row first. He was so bewildered

he didn't question me. He sat three seats in, leaving two spaces between him and the dickie bow guy. Emma sat down next, and then I took the end seat. I figured this way I could block David's escape route, if he did decide to skedaddle.

As I settled into my seat to watch *Mad Dogs*, my ears kind of popped, and suddenly I could hear the Electric's audience laughing along to the movie. I'd tuned in somehow. I wondered if it had something to do with being able to hear Seymour Janks before, or if it was simply that I'd finally channelled into their frequency. The funny thing was, even though I was sitting amongst that audience, and I was able to hear them, they still sounded far away, almost as if they were coming through a transistor radio. It was very strange.

On the screen, Harold Lloyd was banging and clattering around a dusty old manor house. He wore his signature straw hat and round glasses, and was as deft and as natural at physical comedy as ever I'd seen him. He certainly had the Electric's audience enthralled anyway. Every gag, every nuance in his performance, had them falling over themselves, and it was easy to see why; the film was a masterwork of comical grace, and it wasn't long before I was laughing along too.

The opening sequence concerned two builders who had come to the aforementioned house to carry out some renovation work. I recognised one of the actors right away. It was Roscoe "Fatty" Arbuckle. The other man was Harry Langdon, another comedian from the silent era; although not someone I was too familiar with. As you can imagine, mayhem ensued every time this pair tried to carry out even the simplest of tasks. The slapstick was slick and inventive, and soon had us all laughing, even David.

I quickly got up to speed with the film's plot. Lloyd was playing a ghost. His character was Lord Godfrey Skerryvore, a spook who took great pains to haunt the house he had once been master of – the eponymous Skerryvore Manor. Given this set up, Lloyd wasted no time in scaring the bejesus out of the hapless builders. Arbuckle and Langdon crashed and pratfalled their way through one brilliantly crafted set-piece to another, and before long, Lloyd had them racing from the house in comical terror.

It appeared this section had merely been a prologue of sorts, because after Arbuckle and Langdon had had it away on their toes, the film cut to an animated title sequence.

This was set in a creepy, fogbound cemetery, and each credit appeared on a gravestone, or in the case of Harold Lloyd and John Belushi's names, high upon a mausoleum. The classic depiction of a ghost, the white transparent spectre, floated through the graveyard, almost as if he were introducing us to each name that appeared on a headstone. It was somewhat crudely animated, but effective nevertheless. It put me in mind of an old Disney cartoon I'd once seen, also set in a cemetery, where skeletons got up from out of their graves to enjoy a macabre midnight dance. I remember that one frightening me when I was really young.

The list of names carved into the cartoon headstones included Florence Lawrence, Claude Rains, Betty Grable, James Finlayson, and Will Hay, a British comedian I used to watch with my mum when I was a boy. Harold Lloyd wrote the film with Clyde Bruckman, and also directed it himself. Seymour Janks was credited as producer.

After the title sequence, we were introduced to John Belushi's character, Igby Hilliker, a down-on-his-luck rhythm and blues singer, who arrived at Skerryvore Manor licking his wounds somewhat. His latest album had flopped spectacularly, and this had led to an even more disastrous tour of the states. The double punch of failure had sent him scurrying from the public eye, and Skerryvore Manor was the place he planned to hole up for a long while and take stock of his life.

And so, for the first part of the movie, Lloyd watched on in utter dismay as guitars and amplifiers were brought into his house, and Belushi's loud and brash Hilliker character – and his girlfriend, Aishlinn, played by Betty Grable – moved in. Lloyd again wasted no time in *puttin' the old haunt on them*, as he put it, and indeed pulled out all the stops. There were nightly moanings, guitars disappearing and reappearing in random places – one such instrument turning up in a toilet – floating tables and chairs, and clatterings and bangings around the house at all hours.

Only, Belushi and Grable's characters didn't pay these ghostly goings-on much attention. They seemed to sleep through most of these *bumps in the night* – Belushi's snoring often louder than Lloyd's attempts to cause a ruckus – and Grable blamed most of the disturbances on Belushi's oafish behaviour. They were just far too preoccupied by their own selves to even notice the supernatural jiggery-pokery happening all around them. Not one of Lloyd's usual haunting techniques seemed to work on these new interlopers, and before long he was at his wits' end.

The turning point in the story came when Belushi, drunk one night, tripped and fell to his death down the grand staircase. I found this twist in the story unexpected and slightly out of kilter with the rest of the film's tone. However, it served as a catalyst for what transpired to be *Mad Dogs'* main premise – two ghosts battling it out with one another for the house they both want to haunt. It was quite an inspired concept, and was wonderfully executed.

Lloyd and Belushi were just brilliant in the next section of the film. The physical comedy was extraordinary, and one or two of the gags had me crying with laughter. The film played on the cultural clash between its two principal stars, and also displayed some of the depth and range of Belushi's acting abilities.

One inspired sequence concerned Betty Grable inviting two mediums to Skerryvore Manor to perform a séance. The mediums themselves were played by Claude Rains and Florence Lawrence, who, in life, was said to have been the world's first movie star. Lloyd and Belushi, stood on opposite sides of the room, watched as Rains and Lawrence called upon the spirits of the dead. And the spirits did indeed come. Will Hay was the first to be summoned forth, and was decidedly annoyed at being disturbed. He ended up bickering with Belushi about the woes of being deceased. A lot of what he said got big laughs from the Electric audience.

Another spirit that turned up in the sequence was James Finlayson, the master of the double-take and the squinty eye, who had been a regular player in Laurel & Hardy films. In *Mad Dogs,* Finlayson decided that he liked the look of Skerryvore Manor and attempted to stay. Lloyd and Belushi then had to band together to kick this unwanted ghost out on his ear.

This seemed to be another turning point in the film, but that was as far as we got.

About midway through the séance sequence, Elmer Muxloe came into the theatre and began pacing up and down the aisles, peering intently at the faces sat in the dark. A few of the ghosts shooed him away, but still he persisted. He soon quickened his pace, becoming almost frantic, staring at one face after another. It distracted me from the film, which, truth be told, I was a little annoyed about. Then, without a word of explanation, he left again. I turned to Emma, who had also noticed Muxloe's odd behaviour, and gave her a quizzical frown. She shrugged her shoulders. David, however, hadn't noticed; he was still glued to the film. In fact, he looked mesmerised by it, his eyes agleam.

Following on from the séance sequence, Lloyd and Belushi ejected Finlayson unceremoniously out of Skerryvore, and it was here that the film suddenly stopped. The place went up in arms.

I could actually hear ghosts booing and hissing, and it made me laugh. Emma gave me a strange look.

We must have all sat in the darkness for perhaps five minutes or more. Or at least, it seemed that long to me. I was just about to go up to the projector room to see what the hell Muxloe was doing, when suddenly the screen burst into life again. Only, it wasn't *Mad Dogs* playing any longer. It was something very different.

For a start, this film was in colour, and was incredibly grainy and worn. It made me think of Emma's pirated copy of *The Texas Chainsaw Massacre*. There was something dirty about it, sleazy even.

The booing persisted as the Electric's audience realised that this certainly was not the rest of *Mad Dogs*. The dickie bow guy shouted out, "Wrong film, you yahoo!" Some ghosts even got up and left. I heard David say to Emma, "What the hell happened to the film?"

As for me, I got locked into the new film right away. The reason being: it appeared to be about Johnnie Scanlan and Seymour Janks' film *Ghost with a Gun*.

It seemed Muxloe wasn't too concerned with pleasing his audience. Not only did he stop *Mad Dogs* halfway through, but it appeared he'd started the next film several reels in. The matinee had become two halves of different movies.

It was a starkly different picture to the others I'd seen at the Electric, and not just because it was in colour. It was the first film in which I didn't recognise a single actor or actress – they were all *nobodies*, as my dad would've called them. Also, it was shot in an entirely different style to any of the other Janks presentations – if indeed it was one of his. It had a vérité to it. A loose, hand-held, documentary style that reinforced the feeling that I was watching a gritty, low-budget horror movie from the mid-seventies.

And yet, in complete dichotomy to the look and feel of the film, it appeared to be set in Los Angeles in the early part of the century. During the birthing, booming movie years, when Hollywood had sidewalks that ran along and disappeared into open fields, and roads which were little more than dirt tracks, and studio lots that were nothing but bungalows and shacks.

There were two characters standing on one such sidewalk,

which I heard them refer to as Sunset Boulevard. Behind them towered a great scaffolded structure that looked Egyptian in its design. A movie set for sure, but I was astonished by how gigantic it was. It positively loomed over Sunset. I could make out several statues stood high upon great pedestals; they looked to be white elephants rearing up on their hindquarters. One of the men referred to the set as Babylon, and then mentioned the filmmaker D.W. Griffith. Through their conversation I learned that the colossal structure had been built for Griffith's 1916 epic *Intolerance,* which one of the men described as "overblown". They stared at the set for moment. An old jalopy rattled along Sunset, the only vehicle I spotted.

Griffith's great set, a make-believe Mesopotamia seemingly dropped down onto the sleepy, burgeoning Hollywood, stood like a mirage, a grand illusion of a different place and time. It occurred to me then that all films are phantasmal realities; a contradiction that transports us to any given time, or place, and yet only gives a representation of what we're experiencing in 24 frames per second. Celluloid, then, is nothing but the chattering teeth of lies and illusions. Films are waking dreams. The Electric's roster perhaps even more so. Peering into the worlds that Janks and his stellar collaborators had captured were just that: mere representations of what lies beyond this life. I found that to be a startling revelation, for I hadn't realised I'd taken Janks' oeuvre so literally. Perhaps, then, what I had glimpsed in the Electric's films was no more real than Griffith's Babylonian Hollywood. Janks' films were all fiction, after all. Like all cinema, they were mirages; phantom illusions of worlds beyond our own, not actual depictions at all.

Something about this winding train of thought upset me, even though I knew I'd been foolish in blindly believing everything I'd seen. Still, I couldn't help but feel cheated somehow. But they were just movies. Make-believes. Illusions.

Like Janks said, they were just entertainment for the dead.

The other thing troubling me was that the scene on Sunset

had also made me question Janks' *Ghost with a Gun* story. The reason being that the two men standing beneath Babylon were supposed to be Johnnie Scanlan and Seymour Janks. The actor playing Janks looked nothing like him, but that wasn't what was troubling me. Janks had told me that the one and only print of *Ghost with a Gun* had gone up in flames in Atlantic City, and yet this movie had Janks and his director Scanlan planning to show their supernatural opus in L.A. They also made mention of the fire, and said that it'd simply been a ruse to get the film out of New Jersey. The Scanlan character also talked of gangsters trying to muscle in on their newfound box office bonanza. Hence the reason for the arson and subsequent flee to California.

The scene following on from this had Scanlan and Janks preparing for their screening in, of all places, a backroom in the Glen-Holly Hotel. This led me to thinking about another thing that didn't quite sit right with me. Janks had said that *Ghost with a Gun* had been shot in 1900, and yet this film appeared to be set sometime after 1916. Perhaps it was just artistic licence, as many movies so freely play with, but it all just seemed a little strange, especially coming so soon after Janks had spun the yarn. Something didn't add up.

As I sat there trying to figure this latest puzzle out, Muxloe came back into the cinema and started dashing about again, staring at everyone in the audience. This time David noticed. "What the hell's he doing?"

"I have no idea," I said.

If anything, Muxloe looked even more deranged than last time. He went around the entire audience; he even passed us twice, but didn't once look at us. Ghosts were hurling abuse at him – many calling for *Mad Dogs* to be put back on – but Muxloe just ignored them.

Finally, the old projectionist stood beneath the screen and peered out into the gloom. Above him, I caught a glimpse of *Ghost with a Gun* beginning its performance in the backroom of the Glen-Holly Hotel, then the reel ran out and the screen went blank. Just before we were plunged into darkness once more, I saw Muxloe was weeping. Then I heard him cry out, "Where is my son?"

To see the old man so distressed upset me. I stood up and watched as he left the theatre once more. He looked in a real mess. I wanted to call to him, ask him if he was all right – feeble words I knew – but he was gone before I could find my voice. Emma, however, now standing beside me, said, "We've got to go and help him." With what exactly, she didn't specify, but she was right, Muxloe clearly needed some kind of aid. He looked to be at the end of his tether, and it scared me to see him like that. I glanced back at David and saw that he too was already on his feet. Incredibly, he looked ready for anything, and just seeing him like that gave me the shot of strength I needed.

The three of us raced from the theatre, back out into the light.

We bounded up to the third floor. The carpet along the corridor was completely sodden. It squelched under foot. I could hear Muxloe clattering about in the projection room. Further along the corridor, the door to Reginald Stokely's old office had been left slightly ajar, by myself and Emma the previous day no doubt. I thought about my dad's drawings lying on the desk in there, and that, in turn, got me thinking about kissing Emma up on the Electric's rooftop. It hadn't quite been twenty-four hours since all that had happened, and yet it felt like days ago. Time stretched and deceived no end.

Through the smashed out windows, I saw clouds like anvil heads rolling off to the west. The trees glistened, and I could even make out the sound of them dripping heavily. The breeze was cool, and there was still that metallic scent of charged sky lingering. It was the sort of wonderful air that made you think of nothing but living.

We came to the projection room. The door was open. Inside, Elmer Muxloe was frantically rifling through a pile of film cans. He looked at us. His eyes were afire. It unnerved me to see him like that.

"Well, don't just stand there gawping," he said, "help me look through these cans."

A worrisome look passed between the three of us, but then we shuffled into the room and joined Muxloe in rummaging.

Emma asked, "What are we looking for, Mr Muxloe?" but Mr Muxloe didn't answer. In fact, he didn't even appear to hear her; he just checked the labels on individual cans, before casting them aside with absolutely no care whatsoever. It hurt my heart to see these incredibly rare and precious films being treated so badly. And it astonished me that it was Muxloe being the saboteur.

Spools of film had spilled from a few of the cans and lay unravelling on the dirty floor. I began to collect them up, as carefully as I could, and found empty cans to house them in. I was almost certainly putting the reels away under wrongly marked lids, but I wasn't too concerned with that, I just wanted to get the celluloid up off the floor.

I reached across the pile and picked up a can marked *London After Midnight, Reel 2*. I knew the title. I also knew that it was a *real* film. The film Molly Lévesque had died watching.

I'd owned a large, coffee-table-sized book since early childhood. It was called *A Pictorial History of Horror Movies*, by a guy named Denis Gifford, and, as the title suggested, it was packed with pictures from a vast array of fright films. I used to pore over it for hours and hours, trying to imagine what each and every film must be like. Several such pictures were from *London After Midnight,* and showed Lon Chaney as one of the most terrifying-looking vampires I'd ever seen (second only to Max Schreck in *Nosferatu*). Being not only a masterful actor, but also a genius of make-up artistry, Chaney wore sharpened dentures, giving him a hideous shark-like rictus, and had wire loops placed in his eye-sockets, which were apparently tightened before each take in order bulge out his eyes (these were the kind of titbits I'd learned from Gifford's book). This was all topped off with a lopsided, beaver top hat. The effect was certainly terrifying. When I was really young, I would get nervous turning to the particular page in question, knowing that Chaney would be there, staring out at me with those horrible eyes. Often times I'd skip the page altogether.

I pried open the can and found the reel inside. I noticed Muxloe staring at me.

He said, "What you got there?"

I said, "*London After Midnight*, Mr Muxloe."

He reached out his hand. "Give."

With reluctance, I handed it over. He then wasted no time in going about the business of threading the reel through the projector. His hands moved with ease and precision. The three of us simply stood and watched. Muxloe began to mutter to himself as he went about his work, but I couldn't make much sense of it. I picked out the odd word, but nothing more.

Finally, Emma said, "Have you been here all along, Mr Muxloe? Changing the reels, I mean..."

"Uh-huh," he said, but gave away nothing more.

"How long have you been coming here?"

He completely ignored that question. Instead, he locked the film against the final guide, and then turned to us. "This picture was released in 1927, and was one of ten pictures that Chaney made with director Tod Browning. This being one of their biggest hits. It is, however, in the eyes of the world at large, a "lost" film. The last *known* print was destroyed when a fire broke out in a vault on the MGM lot in 1967. Countless silent pictures were lost, including this one. It has since become one of the most famous and eagerly sought-after lost films in motion picture history. Why? Perhaps because of the magnetism of Chaney, or..."

David cut him off. "So you're sayin' that this film doesn't exist anymore?"

"Well, not any prints that anyone knows about. I'm sure it'll be discovered one day… up in somebody's attic or something, gathering dust. But yes, movie history has deemed this a lost film."

"And yet, you've got a copy…" said David.

"Well, only partially… just one reel. The other reels broke down over time. It's one of the great ironies, really. When films came along they were perceived as immortality, and yet celluloid is as fragile as life itself."

"But why haven't you told anyone?"

"Told anyone what?"

"That you've got parts of a film that people think is lost?"

Muxloe looked at David as if he'd just asked the stupidest question possible. "Because we don't want any unwanted eyes on this here picture house, young fella. The Electric already has its audience."

And with that, the old projectionist turned his back on us and sparked his flickering, chattering machine into life. Something about his wild hair in that delicate, quivering half-light put me in mind of Doctor Frankenstein in an old Universal monster picture. The mad projectionist going about his diabolical work!

There was no music on the film, no sound whatsoever. *London After Midnight* was completely silent. The projector whirred and chattered away, giving life to the movie – Frankensteinian in itself – and I peered down through the view-hole to the screen below.

Chaney, dressed as the vampire that had so frightened me as a child, held aloft a lamp and led a pale and dark-eyed young woman through a creepy old house. The film wasn't exactly black and white; it had a brown texture to it. Also, either the frame rate was dropping out, or the film itself was running slightly slower than it should. Chaney and his companion (who I later found out to be an actress named Edna Tichenor) moved almost in slow motion. This only added to the eeriness of the picture.

Muxloe came to stand next to me and peered down to the screen below. As far as I could tell, the rows were now empty of ghosts.

Muxloe said, "My son loved this picture. He always liked the spooky ones." He sighed, then added, "But still he won't come. What will it take?"

As he said this, something occurred to me.

"Mr Muxloe, I have the reel you left in your old car."

He looked at me in astonishment. "Where?" he said.

"I have it here… in my rucksack."

At first I thought he was angry with me, but then his face softened.

"I thought it would be best to destroy it," he said, his eyes glistening in the flickering light. "I thought it would be best…" he repeated, this time seemingly to himself. He appeared to me an altogether different man to the one I'd met the previous day. This version of Elmer Muxloe was like a shadow; a pale imitator of the somewhat imposing character I'd thought him to be.

I said, "Would you run it for us?"

Muxloe glanced at the screen below – and at the rows of empty seats – and said, "Yes, Sam, I will."

As Muxloe changed reels yet again, I asked him, "The film you put on midway through *Mad Dogs,* what was that?"

Without looking up from his work, he said, "Something called *Illusion City*. A labour of love for Janks, I believe. It's about the first film he shot that captured... you know... *them*."

"I know," I said. "He told me about that."

I sensed David and Emma look at me, but I remained focused on Muxloe. He stopped what he was doing and turned around.

"You spoke to Janks?"

"Yes."

"When?"

"Here. During the storm."

"I guess that explains why I didn't hear you. So you talked about..."

"That film of his, yes. *Ghost with a Gun*."

"Really? Well, he's been searching for that filmette for years and years."

"He doesn't have it?"

"No. That's what *Illusion City* is about. Although I'm sure he took a great many liberties with the actual events, mind. Y'know, make it more exciting... as they do. It is a movie after all. Never let the truth get in the way of a good story, that's what they say..."

"So, he *didn't* show *Ghost with a Gun* in Hollywood, like in the film? 'Cause it doesn't make sense. He told me the print was destroyed in a fire in Atlantic City."

"Well, he thought it had been... For a long time, he thought that. Look, I don't know the ins and outs, kid. You'll have to ask Janks for yourself."

"If I ever see him again," I said, quietly.

Muxloe gave me an odd look, and I thought he was going to say something more, but instead, he just turned around and continued lining up the reel.

With his back to us, he said, "You should go back down. I'll be running this footage right away."

There was a coldness to the way he said this.

Elmer Muxloe's reel turned out to be *behind the scenes* footage, shot on the location of a Janks production. It was in colour, and had no sound. Plus, it was shot on super 8, so it was incredibly grainy and raw. It did indeed have a vérité to it, certainly more so even than *Illusion City*, but that wasn't all. Incredibly, the footage felt more *Electric* than any of the other films. That certain *quality*, so intrinsic in everything from *When the Night Came Fallin'* to *A Murder of Crows* to *Mad Dogs,* was, if anything, even more intense. Almost unbearably so. Perhaps that had been why Muxloe had wanted to be rid of it? Maybe he thought it was just too damn *Electric*. Yet, something about that theory didn't add up. Leaving the reel in a car he sold to Albert Looms seemed like quite a game of chance. Corpse cars were always pillaged. Emma could've testified to that. So why had he done it? Had he wanted us to find it? He'd mentioned something about the *item* in his car when Emma and I had called to his house. It'd been one of the first things he'd said to us. Perhaps it'd been a trail of breadcrumbs? I never did find out the true reasoning, but I came to believe that Muxloe, either consciously or subconsciously, had wanted that footage to be found. He wanted the Electric's mysteries to be passed on. I'm sure of it. I'm just glad it was us.

When the footage began, there was only the three of us in the cinema, but by the time it finished ten minutes later, the place was once more brimming with ghosts. They came in their droves, and sat down all around us. I spotted the dickie bow guy, and the Technicolor tramp. Both of them gave me a nod, which I returned.

The ghosts were drawn only to the films made for them, it seemed. *London After Midnight* held no attraction because it was a *real* film. Everything else that played the Electric, however, was supernatural. There was no question of that.

The behind the scenes footage was nothing short of incredible. The location was a desert town – which didn't surprise me – where a film crew were busy working under a blistering sun. The township itself was very strange indeed. On the surface, it looked like an old ghost town, like something from a cowboy movie – dirt roads and wooden boardwalks, bordellos and saloons – yet the buildings themselves seemed to be an amalgamation of wooden and brick structures, with oddly futuristic design flourishes. There were neon signs, and mirrored glass, and strange metal statues, which glinted in the sun and lined the main street, almost as if they were on guard. Some of them put me in mind of the robot from *Metropolis*; others were just bulks of silver. A dragster – which looked like a souped-up Plymouth Fury – rolled along the main street. (At fifteen, I knew the car right away, mainly because of Stephen King.) I also noticed several motorbikes lined up outside a saloon, like metal horses.

There was a hive of activity going on. The crew were busy preparing for a shot. The camera and lighting departments scurried about, and script supervisors and assistant directors rushed here and there. It looked for all the world like the usual hubbub of movie making, yet I knew just by its *texture* that it was very different indeed. Every ounce of my being seemed to respond to it. I sweated profusely, yet felt bone cold. Gooseflesh riddled my arms and legs, and I could feel my right hand shaking terribly. Ghosts drifted into the cinema by the dozen, yet I hardly paid them any mind – save for my brief nods to dickie bow and TT, that was.

I caught a brief shot of the clapperboard. It read:
PROD: RAVENS' BOWER
DIR: WILLIAM DESMOND TAYLOR
CAM: KARL FREUND
SCENE: 153 / TAKE 2

The director, Desmond Taylor – a filmmaker I later found out was murdered in 1922 – was standing out on the dusty main street, talking to his lead actors. One was John Garfield; the other was an impeccably dressed black man. This was Canada Lee, the actor Janks had made mention of. These shots were brief however, as the camera kept cutting. The operator, whomever that was – perhaps Janks himself – seemed to only film intermittently, and then for just short periods of time. This meant the footage leapfrogged around.

In quick succession I saw Canada Lee standing out on the main street, levelling a gun at John Garfield – as William Desmond Taylor sat watching from his director's chair, over by the camera; then there was a shot of Seymour Janks, resplendent as ever in his white suit, talking with Canada Lee on the boardwalk; Jayne Mansfield in a bustling barroom, singing a song I couldn't hear; the camera crew laughing and goofing around as they set up a shot out in the sands; Garfield stood by a huge arc light, talking in silhouette with Mansfield, and finally, Seymour Janks on the edge of town, looking out across the endless desert sands.

Then the film ran out.

As soon as it stopped I felt a huge jolt to my senses, as if I'd been snapped from a spell. Yet, even though my nerve endings calmed, my hand continued to shake uncontrollably. I held it at the wrist to try and steady it. Emma noticed this and asked if I was okay. I said I was, but she didn't look very convinced.

I closed my eyes for a moment. I could hear the ghosts muttering away, sounding far off, like voices carried along the wind. David and Emma were talking beside me, something about the *strangeness* of what we'd just seen, but I tried to block them out.

Front and centre of my mind, I fixed the image of the Electric cinema, with all its ghosts, sat in row after row, watching the movies made for them. I thought of the drawing I'd attempted the previous day, the one old TT and Albert Lévesque had admired. I thought I could do it again, and try and get it better. With all ghosts now filling the cinema, I could actually capture them in time. In pencil. Perhaps not as grandiose as capturing them on film maybe, but it was all I had.

As this idea fixed in my mind, my right hand began to steady a little. To steady it completely, I knew I needed to draw.

There was something else I needed as well.

I stood, then shouted up to the projection room. "Elmer!"

His face appeared in the view-hole.

"Elmer, run *When the Night Came Fallin'*."

It would be the first and the last movie I ever saw at the Electric.

There is a moment in Frank Capra's 1946 classic, *It's a Wonderful Life*, that struck me greatly in the years after the Electric cinema. It comes just after the angel, Clarence Odbody, played by Henry Travers, leaps into the icy cold river which Jimmy Stewart's George Bailey was himself about to commit suicide in. Bailey then dives in to rescue Clarence. But of course, it's really Clarence who rescues him. The scene immediately following this one has George and Clarence drying off in the Bridge Toll House. The tollkeeper sits and listens with growing alarm as Clarence mutters away. George, on the other hand, is hardly listening to the angel at all. It's a great scene. It's also the point where Henry Travers says a line of dialogue that really knocked me for six. He shakes off his copy of *Tom Sawyer* and says, "… Oh, Tom Sawyer's drying out, too. You should read the new book Mark Twain's writing now."

Well, the tollkeeper damn near falls off his chair. As did I when I heard it.

Capra uses the line as a kind of throwaway gag, but it certainly resonated with me. Like Clarence suggesting George Bailey and the tollkeeper read Mark Twain's new book, I had seen a film – or at least parts of a film – that Humphrey Bogart had made since his death in 1957. Likewise, I had seen Lon Chaney, Harold Lloyd, Jayne Mansfield, Bela Lugosi, John Belushi, and scores of others, all performing in films made beyond their passing.

The Electric gave me these wonderful visions, and set me on a path that would shape the rest of my life.

I sat directly beneath the screen, paper and pencil set out before me. Flickering light spilled from the projection room and illuminated the audience in that magical silvery glow of film. The score rumbled. I glanced up and saw the sand dunes, and Bogart's face coming into frame, filling the screen. The Electric's audience settled into the film, and I picked up my pencil.

Before I set it to the paper, however, I spent a little time just soaking in the faces before me. I saw the Technicolor tramp sat in his usual seat. He gave me his customary nod. There was the greaser and his pretty Sandra Dee girlfriend sat a few rows from the front – I hadn't seen them since Emma and I had first watched *When the Night Came Fallin'*. I noticed the dickie bow guy chewing the ear off a very attractive black lady – she was only half listening to him – and a group of teenagers behind them, necking like it was going out of style. (Seems some things never change, even in death.) David and Emma were still seated further back, obscured by darkness. I knew I wanted to include them in my drawing.

In the front row, there were two ghosts that really caught my attention. Engrossed in the film was Albert Lévesque, and beside him, her arm threaded through his, was the lanternist's slight and pretty wife, Molly, the creator of the Electric cinema.

I must have watched them for five minutes or more. I just could not avert my eyes. Molly held onto Albert so sweetly it made my heart ache. He, in turn, held her hand as if he never wanted to let it go. Every now and again, he would glance down at her, and she would look up at him, the film-light casting shadows across their skin, and they would kiss. I thought then that it was like something out of a movie.

Lévesque, the magic lanternist, who'd travelled the world performing his phantasmagoria shows, had once found himself with an audience of the dead, in the very place the Electric came to be built. Shadow plays and lantern shows gave way to film; the moving miracle of captured image. And Molly Lévesque moved with those rushing times, outliving her husband and building the grand picture palace, the Electric, on a secluded scrap of woodland, for her *unique* audience. Then Seymour Janks brought his special talent to Molly Lévesque's movie house, which in turn, led him to make his own pictures for the Electric.

There were many details missing, gaps and contradictions in the timeline, but I could piece together the events, or at least a version of the events, that had led to us all congregating in that cinema, on that storm-ravaged Sunday, to watch films made by ghosts.

You could say I knew a *movie version* of the facts; where timelines and events had been changed and embellished. Memory so often belies and alters the truth. It's history in distortion. Much like a movie.

I knew that Reginald Stokely had commercialised the Electric in an effort to keep it running. This had brought in Muxloe, and in the course of time, my father. And even after the Electric had closed its doors to the public, and Stokely had long gone, Elmer Muxloe continued to show Janks' films to the lingering dead. It occurred to me that Muxloe must still have been paying for the building, keeping the juice running through the wires, in order to continue projecting those glorious movies.

Still, a great many things didn't add up. Some I would come to learn in time, others remained as mysterious as the Electric itself. But for me, there remains a kind of gladness that I never did learn every secret, figure out every puzzle. I was, and still am, grateful for the glimpse I was allowed. And the richness it brought to my subsequent life, and work.

Back then, when I drew my last picture in that place, a lot of the jigsaw fell into place. And I have hardly revised it since that day.

Above me, Bogart was telling Jean Harlow, "… me and the boys had a change of plan." The gunfight with Victor McLaglen was about to begin.

At that moment, I thought, *my dad would've loved this movie*

– *femme fatales* and double crosses, and Bogart stamping out bad guys. It was quintessential Bogie, and I just knew my old man would have lapped it up.

My pencil connected with the paper, and the film, and the room, seemed to zone out. I immediately became lost in my creation. I sketched the faces that peered up at the screen with a speed and fluidity far beyond what I thought myself capable of. My hand, now as steady and precise as a true artist's, worked its magic across the paper. The ghosts knew I was there, and they also knew what I was doing, but I felt a kind of *allowance.* A licence and acceptance. I also felt that they would not have acquiesced to this for just anyone. Of course, I didn't know that for sure. Not one of them told me this was the case, but still, I did feel it very strongly indeed. And if the Electric had taught me anything, it was to trust my instincts. What was *felt* in that place was perhaps truer than any word could be.

I drew Albert and Molly Lévesque first. Bogart and McLaglen were locked in a gunfight above me, but I hardly noticed. Albert turned slightly, and gently kissed Molly on the forehead, and that's how I drew them.

As with my first versions of this scene, I captured the *essence* of the ghosts, rather than a detailed representation. This allowed me to work fast, moving from one face to the next in rapid succession. Before long I had the entire front row completed; then, without pausing for breath, I moved straight onto the second.

It was then I noticed a man I thought I recognised.

The longer I looked, the more familiar he seemed to me, but I just could not place him. I sat and stared, my pencil quivering in my hand. He was very well dressed, in a deep black suit and white shirt, and his eyes captivated me. I felt that I knew them, that I'd seen them before. I was so sure of this that I returned my pencil to the paper and, for the first time, drew those eyes in fine detail.

On the screen above, Bogart was still under siege from

Victor McLaglen. I was *in* the drawing; so fixed on its creation that the world around me almost ceased to be.

I finished the eyes, and then stared at my work. I glanced up and checked the eyes of the ghost against those in my picture. They were an exact match. It was then I realised where I'd seen them before.

I stood up and shouted across the cinema, "Elmer! He's here!"

Elmer Muxloe walked along the aisle, and came upon his son.

I watched from my place beneath the screen. Elmer's son stood slowly and faced his father. The old projectionist placed a hand on the ghost's shoulder, then embraced him. They stood like that for a long time.

I felt a tear fall from my face and hit the drawing. I wiped my eyes, then returned my pencil to the paper.

Elmer and his son sat down together, and watched the screen. I drew this.

They seemed perfectly at ease with one another. They didn't speak, or hardly move even – save to look at each other every now and again – they just sat and watched the Bogart movie, as I used to with my dad. At one point Muxloe placed a hand on his son's head and ruffled his hair. That's when I really began to cry.

I struggled to compose myself, and eventually hid my face in my hands.

I peered through my fingers and saw the Technicolor tramp staring at me from the silvery shadows. Something in his face immediately put me at ease, and I managed to get a handle on myself.

I returned to my drawing, and the preternatural flow leaked from my pencil once more. I drew the greaser and his girlfriend, then a large, bald man with a walrus moustache. I worked fast, capturing each ghost in turn.

Then I came to the Technicolor tramp.

My pencil hovered over the paper, my eyes fixed on that wild looking guy, flaring with colour. I thought back to the night I first discovered the Electric, and how I'd fled when I first laid eyes on old TT. I looked down at my drawing, and without any real understanding as to what I was doing, I left the Technicolor tramp's seat empty. I moved onto the next ghost – a Chinese lady – and drew her instead.

I drew furiously. On the screen above me, Humphrey Bogart and Jean Harlow were encamped in the saloon; a great sandstorm was raging through the town. I only glanced up once, then returned in earnest to finish my picture.

The final two faces I drew were Emma and David's. Emma noticed my attention turn to them, and she waved. They looked considerably duller than the ghosts – half lost to darkness, and without the supernatural vibrancy to light them. But make them out I did, and I detailed them with great care.

When I was done, I sat back against the wall, the bottom of the screen just two or three feet above me my head. The sandstorm whistled and moaned on the soundtrack. I heard Bogart say, "Looks like we're holed up for the night, sweetheart."

I closed my eyes for a moment. I thought back to a long ago afternoon when my dad and I had watched *In a Lonely Place* – the one where Bogart had played a washed-up screenwriter embroiled in a murder. I'd been sat in the chair, while dad had been sprawled out of the sofa. At one point I looked over and saw that he was staring right at me. He said, "You like the film?" and I'd said, "Yeah, it's a real good one, Dad," and he gave me this smile that I've never forgotten. At that moment, he looked like he really cared for me, and I remember it making me feel really good. I carried that smile for a lot of years.

I opened my eyes and looked directly at the Technicolor tramp. There was an empty space right next to him – the other side of the Chinese lady – so I decided I was going to go over there and watch the rest of the movie with him. Maybe I had a sense that something was ending; that these were the last moments in the Electric cinema, or perhaps it just felt right to sit and watch that Bogart movie with the first ghost I ever saw. Whatever possessed me, once the thought had entered my head, I couldn't get over there quick enough.

I rolled up the drawing and slipped it in my rucksack, then bounded up the aisle. Old TT saw me coming and offered out his hand to the empty seat. The invite filled me with warmth I could not have expected, and I couldn't help but smile.

I had to shuffle past several ghosts to get to the seat, but none of them kicked up a fuss, and I even managed to avoid treading on any feet.

I sat down. On the screen, Bogart was turning over tables and using them to board up windows. The sandstorm was howling. I turned to the Technicolor tramp. I was going to ask him what he thought of the movie, but my voice choked as soon I saw him. Gone was the wild hair and great forest of beard. The man was no longer who I'd come to think of as the Technicolor tramp. The man was John Stephen Crowhurst.

My father.

My father took my hand in his, and we sat like that, watching Bogart's strange and wonderful movie.

I looked down at his hand; a hand that had once held my mother. A hand that raised me, held me firm, steadied me against the world.

A hand that had clutched at his heart as it so suddenly gave out.

He held onto me so tightly, as we sat in that dilapidated old cinema, that if I really try, I can still feel that hand in mine.

If I imagine hard enough.

On the screen, Bogart and Harlow were holed up the saloon as the sandstorm continued to rip through the town. On the other side of the street, Victor McLaglen lay in wait. The dialogue crackled between Bogie and Harlow, and sure enough, he got the dame. He pulled her to him, and they kissed as the storm rattled and howled at the saloon.

I felt my dad look at me, yet, if truth be known, I found it difficult to look at him. I just kept staring at his hand in mine, as if that was the most of him I could handle. I kept trying to think of something to say, but everything I thought of just seemed lame. What I truly felt was so great, I just knew I couldn't articulate it. I was afraid that if I even attempted to open my mouth, I would just turn into a gibbering wreck.

In my frustration, at what I felt were my own failings, I suddenly found myself angry at my father. He'd been at the Electric all along, hidden behind a disguise. This alone enraged me. I just couldn't make any sense as to why. Later, I came to understand that he had done so in order to keep his distance; to allow me to discover the mysteries of the Electric in my own good time. Disguised as what I'd come to think of as the Technicolor tramp, he had made a very difficult passage of understanding, and accepting, a little easier. And it had worked, too. By the time he revealed himself to me, I'd become at ease around the ghosts. If he had been himself on that first night of my discovery, I may never have gone so far, and so deep.

But I couldn't see any of that then. I was just angry. I saw it as kind of sick game he'd played, and I couldn't understand it at all.

It wasn't just that, though. I was also angry at him for dying.

I thought back to the laugh I'd heard, when I'd been idling by the river that first evening. Had I just happened to catch it riding along the breeze, or had I been meant to hear it? Had it been to lure me to the Electric? It seemed unlikely, and yet, as soon as the question arose in my mind, I found it difficult to shake. I suddenly realised that my father had known I would come to the Electric that night. Why else would he have been sat there alone in his elaborate disguise? He had been waiting for me.

Finally, I looked at him.

All of me, my entire being, pulsed with that *Electric* surge. I felt a great pressure pinning me to the seat. My father smiled, and all that anger, all that hurt, faded out like the end of a movie.

He said, "Be all that you can be, Sam. You can do great things."

I don't think I've ever felt more alive than in that moment.

On the screen, the image flipped as the reel ran out. The last shot I saw was of Bogart loading his guns. The sandstorm dying away.

I never did see the end of that picture.

The cinema was plunged into darkness. I felt Dad squeeze my hand, then let it go. Right away, my hand felt utterly empty.

He stood up, then glanced down at me. It was my first really good look at him, standing tall and proud. Light blazed from him. Everything was heightened.

His attention turned from me however, to someone over by the auditorium doors. I stood and saw Elmer Muxloe. There was no one else in the cinema. I couldn't even see David and Emma. Muxloe then gave a nod, not to me, but to my father.

Then the old projectionist turned and walked out, and my father... he gave me one final look, and then was gone.

Before I left the Electric for the final time, I went up to Reginald Stokely's office. There I collected up my dad's drawings – the one of Bogart, the other of the windmill, set against the hailstorm sky, and finally, the scene of Lévesque's Phantasmagoria show. I rolled them up and added them to my rucksack, alongside my own picture. Then I stood for a moment. The place was utterly still. As empty as only a derelict building could be. The ghosts had gone. My father had gone. Even Muxloe and my friends had gone. For the briefest of moments, I felt so completely alone that I had to fight to bite back tears. But then it passed, and I walked out of the room and closed the door behind me.

I glanced into the projection room on my way back down. Muxloe had tidied up a little it seemed, and had stacked the film cans neatly into a corner. I did think about taking one or two, but right away decided against it. It didn't feel right to remove them from the Electric. So I closed that door also, and never saw any one of those films again.

Down in the lobby, I paused to stare at my drawing, which still hung over the *Mad Dogs* poster – my second attempt at capturing the Electric's audience. It was certainly cruder, and less populated than the new version, but that wasn't to say it didn't have a certain pull to it. I came to learn in time that all my drawings of the Electric possessed that certain *quality*. (The strongest being the one I drew that very afternoon, before the cinema's audience of ghosts, which I still have to this day.)

As I stood staring at my own picture, I noticed the face I'd drawn where the Technicolor tramp usually sat. It was crudely sketched, and was, at first glance, difficult to make out. But as I stared, it became obvious to me that it was my father.

I guess part of me had known he had been there all along.

I walked through the copse in a daze. I stopped at one point and looked back through the trees. I could make out the letters on the marquee. Just a few days before, they had been my first glimpse of the Electric, pretty much from that exact spot. I stared at the letters, A and M, as I had done that first night, and began to cry.

David and Emma were waiting for me by the shack. Or at least, what was left of the shack. Most of it lay in pieces, scattered across the field. My bike lay by David's feet. Emma stepped towards me as I came stumbling out of the tree line. Behind her the sky was bruised, and light was gently fading. I wiped my eyes and tried to smile, but my attempt felt pitiful.

"Hey," she said, softly. "We thought you needed some time alone... with... you know..."

"You okay, Slaughter?" said David.

I looked at them standing in the gloaming. That beautiful half light made diamonds of their eyes. All I managed to say was, "I'm good."

I walked over to the mud patch that had once been the shack's floor, and kicked over a few pieces of wood.

As I did this, David said, "Muxloe upped and disappeared on us."

"He got what he wanted," I said, toeing more rotten wood. My feet were soaked, but I didn't care.

Emma said, "Did you get what you wanted, Sam?"

I looked at her. A star had revealed itself in the purple sky. Emma's hair fell about her face. She tucked it behind her ears. I felt lost by her question, so decided to ignore it, and continued to kick around in the mud.

I turned over what looked to be a long length of roofing, and there, crushed into the mud, was the torn poster for *When the Night Came Fallin'*.

It was sodden and fragile, but I prised it from the mud and, as carefully as I could, put it in a front compartment of my rucksack. Separate from the drawings.

While I did this, David asked, "What is that?"

"It's part of a poster," I said. "For the Bogart film."

"Were you looking for that?"

"Yeah, I guess. I saw it the first night I came here. It should dry out."

I came away from the shack's muddy ground, and wiped my feet along the grass. Emma came up to me and kissed my mouth. It was brief, and tender, and perhaps one of the most memorable kisses of my life. It was also our last.

She held me then. I glanced over at David, fully expecting him to be mocking us, or perhaps just looking uncomfortable, but he was doing neither one of those things. Instead, he was smiling, looking genuinely pleased for us. It felt good. I held on to Emma, burying my head into her neck. I took in her smell, her touch, everything that she was.

The three of us walked back to town. We didn't say very much, nor did we rush. Emma held my hand most of the way. David pushed my bike. The sky darkened, revealing more and more stars. By the time we reached the old train line, it was full dark.

Emma stood before me, both her hands in mine. David hung back a little.

"I'll see you at school tomorrow then," she said.

"Sure," I said. "It's gonna be weird going back."

"Yeah," she agreed.

I think the strangeness of returning to the flat, humdrum of school life was something that concerned us all. Particularly Emma and I.

She said, "How can we just carry on now? After what we've seen…"

"I don't know," I told her, truthfully.

I held her against me for a moment, but then she gently pushed me away.

"I've gotta go," she said.

Emma turned and hugged David, then without another word, she made off down the line. We watched her go. The moon hung low above the treetops. It lit the tracks in silver.

David and I came to the end of his road. We stood under a streetlight and lingered for a moment. I guess neither of us knew how to part ways.

Finally, David grinned and said, "It's cool you and Em hooked up."

"Yeah?"

"Yeah. It's been on the cards all summer."

I didn't know what to say to that. I jumped on my bike, but didn't ride off right away. Instead, I said, "I know what I want to do with my life, Dave. I'm gonna be an artist. I'm gonna draw and paint… create characters and worlds… I just can feel it. It's what I've gotta do. I need…" I faltered, my voice too shaky to continue. David remained silent, allowing me the time I needed to say what I had to say. Finally, I managed, "I need to be all I can be."

David stared at me for a moment longer, then said, "Well, go for it, man. You're good enough. Your stuff's always blown me away. You could be like… what-ya-call 'em… a concept artist or somethin'. You know, like for the movies."

"Yeah," I said. "Or I could do comic books, or… be an illustrator…"

"The movies would be best."

"Yeah, I guess."

We fell silent. A car turned down Dave's street; its lights splashed over us.

"I'll see ya tomorrow then," David said.

"Yeah. I'll call round for you."

And that was that. I stood on my pedals and rode off into the night.

When I got home, I took another long shower. My second of the day. I stood under the water, watching the dirt of the Electric wash down the plughole. My mind felt numb. As I came out of the bathroom, I saw my mother on the landing. She looked good, happy even. I told her, rather cryptically, that everything was going to be okay. She looked at me puzzled at first, but then took this in good grace and smiled, saying, "I know, Sam. We're going to be all right."

And we were.

In my bedroom, I emptied out my rucksack. I laid the half poster for *When the Night Came Fallin'* on the windowsill to dry out. It was strange seeing it in my room. Then I took all of my dad's drawings and hid them under the bed. I didn't want my mother finding them and getting upset, and no doubt asking a lot of questions. Plus, I'd come to think of those drawings as being just for me. They were my final connection to him.

I had a few copies of *Playboy* hidden away under the bed, which Mum had never found, so I knew my dad's pictures would be pretty safe, at least for the time being. I knew she never ventured beneath my bed, and even if she did, there was so much other junk stashed under there, she'd more than likely make me clean it out before she did anything.

After this, I placed my latest drawing upon the desk. I stared at it for a long time. Finally, I sat down, and took out a pencil. Then, in the two empty spaces I'd left where the Technicolor tramp usually sat, I drew myself and my dad. I detailed us both very carefully. When I was done, I rolled it up and hid it beneath the bed with the others. Then I lay down, and was asleep in seconds.

That night I dreamt of movies. *Electric* movies.

And so began the longest school day of my life. I called for David in the morning – his next door neighbour, old man Travis, watched me with his bottle-ends from behind his twitching net curtains – and we traipsed to school together. The sky was overcast and low. We didn't say very much along the way, and when we did speak, we avoided any mention of the Electric, and we certainly didn't speak about my dad.

The familiar iron railings and brick and glass of our drab school loomed large in our sights as we approached the gates. I marked out several of the classrooms which I knew I would come to know well again over the coming year. The prospect of which seemed insurmountable on the threshold of that grey morning.

The previous year, Emma had often waited for us at the school gates, but she wasn't there that day. I left David without saying much of anything and headed off to my first class. Kids rushed past me, some laughed and yelled, but most, by and large, appeared subdued – shell-shocked to have been yanked from a long, hot summer and thrust back into the grey blocks of monotony.

After I'd been marked in on the register, I drifted through the morning in a daze. Being the first day of the new school year, the Powers That Be, in their infinite wisdom, had thought it wise to subject many of us poor minions to an hour-long dose of maths. Mr Borg headed this particular torture session with about as much enthusiasm as us students. He didn't appear to want to be there, and neither did we, but sit it out we all had to. So that first hour ticked by like an age, and I struggled to keep myself awake.

After that joy was over with I was plunged headlong into woodwork, where I spent most of the lesson pretending to sand down a chair.

It wasn't until lunchtime that I finally saw Emma. She was standing with a friend of hers, a girl named Donna, in the cafeteria line. I came in with David, Rhys, Ben, and another mate of ours called Doy. She saw me right away.

After we'd all eaten, we went down to the Triangle. The Electric never came up, but I knew the three of us were all thinking about it. Before long, Ben and Doy were goofing around and got us all laughing. It was good. It took out minds off things. David became preoccupied with trying to engage Donna in conversation, with little success, and Emma and I sat on the grass and got wet backsides.

There was a moment, just before the school bell rang out, where I felt like a kid again.

As we walked to our classes, David and Emma and I made plans to meet up after school. Each of us knew where we'd be going, but not one of us said it out loud.

The afternoon dragged on. First up was English, where we were subjected to almost an hour of adverbs and verbs – the only shining light was that we were given *Lord of the Flies* to read – and then it was onto art.

And it was here, during the final lesson of that first day, where I actually engaged in the subject at hand.

Our art teacher, Mrs Wood, gave us the task of drawing, or even painting, something that had happened to us over the summer. I had to laugh.

So I drew the Technicolor tramp.

The pencils at school were not the fine leads I had in my arsenal, but I think I did a pretty good job at capturing old TT's likeness. That is to say, I drew my father hidden behind all that wild hair.

When I handed it in, Mrs Wood sat mesmerised by it. She asked me who it was, but I skirted around the question. She took little notice of what I was saying anyhow, she was locked in on TT's face. I knew then that my work had a power to captivate. I'm sure she felt a touch of the *Electric*.

I felt my right hand twitch as Mrs Wood traced her finger down my father's hidden face.

We knew something was very wrong the moment we crested the field.

For starters, the scattered debris of the shack had been cleared away. Nothing remained. Even the earth, which had served as the shack's floor for who knows how long, had been overturned and bedded down.

But that wasn't what caused the fear to pass between us. That was ignited by the sound which drifted along the breeze: The rumble of heavy machinery at work.

The three of us ran down the field. Over the treetops, I caught sight of something moving. Something swinging. I felt my stomach lurch. As we approached the copse, I could hear hydraulics wheezing and droning. I also heard a heavy dull thud. The air seemed to carry this in deadened delay and echo it around the field. I glanced at Emma and David. They both looked frightened. I suppose the realisation of what was happening beyond the trees was sinking in fast. As for me, however, I just felt numb. It wasn't until later that I became feverish with loss. But that came in the days and weeks after.

At the tree line, we staggered to a stop. Beyond the copse, great machines rattled and men hollered. I looked to the patch of freshly churned earth. I recalled that first night, when I'd stood in the shack's doorway, and watched the sun bleed across the horizon. It seemed like a lifetime ago, *and* yet mere moments since. The trickery of time marked by experience.

David asked, rather solemnly, "Are we going to see?"

"Yes," I said.

Emma grabbed my arm. "Are you sure?" She seemed on the

border of tears.

"I have to see it with my own eyes," I said, and headed into the trees.

From the point on the narrow path where I usually spied the marquee through the trees, I glimpsed a great, hulking yellow machine. The marquee, with its barren and wordless letters, was completely obscured. If it was even there at all. It did cross my mind that maybe it had already been reduced to rubble.

The drone of machines was eerie in the copse; the unnatural amplified against the natural.

Emma and David followed me along the path. Not one of us spoke. At the tree line, we battled our way through the low branches and sprawling undergrowth to stumble out into the clearing. Then we saw it.

The Electric had been eaten in half, and its insides stood exposed; a brick and plaster carcass belching out dust plumes like death rattles. The marquee was indeed gone. The lobby was gone. Even the grand staircase was gone. All that remained was the theatre itself, exposed to the world like a tear in reality. Through the dust clouds, I could make out the rows of seats, and the screen itself. Above, the projection room's outer wall had been completely destroyed, leaving it exposed also. The projector was still in there. I thought my legs were going to give out, but somehow I managed to remain standing. Emma began to scream.

There were two great machines either side of the building. One was an excavator – the yellow beast I had glimpsed through the trees – which ran on caterpillar tracks (these seemed bigger than most cars) and tore at the Electric with a monstrous jagged claw. Something about it made me think of a dragon. The other machine was a crane, from which swung a great wrecking ball. Emma screamed again as this destroyed another section of outer wall.

Several of the workmen turned in our direction. One of them, a burly sort, shouted over to us, "Hey, kids! Get out of here!" He waved his hands if as shooing away a pack of dogs. We remained stood where we were, however, galvanized to the Electric's fall.

Emma hyperventilated through a blur of snot and tears. I watched the Excavator tear out a row of seats.

I heard David say, "He's coming over."

Everything seemed so unreal. There was a moment, just before the big guy got to us, when I actually thought I was dreaming.

The wrecking ball continued to pound at the Electric. The noise was tremendous. At the same time, the giant steel teeth of the excavator tore at row after row of seats. I watched as the Technicolor tramp's row was ripped away and tipped out onto the rubble. Those seats had been there for over sixty years.

The guy who came over wore a hard hat and a high visibility jacket, and was vastly overweight. He had a walkie-talkie in his hand, and an air of superiority that I'd often see on adults when they spoke to us. I took him to be the foreman.

"You can't be here." He had to shout to be heard over the noise. "This is a dangerous site."

"Why are you pulling it down?" said David.

"It's been condemned. Place is structurally unsafe."

Behind him, I saw the wrecking ball swing straight through the projection room. The projector itself was obliterated.

That was the moment Emma began to cry out. "I want to see my mum." Hearing her so stricken made me gasp. She screamed it again and again, her voice cracking and shrieking. "I want to see my mum. I want to see my mum." She had both hands pressed to her head and she shook in spasms. David backed away, truly disturbed by what he was seeing. Even the foreman backed off. He too looked horrified.

I didn't know what to do. All I managed was, "Emma, please don't…"

"Please don't what…" she spat back at me.

I went to put my hand on her shoulder, but she knocked it away.

"What? Don't you want me to make a scene?"

"Emma…"

"Fuck you, Sam."

I staggered back.

"You got what you wanted," she cried. "You saw your dad. But now I'll never get to see my…" she faltered, the rage rushing from her in an instant. "I'll never get to see my mummy," she said, finally.

She covered her face with her hands, and wept into them.

I looked over to the Electric. All that remained now was the cinema screen, and the outer wall behind it. At the sight of this, I too began to cry.

I went to Emma and gingerly put my arms around her. She didn't fight me this time; instead she buried her head in my chest and sobbed.

I heard the foreman say, "What the hell's the matter with you kids? Get outta here!"

I whispered to Emma. "I'm so sorry, Em. I'm so sorry."

She looked up at me. "All those films, Sam…"

"Christ! Be it on your own heads," yelled the foreman, exasperated. "Just stay well back, okay." He traipsed off, barking orders into his walkie-talkie.

I took Emma's hand in mine. David came and stood the other side of her. He took her other hand. And like that, the three of us watched the wrecking ball raze the last of the Electric to the ground.

It swung out, riding high into the sky, then came back down and smashed straight through the screen and out through the building's back wall. The impact cracked around the clearing, and the entire wall came toppling down, kicking out great plumes of dust and brick and age and history.

And that was it. There was nothing left.

That is what happened to my friends and I in that long-ago summer of 1985. I still live with it to this day. The years have stretched out – time playing the trickster as always – but no matter how far I travel, both geographically and mentally, part of me still exists in that long-ago land of childhood, where old cinemas played movies made by ghosts, and my friends were the best I ever had.

After the Electric was flattened, the rubble was cleared away over the next few days. A week or so later, you would never have known it was ever there.

David and I returned every day after school. We'd sit and watch the excavator load up these big open-back trucks with great mounds of rubble. The trucks would come and go along the dirt track, one after another, belching out black smoke and hissing their air pressured brakes. Emma didn't come along with us. As far as I know, she never went back to the site of the Electric after that night we saw it destroyed.

She drifted away from us entirely. Both David and I made every attempt to hang out with her still, but she would always make some excuse. Before long, we just stopped asking her altogether. That's the way it is when you're kids. Friendships seem to play out in intense bursts, but hardly ever sustain themselves.

In the middle of that final school year, I heard Emma was seeing some guy from across town. He was older than her and had a car. She died in that car, along with her boyfriend, the following year. It was the usual story. He lost control and crashed headlong into an oncoming vehicle. Five people were killed in all. Emma being one of them. She had been just days away from turning seventeen.

I've never forgotten her.

David and I did remain friends. We were pretty close right into our mid-twenties. After that, it kind of tapered off a little, but I do still speak to him on the telephone from time to time, and I probably see him once every couple of years. Whenever I go back home.

He's married now. He met Sally in college, and they're really good together. They have a houseful of kids. He works in construction.

He tells people that I'm his famous friend from way back when. Whenever we get together, we always get drunk and talk about the past. We've only spoken about the Electric once or twice though. Last time we talked about it, I told him I was searching for *Ghost with a Gun*. He didn't say much about that.

From time to time, I'll send his kids artwork and story-boards from some of the movies I've worked on, and he sends me a Christmas card every year. It usually has a bad joke written inside. He still calls me Sergeant Slaughter.

I never saw Elmer Muxloe after that last day at the Electric. David and I went to his house a few times and banged on the door, but he never answered. I heard a neighbour found him decomposing in his chair beside the fireplace. He had been dead for two weeks or more. I had been away at college by that point and didn't hear about his death until long after. There were so many things I never got to ask him.

I never did see Seymour Janks again either, but I like to think he's out there somewhere, still making his movies. Also, I never saw my father again.

A couple of years ago, I met an old movie producer who claimed he had seen *Ghost with a Gun* back in the fifties. He got in touch after he happened to see one of my drawings. I had

imagined the scene in which the fake ghost pulled his eponymous gun on his unsuspecting assailant, and the actual ghosts
just fell about laughing. The movie producer must have felt that
Electric charge when he saw it, and he tracked me down right
away.

He told me that he had seen the film in a run-down picture
house out in the Mojave Desert. The film had made him feel,
"*as strange and as marvellous as a lightning storm.*" He also told
me that he saw other such pictures there too, and that the owner
of the cinema had been a strange thin man in bright white suit.

I've been searching ever since.

I often spend nights in my studio. I tend to do my best work at
night. The studio is enclosed in glass, and from here up in the
canyons, L.A. spreads out below me like a vast electrical carpet.
On a clear day, I can see the glimmering dream of the Pacific far
off in the distance, but at night, it's a network of lights.

On the wall in my studio hangs the last picture I drew in the
Electric. The audience of ghosts stares upwards, enraptured by
the silver screen. Emma and David sit up in those rows. As do
Molly and Albert Lévesque, and Elmer Muxloe and his son.
And myself, and my father.

Many people have commented on the drawing. Some can't
look at it for very long, others drink it in, standing before it for
long bouts of time. Some nights I've walked into the studio only
to find a ghost stood there, examining every face, every stroke of
my pencil. I tend to leave them to it.

Emma has never come. Nor has my father.

A few nights ago we had a lightning storm up here. I sat
at my desk and watched it for most of the night. Every time
the sky lit up white, I'd look over to the picture. Seeing those
faces illuminated in that ephemeral light really took me back. It
was as if I was there again; sat drawing those faces beneath the
flickering silver of film. I could see Emma waving at me from
up in the darkness, and the Technicolor tramp offering me the

seat next to him. I suppose a great part of me has never left the Electric. And never will.

When I was fifteen, there was nothing quite like the movies.

ABOUT THE AUTHOR

Andrew David Barker was born in Derby, England in 1975. Like Sam Crowhurst, the first film he saw at the cinema was *The Jungle Book* when he was three years old and he has loved movies from that day to this. He directed an independent feature film entitled *A Reckoning* in 2009 and has since written or co-written several screenplays. *The Electric* is his first novel. He now lives in Warwickshire with his wife and daughter.